WANT TWO FREE BOOKS?

Visit **nikikeith.com** to read *The Perfect Ride* and *The Perfect Daughter*.

KEEP YOUR FRIENDS CLOSE

NIKI KEITH

1

EDDIE

NOW

I silently vowed that I wouldn't knock out Riley's teeth.

"Here we are," Diego declared, rolling his shitty Charger to a stop.

Wes, my twin brother, glanced at me from the passenger seat and picked up on my grim expression. "Oh, lighten up, bro. It's only two days," he said as he pushed the door open.

I hurried after him. "So, did we really have to invite *him*?" I muttered, eyeing Riley leaning on his outdated station wagon—just one look at his handsome features and killer smile made me cringe.

Diego came over and back-slapped me hard on the chest. "We're here to patch things up. Now quit bitching and grab your stuff."

I didn't even flinch. My eyes locked on his as my knuckles itched to knock some sense into his boyish face. I could do without his bullshit, too.

He chuckled and spat a glob on the ground. Disgusting ass pig.

"You heard the man," Wes said, bumping shoulders with me.

It was typical of him to side with Diego—sometimes you'd think *they* were brothers. Fuck it. The sooner I got this over with, the sooner I'd be away from them. I grabbed my backpack and tossed one to Wes. A couple of cases of beer sat beside Diego's duffel bag, just what we needed to set the official weekend from hell in motion.

My eyes flicked to the abandoned cabin Wes and I had discovered when we were thirteen. It was supposed to be our secret—until his loyalty to Diego took over.

Brooklyn's BMW purred up the rocky trail behind Riley, vibrating with muffled pop music. My heart skipped a beat. She would definitely make the weekend worthwhile. I suppressed my grin; if anyone cracked a wisecrack, I'd be scratching that knuckle itch.

Brooklyn's best friend, April, hopped out of the passenger seat in sunglasses, her denim short shorts revealing her toned dark-brown legs and a tube top that barely covered her boobs. The guys craned their necks to take it in.

But not me—I only had eyes for Brooklyn, who sat hesitantly behind the wheel. She, too, didn't want to be around Riley. None of us wanted a party, especially after what we had done. Our lives would be over if anyone ever found out.

My gaze met Brooklyn's. She gave a small wave; I returned a curt nod. Maybe we could sneak away and camp somewhere apart from the others. That was the plan—to use the cabin for our personal stuff and camp out because it was unbearably hot. It wasn't as if the place had much to offer—it didn't even have electricity, though our LED lights and lanterns made up for it.

For Wes and me, having the cabin meant a private sanctuary to escape from Hank. God knew our dad wasn't exactly Father-of-the-Year. Lately, we'd been using the cabin for everything but a haven, though.

"Good—all our besties are here," April said overly cheerily.

Riley knew damn well he no longer had that title with me. Any of us, really. He'd burned us, and I wasn't about to pretend it hadn't happened.

April held up two bottles of vodka. "What do you say we get this party started?"

Wes lunged forward to grab one. "Now, I'm all in for that—a shot party!"

"Uh-uh. You can get the food out of the back," she

snapped, clutching the bottle close to her chest, out of his reach.

Wes scoffed and headed for the cabin. "Like hell I will," he muttered.

Riley, still leaning against the station wagon, laughed. "Can we just get this thing going already? I'll help with your stuff since *I'm* the only gentleman here," he said, flashing a toothy grin.

I clenched my fist. Let Riley be, Eddie.

April fluttered her thick, false lashes at him as if he had angel wings. "Aww, thank you, Riley."

I'd had enough. Clutching my bag, I followed Wes up to the lopsided porch. The slate-gray log cabin featured a family room, a half bathroom with working water (miraculously), and an attic-sized bedroom upstairs that Brooklyn and I claimed since we were the only real couple in the group. Wes and April were on-and-off lovers.

The hot, musty living room came complete with a loveseat, coffee table, and oriental rug courtesy of Brooklyn. A fireplace burned fiercely in the winter when lit properly. The back wall held built-in shelves with a set of cast iron skillets left by the previous owner. We kept them, unsure if we'd ever actually cook our meals on them.

Sandwiches and roasted marshmallows made up the menu for the day.

"Why don't we do this?" Diego suggested, unable to

resist his inner control freak. "Let's split into groups. Wes, Riley, and I can set up camp. April and Eddie can gather what we need for the fire. And Brooklyn can prep the food. There—we're all doing our part."

"Me and *April?*" I spun around and glared at Diego.

"I'm pretty sure they'd have to come looking for you if you're with Brooklyn," Diego replied with an eye roll. "Besides, it's only a few hours until sundown. We've already wasted enough time."

Brooklyn appeared, handing out juices. "I'm fine with prep duty," she said with a shrug and a small smile in my direction.

"Oh, come *on* already," April insisted, shoving the vodka into Brooklyn's hand. "Don't worry—I'll bring your boyfriend back in one piece."

"Creepy, isn't it?" April remarked, nearly an hour later.

"What?" I grumbled, swatting away a low branch that barred my path. The heavy, humid air had me sweating profusely. Who in their right mind thought camping was a good idea, anyway?

"It's the isolation. We're completely alone. No one's around for miles," April replied, her eyes shining with excitement.

I smacked a mosquito on my arm. "I'd say it's more

annoying than creepy." I shot a glance at Diego and Wes, impressed by their work. They had managed to set up one tent and were strutting around as if it were the Statue of Liberty. I couldn't fathom why Wes was so enthusiastic about the trip. We'd agreed to limit our time with Riley to avoid more drama. Regardless, we were all here—the whole gang.

I bent down to clear a thick branch when a piercing scream sent me sprawling face-first into the dirt.

April laughed. "Told you it's creepy. Diego, you owe me twenty bucks," she said as Diego and Wes approached.

I hauled myself up, my shirt and shorts now filthy and my palms caked in mud. "You're an idiot," I muttered, wiping my hands on my shorts.

April wrinkled her nose at me. "Did you really think I was being murdered?"

Wes snickered. "If you were, no one would hear your screams from miles away."

"That isn't funny," I snapped.

"Aww—why don't you crawl back to the cabin and cry to your girlfriend about it?" Diego taunted.

I narrowed my eyes at him. "At least I have a girlfriend. You're just a third wheel," I added under my breath.

April's jaw dropped.

Diego stepped forward, his jaw clenching. "What the hell did you just say to me?"

"Whoa," Wes interjected as he leaped between us, one hand on each of our shoulders. "Seriously, just go chill in the cabin, man. And tell Riley to get his ass back here."

I kept my eyes on Diego a moment longer before glancing at Wes. "Why isn't Riley with you guys?"

Wes rolled his eyes. "Typical Riley bullshit. He complained of a stomachache and left to get some water. That was thirty minutes ago."

Lazy fucker. I veered away, ducking over a log as I tried to navigate back to the clearing. "Yeah. I'll go get Riley."

Riley. Everything was his fault. Well, not entirely—the events of last Halloween had a lot to do with it—but Riley was the final straw.

The cabin soon emerged into view, and I hurried over, thinking it was the perfect moment to mention to Brooklyn that we should try camping somewhere else. Instead, inside the cabin, nothing but four blank walls stared back at me. On the table lay bread and condiments, untouched.

"Brook?" I called softly as I ascended the creaky stairs. The cracked bathroom door hinted that no one was inside, yet I still peeked in. Nothing. I moved towards a closed bedroom door, about to knock, when the voices behind it made me pause. Brooklyn and Riley were together in there. I held my breath and listened.

"Riley... wait... I don't..." Brooklyn's voice trembled

with panic.

"No, you can't back out on me now. Come *here*."

Brooklyn shrieked.

My heart pounded against my ribcage. I twisted the doorknob, but it refused to open. "Brooklyn!" I pounded on the wood with my fist.

She gasped. "Eddie?"

I tugged harder. "Open the goddamn door!"

Brooklyn screamed, "Let go of me, Riley. Stop!"

I rammed my shoulder against the door repeatedly. "Riley, you piece of shit." Eventually, the old wood splintered and the door burst open. Riley had Brooklyn pinned against the wall with his forearm as he clumsily fumbled with the button of her jeans. "Get off her!" I shouted, grabbing his shoulders and wrenching him around. He staggered, desperately trying to keep his balance, his eyes wild and sweat pouring down his face. What the hell was wrong with him?

I shoved him hard. "What the hell are you doing?"

A sloppy grin spread across his face as he swayed. "Go back outside, bro." He turned again to Brooklyn, roughly seizing a handful of her hair.

"Riley—stop!" I clutched his shoulders, hoping to pry him away from Brooklyn, but he only pulled her along with him.

"Fuck off!" He elbowed me. "Brooklyn said this was

okay."

"What?" Her voice became shrill.

My vision blurred, and I punched Riley square in the jaw. As he staggered and swung at me, I dipped, driving my shoulder into his waist and knocking the wind out of him. Riley grunted and gasped for air, falling backward with his hands outstretched for support.

I lunged with my arm extended, but his ivory fingertips clawed at air. It was too late. Glass shattered. Riley shrieked—and then he was gone. Brooklyn and I rushed to the broken window and watched in horror as Riley fell to the ground below.

Brooklyn screamed, trembling with shock.

"Oh, God… I didn't…" The prickling fear along my neck stole my words. A gust of wind slithered through the shattered window, sending a chill down my spine. It was as if I were caught in a whirlpool: everything spun, morphing into grotesque shapes I could barely recognize.

Then Riley came into focus below, sprawled on a cluster of jagged stones. I stared at him, willing him to move. I pulled myself away from the broken pane, glass crunching beneath my sneakers. Small drops of blood gleamed on my shaking hands. "Brooklyn…" I whispered hoarsely.

She turned away, sobbing silently. I bolted down the stairs.

"What the hell was th—" Wes nearly collided with me

as I surged out the front door.

"It's Riley!" I called, darting from the porch and skidding to a stop at the edge of the rock pile. Riley lay flat on his back, his arms splayed, blood trickling onto the stones. The image seared into my mind as I stood frozen in time. A bird screeched from a nearby tree, jolting me from my trance. "Riley?" I hardly recognized the high-pitched sound of my own voice.

Wes brushed past me to investigate while I hung back. He carefully crawled over the rocks and reached for Riley's neck, then turned to me with a horrified expression. "Holy shit, Eddie… Riley… he's dead."

2

EDDIE

NOW

"I have no idea where Riley could be, Coach Donahue," I said, the words scorching my throat as I gripped the phone so tightly I almost crushed it. The Donahues—Riley's parents—didn't begin calling until Monday evening, two days after Riley had disappeared.

Coach Donahue cleared his throat. "Are you sure, Edward? I know how Riley can be. If he said something to you, I promise I won't be upset. His mother's car is gone, too. I—" he sighed, "—*we* just want him to come home.

I swallowed hard to keep my throat from closing. "Um, I'm certain, Coach. I haven't heard from Riley since Friday night—at Mario's birthday party. If he calls, I'll tell him to phone home." I ended the call and exhaled in a long whoosh, like air escaping an overinflated balloon. Tears stung behind my eyes as I clutched the warm dryer, trying to pull myself together, groaning at the churn in my stomach. I already felt hollow from days of vomiting. I took a deep breath—in and out, in and out. By the third round, my shoulders relaxed and the tightness in my chest eased. Slowly, I opened my eyes. Alright. Back to work.

I reached inside the dryer for the warm, rainforest-scented bundle when I noticed an olive-green shirt that had appeared out of nowhere. My heart rate surged—where the hell had that come from? I dropped the load and prodded the green top as if it were alive. It was Mom's shirt, of course; olive green was her favorite color. Yet Mom had left nearly eleven years ago. So why was it in the laundry? I shook my head and tossed it in the trash. It had to be Hank's doing. Our father, Henry Hawkins—better known as Hank—swore he'd kill us if we ever called him dad. But Wes and I had a different nickname for him: Monster.

After finishing folding the laundry, I quietly made my way up the basement steps, removing the key from around my neck. It belonged to Mom and opened the double-locked knob on the basement door, her refuge. Wes and I each had matching copies, much to Hank's annoyance whenever we locked ourselves in there. He could have changed the lock, but he refused to invest in the crumbling house. The place clung on by a thread, and people assumed it was vacant. The shutters banged against the siding even in the softest breeze, and there was no telling what lurked in the knee-deep grass. I supposed it was partly my fault—whenever Hank got drunk, he'd yell at me to mow the lawn, only to forget about it once he sobered up. I knew yard work, but honestly, I didn't know where to start.

The sick, yellow tint in the hall reminded me of an old hospital room, and a truck commercial blared from the ancient floor-model TV in the den. Creeping into the kitchen, I spotted Hank's shiny brown head in the busted La-Z-Boy, his nine-millimeter pistol resting on the end table. For some reason, he always kept his gun within arm's reach—perhaps as a reminder of his hay-day as a cop.

Hank tilted his bald head back and downed the final swig of his Budweiser. I was grateful he wasn't drinking something stronger. Why the hell was I spying on him, anyway? I cautiously stepped away from the doorway; we had to be careful around Hank's paranoia. Wes had barged in on him before, and Hank had turned and shot at him—the bullet hole in the kitchen wall was a grim reminder.

"Come here, Eddie," Hank suddenly barked, startling me. Did he have eyes in the back of his head? I dropped the laundry basket near the doorway and approached his chair. "What're you staring at?" he demanded, eyes fixed ahead. "I can see your damn reflection."

Right. "I was just passing by," I said, trying to sound

casual. Not that Hank would ever notice when something was off—Wes hadn't been home since Friday, and Hank hadn't caught on yet. Finally, he turned to me, eyeing me with disgust. "Well, pass by the fridge and bring me another beer."

I nodded and began to step away when a news broadcast stopped me cold. "—a local jogger discovered the body this afternoon—" the newswoman announced. I stared at the TV while everything around me seemed to move in slow motion, the reporter's words fading into slurred, indistinct sounds. "—authorities are yet to release further details—" I gulped hard. What did she mean? A body found where? I nearly screamed. Could it be Riley?

"Dumbass." Hank's face loomed as he leaned over the arm of his seat. "Go fetch my beer before someone finds *your* battered body, and bring me a bowl of chips, will ya?"

I made my way to the kitchen on unsteady legs, clutching the counter to steady myself. Just breathe. It couldn't be Riley, could it? That night we'd been so sure that—

I fished my cell from my pocket. I had to reach Wes. But when I called, his number rang once before going straight to voicemail. "Of course," I muttered, hanging up.

"Edward, if I have to come in there..." Hank said, jostling me into action.

I searched every cabinet, finding nothing suitable—

Hank hadn't picked up groceries in ages, let alone a bag of chips. Instead, I found a pack of saltine crackers in the cupboard that would have to do. With another beer, Hank probably wouldn't notice the difference anyway. But my mind kept returning to that mysterious body—I had to get a hold of Wes.

I grabbed another Budweiser and returned to the den, straining to catch the words on the blaring news discussing scattered thunderstorms for the night. Holding the beer and crackers out to Hank, I said, "Here."

"What the hell is that?" he growled, his glare shifting from the pack of crackers to my face.

"It's all we have." My eyes landed on the pistol. Was it loaded? I didn't want to risk finding out.

Hank snatched the items from me and slumped back into his seat, shoving two crackers into his mouth simultaneously. "Don't just stand there watching me. Make yourself useful and change the goddamn channel."

Hank liked to boast about being a boxer back in his day, which was hard to believe given his current state. I glared at the crumbs on his belly; he was such a slob. As I dragged myself toward the TV, something whooshed past my head, hit the wall, and shattered into pieces—it was his empty beer bottle.

"Move your ass." Hank pounded the end table, causing his gun to jitter slightly. A football match flickered on the screen. "That's more like it. You're excused." He waved me off, but as I turned to leave, he added, "Where's the other one?"

"Other one?" I echoed.

"You know damn well who I mean. Where's Wesley?"

That was exactly what I wanted to know—but was Hank just now noticing Wes's absence? My lips parted to speak when Wes answered from behind me.

"I'm right here. What do you want?"

I spun around, relieved to see Wes; I was so glad I could have kissed his cheek. He grinned back, his eyes wide in surprise.

"Where were you?" Hank demanded.

"Out working—where else? Somebody's got to bring home the bacon," Wes muttered.

Hank snorted, keeping his back turned. "You ought to buy a bag of goddamn chips with that bacon."

Wes frowned at me but quickly brushed off the expression as Hank turned in his seat to eye us. With a grunt, he returned to his game.

I grabbed Wes's arm and practically dragged him toward the kitchen.

"Damn, Eddie. I didn't realize you missed me that much," he teased, snatching his arm from my grip.

"I gotta tell you something," I lowered my voice, checking over my shoulder for Hank. "The cops found a body this afternoon." I paused, waiting for a panicked reaction, but Wes simply blinked, urging me silently to continue.

"And?" he prompted.

I raised my eyebrows. "What if it's you-know-who?"

"Are you high?" he replied, squinting at me. "Just because the cops found a body doesn't mean it's *our* body." He punctuated his words with air quotes. "People die all the time, Eddie. It's probably just some junkie who overdosed. Why do you always work yourself up?" His tone was dismissive.

"Well, Coach Donahue called half an hour ago looking for Riley. What if Riley mentioned the cabin to them? We should go back and—"

"No," Wes exploded, glancing over his shoulder before leaning in close. "If we go back there, someone will discover something. Let's just act normal and forget about it. No one will ever find his car, anyway."

I hung my head, not daring to ask further, but needing to hear him say so. "You promise?"

"Hey. Look at me." He placed both hands on my shoulders. I peered into his face—our identical features, brown skin, narrow dark eyes, and thick coarse hair, though mine was tied back in a puffy ponytail while Wes sported low, neat sides with a curly top tipped reddish-blond. People often mistook us for pro basketball players.

"What have I told you? No matter what happens, I'll always protect you, alright?" I nodded. "So trust me when I say no one will find out about Riley." He squeezed my shoulders firmly, easing some of my tension.

When he pulled away, I felt a small relief, yet I couldn't shake the worry. Mom used to say that even as a baby, she could tell my brain was always at work—observant, taking in every detail. That was how she could tell Wes and me apart.

"Okay. So where were you really? You got fired weeks ago. Hank is gonna kill you if he finds out," I jabbed him playfully.

Wes frowned and rolled his eyes. "Fuck that place. I've *really* been bringing home the bacon. Check this out," he said, rummaging in his pocket and pulling out two wads of twenty-dollar bills. "This one's your cut." He held out a roll.

My jaw dropped. "What the hell, Wesley? Where'd you get all that?" I sputtered, though my excitement quickly faded. "Wait—was that from the auto parts you stole?" I recalled the accusation from Wes's former manager at the auto shop.

"What? No. I didn't steal anything. Don't believe that bullshit."

I gasped. "Well, is it *drug money* then?" Many kids at school had gotten mixed up with some mysterious guy called the Candy Man, a drug dealer. But Wes and I had sworn we'd never become that statistic. That's why we took up swimming.

"Damnit, Eddie." Wes spun around, eyes darting to ensure Hank wasn't listening. "Keep your voice down. And what difference does it make how I got it? It's in our hands and we damn well need it. Now take it." He forced the cash into my palm. "There's plenty left over after I pay the bills, so go buy yourself something nice. Haywood High's star swimmer deserves nothing but the best, right?"

"You're forgetting I'm second best, remember?"

"Bullshit. Riley's out of the picture now," he added bitterly.

"I wish you wouldn't say stuff like that," I whispered.

His brow arched. "Need I remind you what he was up to the other day?"

My chest deflated. "Please, don't." Neither of us wanted to relive that, and Brooklyn certainly didn't.

"Anyway," he waved his hand dismissively. "Just treat yourself—buy something nice, or even get Brooklyn a birthday present. She got you that expensive phone, didn't she? Do something special for her." He rolled his eyes. "Just enjoy yourself for once, damnit."

I shifted the wad of money to my other hand. "It's just… doesn't any of this feel wrong to you?"

"Eddie—"

"No, not only that, but I could apply for a job too, you

know."

He scoffed. "Yeah, well, Hank made it crystal clear who he expects to support this crumbling castle when he got me that job." He rubbed at the scar across his brow—a permanent reminder of when Hank smashed his face through a glass table.

I gripped the wad, eyes lowering. "Maybe you should put this away for next month's bills?" I pushed it toward him.

Wes clicked his tongue and swatted my hand away. "Eddie, there's plenty more where that came from."

"Do I even want to know what you mean by that?"

"I got a new job, okay? I crashed at Diego's until it came through. If I couldn't replace the income, I probably wouldn't have come back." He shrugged. "As you said, Hank is gonna wreck me once he finds out they fired me. But as long as cash is coming in, I figured I could stall him a bit. This," he said, raising a fistful of bills, "is just a taste of what's coming." He rolled his eyes. "Anyway, don't worry about it. I'm a big boy."

I slowly grinned. "Well, big boy, I did your laundry today." I motioned to the basket on the floor.

"Oh, wow. Thank you, Mom—" he froze mid-sentence. My smile faded, the image of that green top flashing through my mind. I started to ask him about it but thought better of it; Wes hated talking about Mom. "See," he added, eyeing the basket, "we're like the perfect pair. I work while you do the housework."

"Hey, men can take care of chores too. This isn't the fifties," I replied, giving him a playful shove and flipping my hair.

He dipped his head and chuckled. "Alright. But seriously, your job is to keep your grades up and dominate at the Spring Nationals next year. That's our ticket out of here." He gave my shoulder a poke.

He was right—the Spring Nationals *had* been the catalyst for everything. I hadn't always been on the swim team, which was why we'd committed the first crime.

3

EDDIE

THEN

I blinked at the bulletin board, my breath shallow. That was it—my second chance.

Before I could react, someone bumped my shoulder and then hooked an arm around my neck. "Is it fate or what?" Riley asked, jabbing a finger at the swim tryouts announcement.

"It sure as hell seems like it," I whispered back. Jackson, the team's butterfly swimmer in the medley relay, had transferred to Ridgedale, leaving us to replace him before next month's trials, which would decide who qualified for Nationals. The butterfly stroke was *my* specialty.

Riley squeezed me tighter. "You can't mess it up this time, bro. We need you on the team." Riley, Wes, and

Diego were already on board.

But I hadn't really screwed it up before—they had snatched the chance from me because of...

"Well, well, boys," Mr. Wright appeared beside Riley like the proverbial fly on the wall. I turned, jaw clenched.

Simon Wright, my foreign language and history teacher, was tall and lanky with brown hair brushed over his head, glasses, and a jutting chin. His soft, wispy voice always sent a chill down my spine.

He eyed me sideways. "Swim tryouts again, huh?" he remarked, exuding the unmistakable scent of a tuna sandwich.

Riley puffed his cheeks as though he were about to gag.

Thankfully, Mr. Wright reached into his pocket, producing a tin of breath mints. With a quick jerk, he knocked several into his mouth, crunching as he backed away.

"See you boys in class," he mumbled with his mouth full.

I stared at his receding figure until he vanished into his classroom. Something about the way he said that unsettled me.

A mere five minutes later, Mr. Wright reappeared, striding in front of the classroom. Of course, he paused at my desk—hence why I was forced to sit in the front row.

"Does anyone know what I just said?" he asked, blinking

at me behind his black square glasses.

He uttered something in a foreign language, but it all sounded like gibberish to me.

Brooklyn raised her hand. "Guess what we're doing today? It's…"

"Uh-uh," he interrupted, waving a finger at her. "I want Edward to tell me which language it is."

I glared up at him, face flushing. What was his problem with me? My eyes darted briefly to Brooklyn before Mr. Wright lowered his gaze back to me. Shifting, I grumbled, "Italian?"

"Wrong." He slammed his hand down on my desk. "We covered this last week, Edward. Come on. Try again."

I sighed. "I don't recognize it, sir."

He straightened and motioned for Brooklyn to speak.

"It's French," she replied quietly, her eyes fixed on her lap.

"Correct. Maybe you two ought to be discussing that after school instead of playing hooky."

Some kids snickered.

"Maybe you should play sometime so you won't be so cranky," someone jeered from the back—I'm pretty sure it was Riley.

"Who said that?" Mr. Wright spun around.

"Your dick." That was definitely Diego, and everyone laughed, including me.

Mr. Wright joined in with a chuckle that grew so loud it hushed all our smiles, fading one by one. He staggered over to his desk, clutching his stomach dramatically. "You kids—you really crack me up." After catching his breath, he removed his glasses. "Since it's comedy hour, we're extending today's class by an extra thirty minutes."

Groans filled the room as his eyes landed on me while he cleaned his lenses with a handkerchief. "Oh, and Edward, you'll join me for after-school detention."

I jumped up. "I can't. The swim tryouts are at three o'clock."

"Well, I'm sorry, but you can't go. We need to work on your French. And if you don't take your seat, we'll be practicing French every day after school."

I slumped back into my seat, eyes stinging with tears. How dare Mr. Wright pull that shit on me again? Last spring I had missed the tryouts because he scheduled a meeting with Hank about my failing history test—and Hank had been livid. By the time the meeting ended, it was too late. Punctuality was one of Coach Donahue's biggest pet peeves.

I gritted my teeth and tried to focus on the chalkboard, struggling to stifle my sobs.

As Mr. Wright passed by, his soft voice trailed near my ear, "Remember, Edward—I always have the last laugh…"

"That old fuck," Wes snarled at lunch later. "Who the

hell does he think he is?"

I sighed, utterly exhausted from trying to figure out Mr. Wright's motives.

"Don't go," Wes said firmly.

I blinked at him. "What?"

"As captain of the swim team, I say skip detention and head to tryouts instead."

"Eddie, that could land you in more trouble," Brooklyn cautioned, squeezing my hand under the table.

April lobbed a piece of broccoli at Riley, giggling. "Did you really say that to Wright, though?" She tossed her braids over her shoulder.

Riley's expression darkened as he ran a hand through his brown hair. "I didn't think he'd take it out on you, Eddie. You didn't do anything wrong."

I shrugged. "It doesn't matter now. I'm never making the swim team if Wright's running the show."

Wes threw up his hands. "Why don't you just attend both tryouts and detention? You can show up late to detention. What's he gonna do—drag you out of the pool?"

"I wouldn't put it past him," I said grimly.

Wes rested his chin on his hand. "You know how much this means to us—making the team is our ticket out of here." He leaned closer. "It's our chance at freedom."

Didn't he think I already knew? Wes and I were top swimmers—Coach Donahue even said Wes had Olympic potential. *I* was faster than Wes. If winning Nationals meant getting noticed, I was in. I just couldn't stand another second in Haywood. Yet, Mr. Wright's shadow loomed large.

"I won't make the team. I refuse to see Wright's ugly face any longer than necessary." I looked at Wes. "I'm sorry."

We sat in silence for a moment, poking at our lunches, when Riley finally spoke. "Let's get even, then."

"What are you talking about?" Brooklyn demanded, turning to him sharply.

"I'm saying we get revenge on Wright."

"And how exactly are we doing that?" I asked.

Riley smiled slyly. "Meet me at my house at eight."

"I don't think I like this," Brooklyn whispered.

"Then butt out, Goody-Two-Shoes," Diego snapped. "It's your boyfriend's future on the line."

"That's not what I meant," Brooklyn whined, spinning to me. "You know I care about you. It's just…"

I nodded. "Brooklyn's right, guys. We shouldn't do anything that'll get us into more trouble."

Riley clicked his tongue. "You're all such amateurs. How will we get in trouble if he can't prove we did anything in the first place?"

Wes arched an eyebrow, then shrugged. "Okay. Fuck it. I'm in."

Diego nodded. "Me too."

April bobbed her head while wiping her lips with a napkin.

"April?" Brooklyn's eyes widened.

"*What*? I hate the bastard, and you all do too," April declared. "Besides, it's not like we're planning his murder or anything, right?" She glanced around at everyone.

Riley just smiled.

Later that evening, Wes, Diego, April, and I gathered on Riley's lawn at exactly eight. Brooklyn didn't show. I'd never been to the Donahues' place before—I hadn't expected it to be in such a rough neighborhood. At the corner, a gang of thugs argued rowdily; a couple of houses over, a front door stood wide open with a TV blasting at full volume, while a baby cried and nearby dogs howled. It was quite the cacophony for eight o'clock at night.

"Why are we all dressed in black?" I asked as I crunched on dried leaves approaching the crooked stoop. My eyes flicked to the boarded-up windows. Had Riley not jumped off the step, I'd never have believed anyone actually lived here.

"If you wore what you just had at school, you'd be digging your own grave," Riley replied.

"You idiot," Diego snickered, rolling his eyes. Diego was Latino, with reddish-brown curly hair and a freckled face that tempered his otherwise tough-guy image.

I folded my arms. "Why does what we're wearing matter? What exactly are we doing?"

"We're going to Wright's house," Riley said nonchalantly.

"*What?*" I choked out, eyes widening in disbelief.

"Damn!" Wes laughed.

"What if he's home?" I asked.

Riley shook his head. "He isn't."

"How do you know?"

"Every Thursday from five to ten, Wright spends time in the cancer ward with his wife," Riley explained.

"And how the hell do you know that?" April blurted out with a laugh before quieting as unease swept over us. "I— I'm sorry, Ri," she murmured softly.

I shot Riley a look, but he remained impassive. Everyone knew Mrs. Donahue—Riley's mother—had been undergoing chemo for the past month. How could April have forgotten?

Wes cleared his throat nervously. "So, are we doing this or what?"

"Yeah. Let's take my car," Riley replied. "Diego, your car is too memorable."

"I don't want to leave my car here. Someone might steal it," Diego muttered.

Riley sighed. "Trust me. They won't. Everyone knows

who my dad is, and they never mess with us."

"Well, of course not. Nobody wants that piece of shit car anyway." Diego pointed at the beat-up station wagon, and April giggled.

"Fine. Just park it in the garage. My dad isn't home." Riley's cheeks flushed as he stormed off to his car.

Wes shot a look at Diego, who just shrugged. "Hey. My Charger is my baby."

"How do you even know where Wright lives?" I asked Riley about ten minutes later.

He glanced at me through the rear-view mirror. "I found it online. There's a website that can track anyone down if you have their full name. And get this: His name is Simon Dick Wright."

We all laughed and started making puns for the rest of the ride.

Wright lived about twenty minutes from Riley's place. We eventually pulled to a stop at the end of a narrow alley, our breathing anxious and heavy.

"Here, put these on," Riley said, handing out masks that looked eerily similar to Michael Myers'. "In case he has security cameras," he added when I gave him a questioning look.

"Security cameras?" I echoed, my heart sinking.

Diego sighed. "He isn't *sure* there are cameras. We're just playing it safe."

"Also—no one is to say a word once we're inside," Riley instructed sharply.

"Why not?" April demanded, adjusting her mask. "Can we even breathe in these things?"

Riley sighed yet again. "Because, if there *are* cameras," he emphasized with a pointed look at me, "we don't want them picking up our voices."

"Right," Wes grinned. "All that'll show is five Michael Myers stalking around."

I lowered my gaze to the mask. Their plan was getting more and more ridiculous.

"Eddie, will you just grow a pair already?" Diego snapped, almost reading my mind. "You've missed two chances to join the swim team because of Wright. He deserves what's coming."

Wes bumped me reassuringly. "Look, if you'd rather wait in the car, that's fine."

"Hey..." Riley demanded our attention. "We're not going in there to vandalize or anything crazy. We're here to have a little fun." He reached under his seat and pulled out a stack of dirty magazines. "Let's give our favorite teacher a helping hand."

Unable to hold back, we all burst into laughter.

I raised my mask. "Let's do it."

We tried to exit the car as quietly as possible, yet every breath and scuff of our shoes echoed like a super-hearing nightmare. We parked behind the corner of the house, then slipped on our masks before following Riley to Wright's modest brick home with its white fence. I glanced back—there wasn't a soul in sight.

Wes fiddled with the padlock on the fence until, with no luck, he hopped over. One by one, the rest of us followed suit.

Riley knelt at the back door. "Bingo," he whispered, lifting a spare key from underneath the mat.

We crept through the dark kitchen. It was unnervingly cold, a fitting ambiance for Wright's icy lair.

Diego marched straight to the fridge. Using his hoodie sleeve, he flung the door open. I couldn't help but be curious about the contents inside, peeking into the bright light with my tongue practically holding the question.

Wright had meticulously labeled rows of brown paper bags and containers with each day of the week.

Diego shook his head as he reached for the bag labeled Friday. Calmly, he emptied the contents into the trash, then replaced the bag as if nothing was out of place.

Relaxing a bit, I chuckled and trailed along with Wes and Riley into the den. A lone lamp on the end table cast a dim orange glow over everything, and the stale smell hinted that the windows hadn't been opened in ages.

The furniture looked ancient, as though straight out of a seventies sitcom, and the gaudy floral wallpaper made me want to hurl.

Riley flipped to the middle of one magazine and dumped it on the coffee table. Diego set another atop the mantel between a white and gold candlestick set.

April and Wes had even removed a painting of horses to slip some torn pages inside the frame before re-hanging it on the wall.

If Wright didn't have cameras, what the hell would he make of all this upon discovering it?

Mr. Wright's gaze was stony when we walked into his classroom the following day. When we took our seats, he looked us each in the face, saying nothing.

4

EDDIE

NOW

"Just where the hell do you two think you're going?" Hank demanded on Wednesday afternoon, stopping Wes and me in the hall.

I froze in my tracks. I'd been hoping we could sneak off without Hank noticing.

Wes spoke up. "Haven't you been watching the news? Our friend Riley has been missing for five days now. His family is gathering a search party to look for him. We're going to hand out flyers and stuff."

Hank's brows furrowed as he took a swig of beer. "Riley? The coach's kid?"

I nodded, my stomach tightening. It was sickening to talk about Riley as if we didn't know where he was. I hadn't wanted to attend the search party, but Wes and Diego insisted I'd look guilty if I didn't.

Hank snorted. "What the hell happened to him?" As if he really cared.

Wes threw up his arms. "That's what we're trying to find out."

Still clutching his bottle, Hank pointed a finger at us. "I don't give a shit who you're searching for. You two just better make curfew tonight."

Was he serious? I wanted to frown but kept a straight face. What difference did it make when we got back if he would be too wasted to know, anyway?

"Yeah. Sure. Whatever." Wes shrugged and started for the door.

I pressed my lips together and moved to follow when Hank clamped a hand on my shoulder and squeezed it tight.

"I mean it. I want you back here at nine o'clock."

Wes came over and pulled me away. "Alright. We *got* it. Nine o'clock." He slammed the door behind us once outside. "*Asshole.*"

That evening, the sky was a warm peach as we searched the woods and called out for Riley. Lots of people turned up to help—classmates, teachers, the sheriff.

Wes was right about the body they mentioned on the news. It turned out to be some random person who had overdosed on drugs.

We'd passed out flyers at most businesses earlier. All the while, the Donahues were portraying Riley as if he were an angel sent from heaven.

I shuddered at the thought of where Riley was now. I'd never considered the afterlife before, although Mom had once told me there was a special place in hell for monsters. Would I see Riley there when I died? I couldn't believe I entertained such thoughts now. My priority should have been getting through the last hour without losing it.

It was heart-wrenching watching the Donahues—Mrs. Donahue, the coach, and Riley's sister, Mackenzie, known to everyone as Mack. She and Mrs. Donahue could barely hold themselves together. At the sight of every tall, dark-haired guy, they bolted. I'd slipped away from the group twice just to have a moment alone to cry.

I caught up to Brooklyn. "Hey," I said, falling into step beside her. A bead of sweat trickled down the back of my neck in the humid August air.

Brooklyn kept her head low, her long, fluffy hair tumbling to her waist in massed black waves like silk. Every time I saw her, it felt like the first time. Her ivory skin remained pale despite the scorching summer. She peeked at me with her powder blue irises, tears gathering at the corners of her eyes. Without a word, I pulled her into a tight embrace. Her body shivered underneath mine even in the ninety-degree heat.

"Edward…?" she muttered against my chest.

"Yes?" I replied, nuzzling my chin in her hair and catching a whiff of her orangey clove fragrance—a scent that reminded me of a cozy winter night.

She gazed at me softly. "I can't stop thinking about what happened." Was she really going to discuss it now? I scanned our surroundings—no one seemed within earshot. Brooklyn, however, didn't notice my slight paranoia. "What if I'd just given Riley what he wanted—long before we went up to the cabin?" she whispered. "At least, he'd still be…"

"Stop it," I urged, pulling her closer. "Don't think like that. Regardless of when it happened, I definitely would've confronted him either way, unless you two kept it from me." I stared at her.

"If it meant none of this would've happened—I don't know, Eddie."

"Can we not talk about that right now?" I glanced around again and spotted a man who quickly stepped out of view when he caught me staring. With black hair trimmed to his neckline and a beard, he seemed oddly familiar. I was still watching him when Brooklyn pushed away and exploded in anger.

"Why not, Edward? When is the perfect time? We're already four days too late," she hissed, shoving me.

"Say cheese," April called, blinding us with the bright flash of her camera.

"What the hell do you think you're doing?" Brooklyn snapped as she yanked April's arms down by her sides.

"I'm building my portfolio," April replied.

"Seriously, your portfolio? Don't you realize where we are right now?" Brooklyn's cheeks flushed a deep red.

April's doe eyes gleamed as she tossed her long waist-length braids over one shoulder. "Of course I do. Everyone's raw emotions are perfect for the camera."

"That's disgusting, April. Someone is missing. Who cares about your photo book right now?"

"*I* do. It's material like this that'll get me a scholarship. Not all of us grew up with a silver spoon in our mouths."

I grabbed Brooklyn's wrist as she searched for a comeback.

"I still don't think filming this event is the right call. Not after what we did…" she added softly.

April just blinked, letting her camera dangle from her neck as she folded her arms. "Guess I better keep calling for Riley," she muttered, stalking away.

Brooklyn sighed, her lips forming a thin line as her eyes filled once more. "It just feels so shitty. You can't tell me you don't feel it, too."

I pulled her farther away from the others and lowered my voice. "Of course I do. But what can we do now? It's too late. We made a choice—every single one of us did. I don't understand why…"

"It wasn't the right call." She pushed her hair back with her hands, gripping a handful of it. "Jesus, what did we do? I mean, look at this. A search party?" Her voice broke as a tear trailed down her cheek. I didn't know what to say except that it was true—we *hadn't* done the right thing.

"Edward?" a voice called out. It was Coach Donahue. "What are you two doing back here? We don't want anyone getting lost. Everything alright?"

I cleared my throat, my nerves jangling. How much had he overheard?

"Uh—yeah," I mumbled. "We were just… taking a moment." Brooklyn kept her gaze on the ground, nervously chewing her bottom lip.

Coach Donahue folded his arms across his broad chest. Riley had inherited his dark looks from his dad, and the coach's fine curls still held despite their age difference. His handsome face clouded with a frown as his eyes swept from me to Brooklyn and back. "You two weren't fighting or anything, were you?"

I forced a laugh. "We're okay." I silently pleaded for Brooklyn to speak up, but she continued to keep her gaze low. "We're okay," I repeated. "How are you holding up?"

Come on, Brooklyn.

"Well, I'm managing. I know how stubborn Riley can be. He'd hide for days just to spite me. Now that his mother's car is missing, I can only assume that's what's happened. But I don't know…" He sighed. "This feels different."

Brooklyn turned away, a fist covering her mouth.

"What feels different?" Wes interjected as he appeared.

I turned to him. "Coach was just saying that Riley has a habit of disappearing when he's in a mood."

Wes slowly nodded. "Oh, yeah. Now that you mention it, didn't Riley say something like that last week?" He frowned at me.

What the hell was he doing? "I don't remember, Wes."

"Sure, he did. When practice pissed him off, he said someday he'd just skip town."

"Skip town?" Coach Donahue repeated, looking between us.

Why was Wes lying? Not only had he given the Donahues hope that Riley was still alive, but he also made Coach Donahue feel partly responsible.

"Did Riley ever say where he would go?" Coach Donahue asked.

Wes pretended to think. "Nah. Not that I can recall."

Coach Donahue sniffled. "You guys should come on. We're about to wrap this up. And thank you, Wesley. I'll inform Sheriff Owens."

Once the coach was gone, Wes shoved me. "Why didn't you back me up?"

"Because it was a *stupid* idea!" I shoved him back.

Brooklyn stepped between us. "Cut it out, guys. We have to go."

Wes locked eyes with me. "Riley might not have said it that day, but he'd talked about leaving before. Fuck, don't we all?" he declared, throwing up his hands.

"That's not the point—" I began.

Wes walked away. "Whatever. I'm out."

Brooklyn and I continued in silence until our phones pinged at the same time.

She checked hers. "Unbelievable." She flashed her phone at me—a message from Mario Rossi inviting her to a party starting in less than an hour. My phone displayed the same message. "He's throwing a party while Riley's missing?" she asked. Clearly, not everyone cared that Riley was gone.

"Thank you all for coming today," Mrs. Donahue said a short while later as we gathered by the road, preparing to head to our cars. It was nearly nightfall. The streetlamp bathed her in an eerie glow that made her look ghostly. Her sunken skin clung to her frail bones, and a tie-dyed scarf covered her bald head. "We really appreciate all your help. We're counting on anyone with information about Riley's whereabouts to come forward. Riley should know how deeply we love and miss him," she said, covering her mouth with a tissue.

Coach Donahue carefully took over, holding her gently. Brooklyn shifted under my arm as he made plans for tomorrow's search.

"What is it?" I leaned over and asked.

"I think—I think Mack is staring at me," she whispered back. I turned toward her, but Brooklyn stopped me. "No, don't make it obvious."

I slowly scanned the crowd. It was true—Mack had been looking in our direction but quickly turned when she noticed me. "Shit," I whispered.

"What?" Brooklyn glanced up.

"Do you think Riley said something to her? Something about where he went that weekend?"

Brooklyn pursed her lips as my stomach dropped. How had we not considered that possibility?

"Get home safe and have a good night, everyone," Coach Donahue called out.

I whipped around to Brooklyn. "Come on, let's get to your car," I said, linking my arm through hers. I was desperate to get away. We didn't speak until we were inside the car with the doors locked. "What do you think we should do?" I asked.

Brooklyn gripped the steering wheel, even though the car wasn't running. "I don't really know, Eddie. I just wish we could end it before it goes too far."

"How?" My voice cracked. She was silent for a long moment—then her mouth opened, but no words came. "Go ahead," I urged.

"What if we gave an anonymous tip to the police? Something that would lead them to Riley, so all this searching stops. The Donahues would finally get closure— they deserve that."

As much as I wanted Riley's body to remain hidden, her idea wasn't bad. After they found him, we were certain they'd rule his death an accident.

"Yeah, but I don't think we should make that call without the others," I countered.

She folded her arms. "You mean without Diego, who didn't even have the decency to show up tonight?" Her words dripped with ice, which was ironic since Diego had insisted I take part in the search.

"Yes, *all* of them, Brook. They have the right to be in the know."

She scoffed. "It's not as if they care. I mean, April taking those damn photos? What was she thinking?"

"I don't know—about her future?" I asked.

"Are you defending her? Oh my gosh." She covered her

mouth.

"Babe?" I reached for her hand, but she pulled away. I sighed. "You can't be upset if April wants to move on. At some point, we all have to. Otherwise, what are we keeping this secret for?" I stroked her hair. "I like your idea. I just think we should be fair to everyone involved before making a decision. Like, we should vote on it or something."

"You'll take my side?" she asked sharply, eyeing me.

"Always," I replied, stroking her cheek before we kissed.

When we pulled apart, she squinted past me. "Where's Wesley going?"

"Is that Diego?" I nodded toward the blue Charger parked down the street.

"It is. Diego must've stayed in his car the entire time."

I shook my head as Wes and April climbed into Diego's car. "No. I think Diego's come to pick them up."

Had Wes forgotten about Hank? He had specifically said he wanted us to be back by curfew. I dashed from the car and jogged over, breathless.

"What's up, Eddie?" Diego greeted me from behind the wheel.

I kept my gaze on Wes. "Wes? Where are you going?"

"Why?" he huffed, clearly still pissed about the Coach Donahue conversation.

"Because Hank expects us to be back by curfew, remember?" I whispered.

He turned, his expression cold. "Mario Rossi's hosting a back-to-school party, and he expects me to show up and have some fun."

"You can hop in," Diego offered.

I avoided his eyes. "But you don't even like him, Wesley."

"So?" Wes shrugged. "Why should I turn down free booze?" He and Diego laughed.

I shot him a look, my unspoken warning clear. "I'm serious. Hank won't like that."

Wes widened his eyes. "I don't care…"

I studied his face. Why was he putting on a front? He couldn't be that mad at me—he'd pretend he didn't know what Hank was capable of. He gave me an "anything else?" look, so I backed away.

"Last chance," Diego said firmly. I shook my head. "What about you, Brook?" he asked, looking past me. I hadn't even noticed her approach until she narrowed her eyes.

"Fine. Suit yourselves," Diego said with a shrug.

Brooklyn and I stepped aside as the Charger sped away. I kept my eyes on the blue car until it disappeared into the distance.

"Want to catch a movie until curfew? You could come over," Brooklyn offered.

"Isn't your dad home?" I asked.

She nodded. "You could climb up to my room from that oak tree."

"That's alright," I muttered. I wasn't really in the mood for a movie anyway. I couldn't shake the thought of Wes heading to the Rossi mansion. He despised anyone better off than we were—especially that snob, Mario. One look at Mario's luxuries, a couple of beers in hand, and Diego egging him on, and Wes was bound to lose it. "I have to get to that party," I said out loud.

"Okay," Brooklyn agreed.

"Huh?" I blinked at her.

Her cheeks flushed. "I kinda wanna go, too. Maybe if we catch the gang together, we could make that vote."

There was no chance of that happening tonight, but I didn't dare say so. If it was enough to lift her spirits, who was I to argue? Besides, I needed to be sure Wes made curfew. Otherwise, he'd get his ass handed to him.

5

EDDIE

NOW

"Ed-die! Ed-die! Ed-die!" Brooklyn and the other kids chanted as I swam in the Rossi's pool like it was the Nationals.

I was shirtless in my basketball shorts because a guy from Ridgedale had challenged me to a three-lap race. The rectangular, in-ground pool was about fourteen by twenty-eight feet, but to me it felt no bigger than a bathtub.

On my final lap, about halfway across, Brooklyn's cheers outshone the others, pushing me to pump harder, faster. The chlorine water slashed against my body as I carved graceful strokes through the waves. My lungs burned with anticipation as the tiled edge drew near. With a somersault, I executed a perfect flip turn off the tile for maximum effect.

Brooklyn screamed as I touched the wall. I emerged from the water and wrapped my wet arms around her legs.

"Winner!" she declared, her fists springing up in triumph.

"Not bad," my opponent called from the far end of the pool.

"Not bad?" someone else echoed. "You got your ass kicked, bro."

I wished Wes were there to witness my victory. I scanned the crowd for his familiar face. He couldn't still be upset, could he? Just hours ago, I'd seen him smoking with a purple-haired girl—a clear sign that he and April were off.

"You are too awesome," Brooklyn smiled.

It felt incredible to impress her. Brooklyn was a piano prodigy with Juilliard on her horizon next year—destined for success with her GPA and musical talent, unlike me, riding on winning the Nationals as my first step toward the Olympics.

On impulse, I kissed her. The moment was perfect.

She blushed as I led her to a lawn chair and pulled her onto my lap. Handing me my shirt and a towel, she said, "You know you're making me wet, right?" Her eyes widened before she added, "No. Not literally—" She sighed, burying her face in her hands.

I grinned. "I'll settle for either way you meant it." I

trailed a kiss along her bare shoulder. We were probably the only ones at Haywood High who hadn't yet had sex, yet we both agreed that the right time hadn't come—and it wouldn't be some clichéd prom night, either.

"I have a confession," she said softly.

"Yeah?" I prompted, waiting.

She grinned. "I'm really glad we came to the party. I didn't expect it to be such a relief. Things haven't been great at home, you know."

I frowned, my fingers tracing tiny circles on her shoulder. "What's going on?"

"My dad. He's hounding me about the SATs. Then there's the recital coming up—everything's too much, and my concentration's shot."

"Hey." I cupped her chin, holding her gaze. "You know you can always talk to me." She pulled away slightly. "What is it?"

"My dad is really against us—our relationship, I mean."

"Damn. Why doesn't your dad like me?"

"I don't think it's really you, Eddie. He just wants to control every bit of my life until I go off to college. He thinks I should focus only on my grades and the piano."

"Am I really that much of a distraction?" I laughed. "I want the best for you, too. I've got my own goals, sure— but why does our relationship have to be on hold?"

Her full lips curved into a smile. "You're right. No one

should make that call."

"Not even your daddy?" I leaned in slowly, my eyes dropping to her lips.

"Nope." She playfully popped her p, and when our foreheads touched, we peered deeply into each other's eyes.

"I only want the best for you." I felt I'd even kill for her again if it meant protecting her, though I never dared say it aloud—she knew already.

Our lips melted into a passionate kiss. Just as it deepened, Hank flashed in my mind—our curfew. I abruptly shoved Brooklyn away and leaped to my feet.

"What's the matter?" she cried.

"*Hank.*"

"Here? Where?" She scanned the party frantically.

"We're late for our curfew." I spun and tore through the crowd of partying kids.

Okay—rewind. Hank had been sipping a beer when we left. No telling how many more he'd had since, and though he was likely drunk out of his mind, he'd warned us *twice* to be home. He meant business.

"Wesley?" I shouted, but an overwhelming rap beat drowned out my voice. "Wesley, where are you?" I headed toward the house.

Mario threw a party nearly every week. Just last Friday, I was at the Rossi mansion for his birthday—an immense labyrinth of rooms that practically begged for tour guides.

I stomped through a side door into a hallway. "Wesley, answer me, bro." I wriggled around until I reached the dining hall, littered with kids so trashed they could barely stand. I never understood how someone could do that to themselves. What's the point of a party if you're going to forget it all?

That was something Riley and I shared. As athletes, we didn't drink or do drugs—we had too much at stake, especially with Riley banking on a scholarship. Mrs. Donahue's mounting bills reminded everyone just how underpaid teachers were.

"Wesley, are you in here?" I moved toward the kitchen, where a group of guys were hooting and chanting. I recognized Diego's voice—and if he was there, Wes couldn't be far off.

"*Take it off! Take it off!*" the guys chanted.

Amid their chaos, I heard a small voice say, "no." I elbowed my way forward to see what was happening. Diego and Wes were cornering a petite, dark-haired girl clutching her torn top as if fighting for dear life. It was like a déjà vu of entering that cramped room in the cabin with Riley and Brooklyn.

Diego giggled, reaching for her shirt. "Come on. We won't bite. Give us a tease."

"I said stop it." She slapped him sharply.

Diego, eyes locked on her, took a quick sip of beer

before dumping the rest over her head. "You stupid bitch."

She screamed in surprise.

I rushed over and shoved Diego aside. "Chill out, dude."

"Touch me again, and I'll break every bone in your fucking face." He advanced, his finger inches from my nose. I grabbed it and yanked him closer. Just as Diego swung, Wes leaped between us and caught his arm.

"Will y'all both chill?" Wes snapped.

Diego swore and struggled to get at me, but Wes tugged him out the patio door. Most of the party had dispersed since the show ended. The dark-haired girl remained, arms tightly clutched around her soaked, ripped top.

I handed her my T-shirt. "Are you alright?"

Shakily, she accepted it and slipped it over her head. "Yes. Thank you," she said, finally meeting my eyes. "Thanks for everything."

I blinked—she looked a lot like Brooklyn, only without her mysterious eyes. Her gaze, darker now, gave off a Mila Kunis vibe.

"It was nothing," I said with a shrug.

Her eyes landed on my bare torso. "I'd say it's a bit more than that," she teased, making me laugh.

Brooklyn burst through the patio door. "Hey…" She paused, then slowed when she saw the lookalike in my T-shirt. "Uh, get out here. Wes is getting his ass kicked."

I dashed for the door. "By Diego?"

"I don't know." She threw her arms in exasperation.

A cacophony of music, shouts, and laughter greeted me outside. On the lawn, I spotted Wes locked in a brawl with a guy half his size—Wes was pinned in a headlock.

"You're trying to rip me off? Huh? You think I'm stupid?" the larger guy grunted while struggling with Wes.

Without thinking, I lunged. My weight caught him off guard long enough to loosen his grip on Wes.

As he turned to attack me, Wes threw a quick jab to his stomach, sending him reeling into a nearby group.

Instantly, a needless fight erupted. Soon, we were a tangle of bodies on the lawn—kicking, punching, sprawling everywhere. A bottle smashed against my head. Dizzy, I spun, and before I knew it someone shoved me down onto the prickly grass. My chin collided with a knee as I scrambled to break away. Pain exploded in my face, and defeated, I collapsed back onto the grass, writhing like a fish out of water.

"Alright, all of you! Let me see your hands," boomed a voice. I slowly got to my feet and saw two officers, guns at the ready.

"We're hauling your asses to the station," one officer declared.

I slumped back onto the grass with a heavy sigh. We'd never make our curfew.

Wes gripped the iron bars and stuck his lips through them. "It smells like a sack of balls in here," he shouted, his drunken laugh rough and ragged. "A sack of smelly balls."

I just sat on the cold, steel bench, face buried in my hands, unable to believe the mess we'd made. What if Coach Donahue found out? Would they kick me off the Nationals? Did that mean I now had a criminal record?

"This really sucks," I murmured. Wes blew another raspberry that escalated into a series of farting noises.

"Will you stop?" I snapped, then jumped to my feet. "Look at what you've gotten us into. What the hell was that guy accusing you of, Wesley? And who was that girl in the kitchen?" Wes, still turned away, leaned forward. "Hey? Say something." I jerked his shoulder and he leaned in—only to vomit. "Perfect." I rolled my eyes. "Excuse me, can I please have some tissue?" I guided Wes to a metal bench and forced him down. Leaning in mere inches from his face, I snapped my fingers for his attention. "Just sit still, okay?"

He blew more raspberries as I walked over to the bars, where an officer held out a half-roll of paper towels.

"Don't you try anything funny," the officer warned as I accepted them.

What did he expect me to do—hang myself? I piled some

paper on top of Wes's vomit and handed him the rest to clean himself up.

If only I'd gone to Brooklyn's like she'd offered.

Her face flashed through my mind, and on instinct I reached into my pocket for my cell—only to remember that the cops had confiscated everything upon our arrest. She must have been so worried about me and wondering why a girl, who looked like her, was wearing my shirt. I'd never seen that girl at Haywood High before.

"Hey," I said, leaning so Wes could see. "Did you know that girl—the one in the kitchen?"

"Huh?" he squinted, pulling sheets off the roll one by one and watching them flutter to the floor.

"The girl Diego was picking on—do you know her?"

"Oh—that was just some girl Diego was feeling—I dunno." He shrugged.

I sighed and ran my hand through my hair, glancing down at my bare chest. What time was it anyway? How long were we going to be stuck here?

I inhaled sharply and nearly choked. Wes was right—it did smell like balls. If I confessed the truth about Riley— that I shoved him out the window—I could spend the rest of my life in jail. Did I deserve that after what he tried with Brooklyn? I'd saved her just as I saved the girl at the party. But did that really justify taking a life? I supposed that was what judges and juries were for.

"Hawkins boys?" an officer called as he approached the bars with a key in hand. "Time to go." He swung the door open and waved us out.

I helped Wes to his feet and guided him over. "Why only us? What about them?" I nodded toward the other kids from the party and an older guy who was already there. Did I really care about them? The man was setting us free.

"Your father's here to pick you up. We're still trying to reach your folks. But you two…" He wiggled a finger at us. "You two should be ashamed of yourselves, embarrassing Henry like this." Then he gestured for us to go ahead.

Embarrassing *him*? I really wanted to point at Hank as he emerged near the desk, busy signing papers. He wore an oddly buttoned-down shirt with stained khaki shorts, socks, and flip-flops. Turning toward us, anger radiated from him like poisonous gas. For a moment, I wished I could go back to that stinking cell.

"Daddy!" Wes cried, arms outstretched.

Shit. I reached to stop him—but it was too late. Wes had already rushed over to Hank, who wasted no time expressing his displeasure by punching Wes in the stomach. Wes folded and dropped to his knees. Hank loomed over him and continued to slap him with every blow, while I peered around at the police officers. Would someone step in? Apparently not. Most of them knew Hank's temper all too well. He'd been a cop for fifteen years until some terrible incident forced him to resign when Mom left.

Then a female cop suddenly sprang from behind her desk.

"Officer Dodds, those papers won't file themselves," Sheriff Owens announced as he entered. The cop slumped back into her seat. Placing a hand on Hank's shoulder, Owens said, "Now, now, Hank. Just take it easy. You know how kids are today—they're scavengers!" He chuckled.

Hank straightened, sweat beading on his forehead, and then smiled, pulling the sheriff into a tight hug. "Well, if it isn't the Caterpillar!"

Sheriff Owens's chubby, white fingers lifted his unruly mustache. "I swear this thing only gets hairier by the minute." Owens, with his bald head and heavy-set frame, looked like a character from a Western. Pointing at us as I stooped to help Wes up, he said, "Times really have changed. How can you boys be partying while your friend is missing?"

Wes was too drunk to reply, and I found myself at a loss for words, making us all seem like horrible friends.

"Do you have any idea the man your father was? He used to collar every jackass roaming the streets of Haywood."

Yeah, except him.

"Why don't you ever come around anymore, Hank?"

Hank sighed. "Don't have much reason to, Owens, especially since you let me go," he added.

Owens waved a dismissive hand. "Don't be bitter. That's water under the bridge. No one's talking about it anymore."

Talking about what? They kind of did now, didn't they?

Wes shifted against me. "I got you," I whispered, steadying him while trying to catch every word of Hank and Owens' conversation.

Hank nodded grimly. "Sure. Water under the bridge. Well, why didn't I get my job back?" He clenched his fist, and Owens chuckled as he glanced downward. Hank snorted. "Come on, boys." He clamped a hand on the back of my neck, sending shivers down my spine.

"Wait," Owens interjected. "They have to collect their belongings." He snapped his fingers for an officer to bring our stuff. Soon enough, someone emerged carrying our cell phones and Wes's wad of cash. Why hadn't he stashed that away yet?

Hank gasped when he saw it, then glared at Wes. "Where'd you get that?"

My heart picked up pace when I noticed Wes's mischievous eyes—I knew some stupid comment was on its way.

"The Candy Man gave it to me."

Candy Man? Someone who had any kind of drug you needed. But what did Wes know about that?

"Candy Man?" Sheriff Owens repeated while tugging his

pants up over his enormous belly. "Just who might this Candy Man be?"

"He's only kidding," I interjected quickly. "We keep a candy jar for our savings. The Candy Man thing is just an inside joke between us." It sounded half-plausible, but it was too late to argue. Owens might fall for it, yet Hank certainly knew better—I could see the throbbing vein above his left temple. Yep, he knew.

"Is that true?" Owens turned to Wes.

I cleared my throat, silently hoping Wes caught the signal. Since we were kids, our secret codes were simple— a throat clear meant yes, a fake sneeze meant no.

"N-yes!" Wes nodded, swaying groggily, on the verge of another bout of vomiting.

"Well, you better watch your mouth around here. We're still looking for that damn Candy Man—he keeps slipping between the cracks," Owens warned Hank.

"Yeah, I bet," Hank muttered, confiscating both our phones and the cash. I knew he'd keep the money, but why our phones? I needed to call Brooklyn. "We'll let you get on with your search then," Hank said, starting for the door.

"Alright. You all take care. And don't be a stranger, Hank the Tank," Owens winked.

"Bye-bye, Caterpillar!" Wes waved.

Hank spun toward him. "One more word out of you, and I swear I'll rip your tongue out."

Bile bubbled in my throat as we neared Hank's beat-up truck. The crescent moon hung low like a sideways grin, as if laughing at our night. Little did it know, our night was far from over.

Hank grabbed Wes by the collar and slammed him against the refrigerator. "Where did you get the money?" he bellowed for what felt like the hundredth time. Wes's mouth hung open, blood pooling from his busted lips. I stood back, unable to watch as Hank pressed for an answer. With a hand over Wes's mouth and chin, he gripped his face tightly. "*Where?*"

Wes blinked those laughing eyes. "You said… one more word, and you'd rip out my tongue…"

Enraged, Hank head-butted him. Wes's knees buckled and he slid down the fridge, but Hank yanked him up to knock his forehead into his face again. Wes moaned before collapsing to the floor

When Hank advanced for another blow, I jumped in between. "Hank, stop it. I gave him the money, okay? It was a gift from Brooklyn." I gripped Hank's shoulders and tried to pull him away.

He shrugged me off. "You must think I'm a fool. Goddamn candy jar—Kira thought she could fool me too, and look where it got her. You assholes will end up worthless, just like your mother." His gaze shifted to me, and I took a few shaky steps backward. "It's the tru—" was cut off as Hank's hand clamped around my throat. His grip was so tight my eyes nearly bulged. It felt like the floor had dropped beneath me. He hoisted me high like some cartoonish villain. With my air supply cut off, I silently counted.

One-one thousand… Two-one thousand…

"I was Haywood's finest. Nothing gets past me." A left hook smashed into my liver.

Pain pulsed through my middle and my stomach retched. I clawed at his thick wrist, but the combined agony of choking and vomiting was like a series of bombs exploding inside me.

With a roar, Hank heaved me higher before slamming me down onto the kitchen table—shattering it into splinters. Air rushed back in, and I gulped it greedily, even if only for a moment. But it wasn't long before Hank straddled me and wrapped both hands around my neck again.

"Han—"

"You want to be a liar like your mother?" Hank shrieked, sweat streaming down his face as he banged my head repeatedly against the broken tabletop. Stars danced before my eyes.

"Hey, asshole?" Wes called out. As Hank glanced over

his shoulder, Wes smashed him across the head with a wooden leg. Hank crumpled, falling heavily to his side. "*Come on.*" Wes tugged at my ankle, broke away, and bolted for the basement.

I scrambled on all fours after him.

"I'm gonna kill you," Hank promised as he staggered through the doorway. Wes flipped him the middle finger. And as Hank charged, Wes slammed the door in his face. I leaned against the door, trying to keep pace.

"Hurry," I urged, watching as Wes fumbled with the lock. Finally, it clicked.

On the other side, Hank pounded the door. "*I swear I'm gonna kill you, Wesley.*"

"For sure, Hank the Tank," Wes shot back.

"Don't taunt him like that," I whispered, my throat raw and sore.

Wes kicked the door. "Fuck him." He hurried downstairs and collapsed onto a busted loveseat. Eventually, Hank's thuds faded away and Wes released a muffled groan.

"What hurts?" I asked, hovering over him.

He rolled onto his back, drenched in sweat and blood. "Every fucking thing," he muttered, wincing as his swollen, almost boneless nose—already drying with blood—told the tale.

"I'll be back," I murmured. I moved to the wash sink

and soaked a T-shirt in cold water. Wes needed something for the swelling, but I wasn't about to return to that chaotic kitchen.

"This won't do much but…" I carefully dabbed at his face, wiping away most of the blood and sweat. He winced, eyes squeezing shut. A stray drop of water fell into his hair. His shallow breathing eventually lulled him into sleep. I sat on an old workout bench, watching his chest rise and fall, and soon drifted off—until I was jolted awake by a few droplets splattering onto my face.

Squinting at the sweating pipe overhead, I groggily pulled myself up, feeling as if I'd been run over by an eighteen-wheeler twice. In an instant, images of last night flashed by—Hank's sweaty, enraged face, Owens's bushy mustache, Diego's accusing finger, Brooklyn.

Brooklyn. I sprang to my feet, patting my empty pockets. Where the hell had I left my phone? Then it hit me—I'd left it in Hank's pocket. Slowly, I turned toward the crooked staircase.

Hank's routine was always the same—beat us up and then fall into a drunken sleep. If I was right, and I was sure I was, Hank was out cold somewhere. All I had to do was recover our phones and cash from his khaki shorts.

I crept up the stairs, holding my breath. Unlocking the door, I peeked out. The light was off, though shards of dawn crept in through the window. The refrigerator hummed steadily. I tiptoed closer to the kitchen, keeping my back to the wall. As I reached the doorway, I caught Hank's snores drifting in.

I frowned. Was he asleep in the kitchen? Quickly, I grabbed one of the broken table legs—a makeshift club. He'd threatened to kill Wes. Who was to say he wouldn't wake suddenly, mistake me for him, and blow my head off?

Gripping the club tighter, I edged into the kitchen. There, sprawled on his back with his belly exposed, Hank lay deep in a drunken sleep. Beer bottles and cans littered the floor. I could quickly grab our phones and Wes's money, and he'd wake up with no recollection.

Raising the club again, I muttered, "Here goes nothing." Before I could change my mind, I tiptoed over shards of broken glass, crushed cans, and splintered wood. I silently stalked toward Hank's inert form, prepared to knock him out if he stirred. His snoring—deep then high, deep then high—filled the room.

Then, he froze. So did I. His breathing paused for a moment before resuming its gentle rhythm. I saw our items spilling from his shorts as I drew closer, and with a whispered sigh of relief, I snatched everything up and shoveled it into my pocket. Yet, I couldn't tear my eyes away from him.

He lay there so peacefully, oblivious and vulnerable—so confident that nobody would dare harm big, tough Hank.

And yet, there he was, asleep.

I swallowed hard, gingerly touching my still-sore neck. If Wes hadn't knocked him off of me earlier, he might have killed me. Was that really Hank's intention? My vision blurred and my heart pounded so fiercely it threatened to burst. There was my moment to set us free. I set the club aside and picked up a broken beer bottle, its jagged edge gleaming.

"You can't hurt us anymore," I said aloud. Hank stirred and his eyes blinked open faintly, but I didn't care. I simply smiled.

"What the hell are you doing?" Hank asked, slowly pushing himself toward a seated position. I kicked him forcefully back—my sneaker connecting dead center with his forehead. He slammed onto the linoleum with a heavy thud. "You mother—" he began.

I jammed the broken bottle into his belly. Warm blood sprayed across my face. With a hoarse cry, I stabbed him over and over, ending our night in a brutal, irreversible climax.

6

BROOKLYN

NOW

My cell buzzed, and my eyelids flew wide open early the next morning.

"Eddie." I muttered. I tossed the covers off and grabbed the phone from the nightstand. The charger popped from the wall and clattered to the floor.

I froze, slowly turning toward the door. The last thing I needed was Dad patrolling the house, looking for a burglar. It had already been a hassle quieting my little sister's dog when I snuck back in. JoJo was a small brown-and-white Cavalier Spaniel, and for some reason, he always growled and barked at me like I were a total stranger. Or maybe Dad had trained him to catch me red-handed. Either way, I quickly silenced him with a cookie.

Once I was sure the coast was clear, I checked my phone.

> Can we meet for coffee?

It wasn't Eddie. It was Mack.

I pushed my hair from my face. *Mack?* Why was she sending me a DM, and at four in the morning?

Eddie was right—Riley must have let something slip. I bit down on my lip as I pictured Mack. We hadn't hung out since sixth grade, back when we attended an all-girls school—a school that eventually kicked her out. The rumor was that the Donahues couldn't afford the tuition, but those who really knew Mack said otherwise. They whispered that a teacher had caught her being, as they put it, inappropriate with another student. Shortly afterwards, she vanished.

I hadn't seen Mack again until our junior year, and even then, she and I barely spoke. So why now? Clearly, she suspected something. I recalled how she had looked at me oddly during the search party.

I stared at the screen until the words blurred together.

While chewing on my chapped lips, the metallic taste of blood hit my tongue, jolting me from my thoughts. Should I reply? Nah. Mack was the least of my worries. Where was Eddie? Why hadn't *he* responded yet? If he were still being held in a cell by the time Dad woke up, he'd forbid me from ever seeing him again—after all, Dad was an attorney, and Eddie wouldn't need a lawyer, would he?

I had no idea what was happening anymore. I dropped my head onto the pillow and pulled the covers over my chin. Clutching the phone against my chest, I hoped Eddie would reach out. But he didn't.

That afternoon, my fingers raced across the piano in the sitting room. The piece I'd chosen for my recital was Ravel's Jeux d'Eau—French for fountains or playing water. The sound of water, its sprays, cascades, and brooks had inspired the music. I had selected it as a dedication to Eddie's swimming.

As I practiced, I envisioned his torso plunging through crystal waters, the ripples casting waves across his muscular back and legs. His feet fluttered in time with the quick, quieter notes.

I closed my eyes, trying to hold the vision tighter.

In my mind, Eddie kicked into a long-distance swim as if he were in a race. He swam faster, frantically, revealing that he wasn't heading for a finish line—he was swimming *away* from something.

The passage intensified as the notes quickened, the harmonies flowing from the piano with raw energy and passion. My fingertips glided across the keys in a sweeping glissando, my mind curious about where this vision might lead.

A wispy red cloud chased after Eddie's flickering feet.

I pressed the piano keys, the notes tumbling out nonstop, tinkling like thick raindrops.

"Faster, Edward!" my mind screamed. But it was my fingers that obeyed, even as that red hue swallowed Eddie whole. The piece ended with a deep, dramatic tone.

I bowed my head to catch my breath, the image gnawing at my stomach. That was weird. I had imagined stories while playing for as long as I could remember, but never had the tone turned this dark.

Loud, steady claps made me spin around. "Dad…" I called as I rose to greet him. Dad, of Russian descent, towered over me at six foot six. I went on my tiptoes to kiss his cheek, meeting his piercing, icy eyes.

"That piece lost you, didn't it?" he observed.

I nodded, cheeks flushing. I wasn't sure how much he'd seen. "The notes are tough and require a lot of concentration." Something I seem to be lacking.

"Well, I'm sure you have plenty of concentration, right? When you're not distracted by wild parties?"

I wanted to speak, but I knew I should choose my words carefully. Lie to Dad once, and he'd hold it against you for the rest of your life.

I blinked. "Oh, you mean last night?"

He walked over to the emerald chaise sofa and ran his hands along its golden trim. "I just got off the phone with Riccardo Rossi."

Riccardo? That was Mario's father. Dad had been Rossi's attorney for years.

"He returned from his trip early to find his mansion littered with drunken teens. It appears one of them stole the jeweled urn containing the remains of Grandpa Rossi."

Gross. I struggled to keep a straight face. "That's horrible. That must have happened after I left."

His forehead creased. "So, you were there?"

"Well, yes. I accompanied April. After the search, she was so upset that I thought a party might cheer her up. But it was a bit of a drag, so we left early."

"Were the Hawkins boys there? I mean, stealing an urn with actual remains signals desperation, and I know how badly they could use the money."

My mouth dropped open. "Dad!"

"They encrusted that urn with jewels and rubies worth thousands."

"Eddie wouldn't steal from his own friends."

"But he's stolen before?"

I sighed and headed back to the piano. "Now you're just twisting my words. I'll ask around about the urn. But it wasn't anyone from my group, I know that much." My voice wavered on the last part—I wasn't sure about Diego and Wes.

"There you are." Mom entered. "Look who I found out front."

April waved at me. Despite her being Black, she seemed more like Mom's daughter with their matching happy-go-lucky vibes—something that didn't come naturally to me. Once again, Dad had given me the blues for the day.

"April says you two are in charge of the party plans today," Mom said.

"We are?" I blinked in confusion. Our birthdays were just a day apart—we'd thought it was the coolest thing ever dating twins. But what was April talking about? After Riley died, we had agreed never to throw another party.

Yet, we had partied at Mario's last night—the guilt still nagged at me.

April pursed her purple lips. "Of course. Remember, we're going to browse around for some ideas?"

"Oh—" I nodded. Perhaps she had news about Eddie. "Right." I played along.

Dad scoffed. "As if another party is what you kids need. Anyway, Brooklyn should get back to her rehearsal. We've already interrupted and taken too much of her time."

"Dana," Mom chided. "It's their birthday. Let them plan it how they wish." She turned to me. "You go on, Brook. The piano will still be here when you get back." She winked.

I shot a glance at Dad. Even with his arms folded, he merely shrugged in agreement. I smiled, hurriedly grabbing my purse and following April outside. It wasn't until we were in my silver BMW that I finally spoke.

"Did Eddie send you? Did he lose his phone or something?"

Her face contorted with every word. "*What*? I don't know. They probably just slept in after that wild fight. I'm sneaking you off to get matching manicures and pedicures."

"Are you serious?"

"Can we? Please? Please?" She practically danced in her seat.

If she didn't look so childish, I might have smacked her. I glanced at my chewed fingernails—they *should* look decent for my recital, though.

"Oh, alright." I started the car.

"Mm..." April slurped her berry smoothie about half an hour later.

We had gone to the mall for drinks and then to the nail salon. The manicurists were working on our toes and perfecting our French-tipped nails.

"Either Mario broke that urn and disposed of it, or he

sold it for quick cash," April remarked. "My money's on the latter. Have you seen how obsessed he is with money? I even heard he's selling SAT answer sheets."

I gasped. "How did Mario get those?"

"He's a hacker, I guess," she shrugged. "But I know it wasn't Wes who took that disgusting thing. Besides, if either of them had, wouldn't the cops have confiscated it when they arrested them?"

Right. I mentally slapped myself. I grabbed my phone again—still no word from Eddie. I called Diego to see if he knew anything. Apparently, he hadn't been arrested and knew no more than I did. I suggested we go over to the boys' house, but he wasn't too keen on the idea. He said Hank wouldn't allow anyone into their home.

Come to think of it, I'd never been inside Eddie's place during the two years we'd been dating. Sure, I'd dropped him off a few times, but I had never seen the inside.

"Hey, have you ever been inside the boys' house?" I asked abruptly.

April used her straw to stir her smoothie. "No, not really. I mean, Wes and I were fooling around in the hall once. His dad's truck wasn't in front, so we got carried away before making it to the room." She giggled. "But his dad was actually in the back, and Wes freaked out when he came in. He didn't catch us, though. I just don't think he allows Wes to have company over."

"Weird," I muttered. "Or maybe he grounded Wes."

She shrugged. "Probably. Wes is so badass…and so hung," she whispered, eyes gleaming at the thought.

I almost sprayed the manicurist with my banana smoothie. "*April.*"

"What?" she grinned. "It's true. Well, isn't Eddie? They're like identical twins. I'm sure that counts for identical dicks, too."

I glanced away shyly. "Maybe."

She touched my shoulder. "You haven't done it yet, have you?" She gasped at my silence. "OMG, girl, what are you waiting for?"

"We're not like everybody else, A. We want it to be special." Honestly, I wasn't sure *what* we were waiting for. Eddie and I always messed around, but he backed off whenever we got too close. I shrugged. "Besides, it doesn't matter. It's not always about sex. Eddie loves me."

She rolled her eyes. "Trust me, everyone knows just how much Eddie does."

"What's that supposed to mean?" I asked, staring at her. She glared back, arching an eyebrow. It was obvious she was referring to the Riley situation. I broke eye contact. "Come on—don't turn it into that."

"Anyway… there's another guy who was a beast in bed."

"Who?" I frowned.

"Riley."

I spun my head to look at her, startling the manicurist. "You slept with Riley? *When?*"

"Plenty of times. You know how Wes and I can be—we never last more than a week together."

"So, you cheated on Wes with Riley?"

"Well, no. We were technically on a break, so I wouldn't call it cheating. And it's not like Wes is exactly the poster child for fidelity." She made me laugh. "But seriously—are you saying you'd never be with another guy? Even if he was the sexiest creature you've ever laid eyes on?"

I scoffed. "Of course not. I could never do that to Eddie."

"Seriously?"

"My gosh. No. Never." I laughed, trying to play it cool even though I was lying through my teeth.

7

BROOKLYN

THEN

"I got them," I said, chewing on my lower lip.

"Got what?" April asked as she peered into her locker mirror while applying a fresh shade of purple lipstick. She smacked her lips and glanced over her shoulder because I'd gone silent. "What, B?"

"The uh—lace panties," I whispered, eyes darting around for anyone in earshot. Of course, no one was paying us any attention. Everyone had Mario's party on their mind. Including me. That was why I'd already been to the lingerie store after turning down April's idea before. She'd suggested I wear something sexy tonight, in case Eddie and I hooked up—a notion I was counting on. He'd said something like tonight would be the night we'd never forget.

April gasped and shut her locker. "You're going to wear them tonight?" she grinned, hooking her arm through mine. "Why, you little slut?"

"Shh," I hissed, unable to hide my amused smile. But damn, was I excited. "I can hardly wait," I blurted, lifting my face toward the ceiling. After lunch, we walked back to class. It was Thursday, and later Haywood High was having a Halloween dance. But everyone was looking forward to the after-party bonfire at Mario's. You'd think it was prom the way I was carrying on.

"I'm just glad my dad even agreed to let me go," I said.

April's face twisted sourly. "He's still pissed about that stunt Wright pulled?"

"He gave me a B-minus. My dad has a Nothing-But-A's policy. He totally flipped out. But Mom talked him out of grounding me, so." I shrugged. "Mr. Wright is such a jerk, though." I spun toward her, lowering my voice. "Did you really go into his bedroom?"

April's lips spread wide. "He's such a weirdo. He's got dozens of the same shirts and pants hanging in his closet. I could've sworn he was standing there watching us."

I squealed. "I would've *died*."

"We should've taken six outfits and been Simon Wright for Halloween."

We laughed so hard our eyes watered. "Shh," she

motioned toward Mr. Wright's room. I rolled my eyes and pushed the door open.

"Come in. Take your seats, everyone," Mr. Wright said as he stalked the room, dropping papers on each desk. "We're going to get right to it today—the results of your history essay."

I took a deep breath as I slid into my seat and peeked at my result—a fat red F staring back at me. I opened my mouth, but only a high-pitched squeak emerged. Clutching my paper, I spun toward him. "Mr. Wright, I don't understand. What did I do wrong?"

"Everything. Your paper is eighty percent fluff." He glanced over his shoulder. "You're welcome to a chance at rewriting it. By tomorrow morning, of course."

I sighed in relief. "Thank you so much, Mr. Wright."

"No problem. I need it to be twenty-five hundred words this time." He stomped on my hope.

"Um, sir, this one is only a thousand words."

He smiled. "Good—you can count."

I laughed nervously. "But I have piano lessons after school."

"So write your paper tonight, Brooklyn." He rolled his eyes impatiently.

"Yeah, but it's the Halloween dance tonight, and—"

He stared at me. "You're a smart girl. At least, I believe you are. I'm certain you know your grades are more important than partying. Or must I schedule a meeting with your parents?"

"No, sir." I slowly sank back into my seat, defeated.

"Great. Oh, and Brooklyn, because of our little conversation, you've got detention after school."

"Well, well. Look what the cat dragged in," Diego teased as I entered detention later.

"Hush your mouth, Diego," said Mrs. Humphrey, the English teacher. "Take a seat, Brooklyn."

I sat behind Diego, the only other student in the class. I began working on my homework since I couldn't research my essay. Twenty minutes later, upset about Mr. Wright, my mind was in a jumble. I needed a break. I slammed my pencil with a frustrated growl.

Luckily, Mrs. Humphrey had stepped out for a meeting.

Diego laughed. I really wasn't in the mood for his wisecracks. I closed my eyes and counted to three—just take a breather, Brook. The thought sounded serene in my head, but I felt like crying when I opened my eyes. I still had another forty minutes of detention, I wouldn't make my piano lesson, and I'd made no progress on that stupid essay. And oh—let's not forget—I was kissing the party goodbye. I hadn't even broken the news to Eddie yet.

"What's so funny?" I glared at Diego from the back of

the room, swiping furiously to stifle a tear.

Diego turned to face me. "You're taking this way too seriously. Are you actually doing homework?"

"Trying to, yeah. Aren't you?"

He held up his notebook. It was a sketch of Mrs. Humphrey, with wiry curls and glasses, riding a fire-breathing dragon. The artwork was fantastic.

I struggled not to smile. "You could get into trouble if someone sees that."

His lip curled into a sneer. "I am trouble."

"Whatever you say." I returned to my book but stole a glance at him as he rummaged through his backpack. He pulled out a bottle of scotch. My eyes flicked to the door in alarm. "What are you doing? If you get caught—"

"Will you calm down? I can hear Humphrey's heels miles away. Here, why don't *you* have a sip to take the edge off? Or are you too afraid?"

My eyes narrowed as I stuck out my chin, snatched the bottle, and, without thinking, took a long swig—ignoring the burn in my throat.

"Whoa—whoa." Diego's eyes went as wide as softballs. "You only need a swig." He quickly stripped the bottle from me.

I licked my lips. "You were saying?"

He gave me a brief salute. "Nothing, Serge." I laughed, feeling warm and tingly from head to toe. Diego took his shot and tucked the bottle away. "So, what's the matter?"

I blew a sloppy raspberry before explaining how Mr. Wright had ruined my life.

Diego shook his head sympathetically. "Wow. Global warming is nothing compared to your drama."

I shoved him. "I'm being serious. My dad will kill me. My timeframe is so limited. Plus, I really want to go to that party." My voice broke.

Diego clicked his tongue. "Well, I have one solution, but I'm not sure you'll like it."

I rested my chin in my hands. "I'm so goddamn frustrated I'll try anything." Diego drummed his thumbs on the back of his chair in thought. I cleared my throat. "So, let's hear it. We don't have all day—I most certainly don't." Diego rifled through his bag and produced a tiny zip-locked bag containing one pill. "What's that?" I asked, staring at the oblong white pill.

"Speed. It keeps you energized and alert—and—"

"Meth?" I squeaked, the whiskey curdling in my stomach.

He rolled his eyes. "I said you wouldn't like it."

"What are you even doing with that? That stuff's dangerous, Diego. If Coach Donahue finds out, he'll kick you off the swim team. Expel you even."

"You think I don't know that? Besides, I don't use it. Coach tests the team once a month, remember?"

"Then why do you have it?"

"Because I don't have a rich daddy." He mimicked my tone.

I couldn't argue. Diego's parents had died in a car accident, and to avoid foster care, his grandfather had taken him in. But his grandfather had little, and wasn't prepared for a kid around. Diego had to move into the tiny attic space. Wes told Eddie that Diego's grandfather was ailing, and if something happened, Diego planned to live on his own somehow.

"The kids who think they can buy their way through life are my biggest customers. They know the dangers of drugs, yet they risk it anyway." He shrugged nonchalantly. "The money's good."

"But—what if someone dies?"

"That won't be on my conscience. I'm not forcing anyone to do anything."

I pushed my pencil back and forth. "Would you say that if I were one of those people?"

He glanced up with a scowl. "Hell no. And you're not one of those people. This will be a one-time thing, so you can ace your stupid essay and still party tonight." He slid the bag across the desk. "It's on the house."

I blinked at it, confused that something so tiny could hold such power. Wait, was I actually considering that?

Chewing on my lip, I checked the clock. It was a quarter

to three. Maybe my piano teacher wouldn't mind if I was a bit late.

"Don't worry so much. Wright threw you a curveball. You can beat him at his own game. Try that just once and show him what you're made of. I'm sure he'll never mess with you again."

I clamped a hand over the bag and quickly shoved it into my pocket. "Look, this doesn't leave this room," I said through clenched teeth. Diego laughed. I grabbed a fistful of his shirt. "I mean it. No one is to know about this, Diego."

"Alright, alright." He threw up his hands, still grinning comically. I tugged him closer, catching a whiff of his musky cologne. His goofy grin faded as his eyes fixed on my lips. I released his shirt just as he cupped my chin and pressed his mouth to mine. A few seconds later, he pulled away. "There. We sealed the deal with a kiss."

My heart raced as I tried to keep my breathing steady. "That—can never happen—" I hiccupped, cheeks flushing.

Diego arched an eyebrow. "Did you like it?" His goofy grin returned. "Yeah. I thought so." He straightened up in his seat. That's when I noticed Riley watching us from the doorway.

8

BROOKLYN

NOW

"We look fantabulous!" April chirped as we left the nail salon, the mall alive with music, chatter, children laughing, and babies crying. I could barely hear my own thoughts.

Eddie still hadn't returned my calls. I held the phone to my ear, listening as it rang endlessly on his end before finally slipping to voicemail. I nearly wanted to throw it—I was that pissed.

"Where the hell *is* he?"

"Well, at least I know your cell works," a voice remarked. I spun around. It was Mack, standing behind us with her arms crossed, clad in a yellow-and-white apron from that pretzel place. Her dark hair was tucked under a matching hat, and her dramatic, smoky eyes narrowed.

"*Mackenzie*," I sputtered. "I meant to text you back, but something else came up."

"I can tell." She gestured at our fresh manicures. "But do you have a minute?"

"What do you want?" April interjected sharply, her tone taking me by surprise.

"To talk to Brooklyn. Are you deaf?" Mack snapped back.

April looped her arm through mine. "Sorry, but we're busy." She turned to pull me along.

"What are you doing?" I whispered, slipping away from her grasp.

"We shouldn't be talking to her after what happened," April murmured.

My God. I rolled my eyes. "Ignoring her doesn't solve anything either. Just meet me by Lips and Heels in ten minutes," I called back as I turned to face Mack.

April let out a choked sound and reached for me. "*Don't*."

"Ten minutes," I repeated over my shoulder. Mack and I fell into step as we headed toward the water fountain.

"What's chewing up your friend's ass?" Mack asked.

"Never mind April—she's in a rush to shop," I lied and forced a smile. Mack didn't return it. "I really meant to text back," I added, wondering if I should've just apologized.

After a few moments of silence, Mack settled on a bench and finally looked up at me. "Remember that hiking trip when you and I wandered off to chase a bigfoot rumor?"

I squinted and laughed. I hadn't thought of that in ages. "Mrs. Bernstein was so angry with us."

Mack smiled, tears glistening in her eyes. "I miss those times. I thought we were great friends."

I realized how lonely she must've felt without Riley. They weren't exactly close, but he was still her brother, and I hardly felt I was the right person to fill that void— especially not after everything. Still, I couldn't just ignore her. I brushed my hair behind my ear. "Times have changed, I guess. No one said we couldn't still be friends. It's just...right now, I've been really busy with..."

She shook her head. "Look, I get it, okay? I don't fit in with your clique, and I don't want to. But right now, I need your help."

I nodded. "Sure. Anything."

"I need you to help me investigate my dad. I think he killed Riley."

9

EDDIE

NOW

I sat on the basement stairs, my mind blank. I'd just killed my father. I watched as the anger drained from his eyes while he took his final, blood-curdling breath.

I jumped to my feet and staggered down the remaining steps. Wes was still sprawled on the battered sofa. "Wesley?" I gently tugged his shoulder.

He rolled over slowly, blinking away sleep. Even though the swelling on his face had subsided, his cuts and bruises still looked horrific. "What the hell?" he mumbled, peering at me. "What's going on?"

I took a sharp breath, my voice croaking, "I killed him."

"Killed him? Killed who?"

"Hank."

Wes scoffed and turned his back to me. "I want to kill that bastard too, but that's just wishful thinking."

I broke into sobs. "Hank's really dead, Wesley."

He slowly turned to face me, propping himself up on one elbow. "Damn—really?" Then he hoisted himself off the couch. "What happened? Hey—just breathe, alright?" I nodded, licking my lips as I struggled to steady my breathing. My insides felt like they were jittering like frogs. Trembling, I gasped for air as Wes gripped my shoulders and studied me with his clear eye. "What did you do?"

"I—I woke up. I wanted to call Brooklyn but couldn't find my phone. So I went upstairs to get it from Hank. I grabbed yours too. And your roll of money." I reached into my pockets to confirm—the items were there. I squeezed my eyes shut as tears wet my face. "Hank was sleeping on the kitchen floor, and I *stabbed* him. I just couldn't stop. Wes…there's blood everywhere."

Wes frowned. "Where exactly?"

"All over the kitchen floor, on the cabinets, on me…"

"But I don't see any," he whispered, shaking his head while eyeing me.

I extended my trembling hands and gasped—they were clean. "But…" I started.

Wes folded his arms. "Were you dreaming?"

"No. How did I end up with these?" I said, producing his phone and money.

"Whoa! You took that straight from his pockets?" He grinned, collecting the items.

I sniffed and wiped my face with my hands. "Are you even listening? Come on—I'll show you." We headed upstairs, and I hung back as Wes neared the kitchen.

"Is he in there?" he whispered, pointing. I nodded, biting the inside of my cheek. My feet felt rooted in place. I couldn't bring myself to face what I'd done. When he slipped into the kitchen, I held my breath. Seconds later, his sick moaning yanked me out of hiding. Wes wailed, *"It can't be."*

I staggered into the room, mouth hanging open. Hank was gone. I scanned the mess—the crushed cans, scattered bottles, shattered table—but there was no blood, no body.

Wes's laughter came from behind me. "Gotcha," he declared, pointing at me.

I swatted his hand away. "It isn't funny. He really was…"

"Must you two be so damn loud?" Hank grumbled, making both of us jump. I moved closer to Wes, facing Hank as though he were a ghost. He was slumped against the refrigerator, his head lolling slowly, looking half-awake. "Well, don't just stand there. Come help your old man up!" Hank stretched out his arms.

Wes and I quickly rushed over and grabbed his hands. Lifting him was like hoisting a dead body. He groaned before finally rising. He gave Wes a sideways glance and chuckled hoarsely, "You look like a raw rib-eye steak."

"Ha-ha," Wes sneered.

Hank hobbled to the doorway. "I better shower. I smell like piss."

We watched him go. "Yep. He's good and dead to me," Wes rolled his eyes.

"But I don't understand. How did I end up with our stuff back?" I whispered.

Wes shrugged. "Sleepwalking, maybe? You used to do it a lot after…"

I slowly nodded, remembering the time after Mom left. But that was ages ago. Why restart now?

That evening, Brooklyn rushed over with open arms, her voice filled with worry. "Eddie, I was *so* worried." She'd sent an urgent text for the group to meet at the park behind the school.

I squeezed her tight and kissed her. "I'm so sorry. Hank had my phone." I stroked her hair, drawing her closer.

She pressed her forehead to my chest. "I thought something had happened to you—I was terrified."

"Well, they definitely did a number on *you* at that party," April commented to Wes, frowning at his bruises.

He ignored her. "What the hell is this about?" Wes snapped at Brooklyn.

"We have to wait for Diego," she insisted.

Within seconds, his Charger roared down the street. "Alright. We're all here…" Diego called as he stepped out of the car. "What's so urgent?"

Brooklyn brushed her hair behind her ears. "We have a problem, guys. Mack came by. She thinks Coach Donahue killed Riley."

My hand flew to my mouth—I felt like I was going to be sick. We all stood in stunned silence for a beat until Diego burst into laughter.

"Dude?" Wes frowned at him.

"No… It's perfect. Don't you see? If she goes to the police with those claims, it throws them off our trail."

April nodded. "Well, that's one way to look at it."

"Guys, come on," Brooklyn said, her voice breaking. "That's sick, and you know it. Coach Donahue is innocent. We all know he is."

I stepped toward her to offer comfort, but she buried her face in her hands.

"Wait a minute," Wes interjected. "Why the hell is she telling you instead of going to the cops?"

Brooklyn sniffled. "She wants my help investigating him. You know—collecting evidence and all that."

"Evidence? From where?" I asked.

She shrugged. "I don't know—maybe at his home or his office. I just can't do it."

"Yes, you will," Diego stated firmly.

I turned to him. "*What*? She said she doesn't want to—"

"I don't care. If she plays along with Mack, she'll be our inside person to mislead them."

"Inside person? What are you talking about—?"

"Wait," Diego said. "From where I stand, we couldn't have asked for a better plan. I don't give a damn who feels guilty—I'm not going to jail for this. Sure, you might've done it, Eddie, but we all helped cover it up."

"I might've done it? Don't stand there and act like this is the first crime we've covered up. What about Mr. Wright?"

Diego scowled. "It's not like you were ever completely against it, Mr. I-Didn't-Make-The-Swim-Team. If the police start looking into any of us, you have the strongest motive in both cases."

I hesitated. Diego was right. Gasping, I turned away, tugging at my hair. I was completely screwed. How hadn't I seen it before?

"Shut the fuck up," Wes spat, as Diego laughed teasingly.

"Nobody's investigating anyone, but this whole Mack situation… Brook, just go along with her for a while. If it gets too weird or uncomfortable, just back out. I'm sure you can come up with an excuse." He fixed his gaze on her.

She nodded and then turned to me. "It'll be alright, Eddie," she promised, though I found it hard to believe.

10

EDDIE

THEN

"Just who the hell do you think you are?" Coach Donahue barked as he stormed into Mr. Wright's class on Friday, Halloween Eve.

Mr. Wright looked up from his desk and peered over his glasses at the intruder. "Excuse me? I'm in the middle—"

"I don't give a flying shit what you're doing. How dare you go behind my back and have my best swimmer pulled from the team!"

My ears perked up. Best swimmer? Who—Riley or Wes? If Coach was that worked up, it had to be Riley. Then I realized: Riley wasn't in class today. I stole a glance at the two teachers, silently praying it wasn't Wes. Hank would kill him. I still hadn't even told Hank I'd missed tryouts, and Wes's excuse about a delayed test was already on thin ice.

My heart sank as Mr. Wright uttered the name I'd hoped he wouldn't.

"Wesley failed his—"

Coach Donahue raised his hand to cut him off again. "He could've taken a makeup test. You did this deliberately to sabotage my race."

Mr. Wright exhaled a huff so forceful it might have fogged his glasses. "I don't know how *you* do things, Donahue, but Wesley's run out of favors and makeup tests. If his grades don't improve, I'm going to have to fail him. You'd better be glad the principal and I only dropped him from the team. And besides, this isn't something we should be discussing in front of my students."

"Then let's take it to the hallway," Coach Donahue roared. "This is far from over."

Placing both hands on his desk, Mr. Wright pushed himself up. "Really, Robert? Do you want to do this?" Coach Donahue didn't reply. He simply turned and headed for the door. Mr. Wright shot a pointed look in my direction. "Carry on. This should only take a few minutes," he said, trailing after the Coach. The door shut hard behind them.

I gulped and glanced at Brooklyn. "Where's Wesley?" I

whispered.

She shrugged. "I don't know. I think he left," she whispered back.

My stomach sank further. What the hell was happening? And why was I only just finding out now?

The door flung open again. "You can bet I'll speak to the principal about this on Monday," Mr. Wright called over his shoulder.

My brows dropped. I'd never seen two teachers argue like that before—it had to be serious.

"We're wearing those tonight," Riley declared on Saturday, brandishing a plastic bag. It was Halloween, and he had sent a group text calling for everyone to meet at his place after midnight. He and Wes had already ditched school yesterday. I caught a ride with Brooklyn and April, who waited in the car as I approached the group to find out what was happening. Riley shoved the bag toward Diego.

"Halloween masks?" he said as he pulled out a zombie mask and a clown mask. "We're too old to trick-or-treat, aren't we?"

Riley rolled his eyes. "Let's just get going."

Wes kept his arms folded, staring straight ahead. I tried to talk to him about what had happened, but he offered nothing. Besides, it was simple enough: Mr. Wright had pissed on our lives yet again.

"Where are we going?" I asked, noting the unusual quiet from Riley and Wes.

Diego tapped my arm. "Are you in or out?"

I glanced back at Brooklyn and April in her BMW, ready to follow.

I hopped in with the guys. Within five minutes, I realized exactly where we were headed—to Mr. Wright's house. I laughed nervously. "What are you guys planning?" I pressed. No one responded. "It's Saturday. Wright can't be in the hospital tonight. Besides, visiting hours are over." Still, silence. I continued, "I'm sure Wright changed the locks after our last encounter anyway."

Riley and Wes exchanged a brief glance but still wouldn't speak. Why were they acting so weird?

Then Mr. Wright's Jeep came into view in his driveway. He was definitely home.

"*Whoa.*" I grabbed Riley's shoulder and pointed at the windshield. "If he's here, what are we doing?"

Riley shrugged me off. "We're going in like before. Only this time, Wright is in for the scare of his life."

I looked at Wes, who wouldn't meet my eyes as he shifted his gaze toward the window. "I—I don't know about this. What if—"

"What if nothing, Eddie," Riley snapped, his dark eyes flicking to me through the rearview mirror. "It's time that piece of shit learned he doesn't own us. He doesn't get to play chess with our fucking lives."

"What am I going to do now?" Wes murmured. "I'm not going to get a scholarship for swimming because no one will ever know if I'm any good."

My shoulders slumped. We were both counting on our athleticism to get us into college. "We could be in even more trouble breaking into his home," I argued. "He could call the cops on us. Shouldn't we rethink this?" I wished Brooklyn were there to back me up, but her car was right behind us. Had they already filled her in on the plan?

"According to Wright, we're always in trouble," Diego observed.

"Exactly," Riley agreed. "We never do anything right by his standards. So what's the point? Yeah—we're going inside wearing these masks. So what if he suspects it's us? He won't be able to prove it."

"Who knows? Maybe after this, he'll leave us alone," Wes said. "Although it's too fucking late. The damage is already done."

I folded my arms, defeated. There was no talking them out of it.

Riley shut off the engine. "I want the skull," he said, reaching behind the seat for the bag.

Wes grabbed the jack-o'-lantern mask, and Diego took the zombie one. Naturally, I ended up with the clown mask. It wasn't even a horror clown mask—just a happy-faced, rosy-cheeked kiddie clown with tufts of red hair.

I rolled my eyes. "And what about the girls?" I asked. Brooklyn's lights were out, and neither she nor April had gotten out of the car.

Riley glanced at them. "They're not coming inside. April's hopping behind my wheel so she and Brook can be our getaway drivers." Suddenly, it sounded like a heist.

"Let's go." Wes couldn't be any more impatient.

I pulled on my gloves and mask and followed the others down the alley. The air was chilly and damp from the earlier storm. Unfortunately, I wasn't dressed warmly, and the stupid clown mask made my vision blurry. I stayed low, close to the dark silhouette leading the way as we sneaked to Wright's house.

This time, instead of slipping in through the back as before, we circled around the front. I wasn't sure what was about to happen and wished more than ever I could talk the guys out of it. The moment Riley calmly rang the doorbell, I knew I should have stopped them. But my brain went blank and my body just followed.

After a few beats, a bewildered Mr. Wright cracked his front door, squinting as if to ask which crazy person would be out at this hour.

"Trick or treat, motherfucker," one of the guys called as they shoved their way inside.

"Hurry up. Shut the door," Wes whispered to me. I stumbled in behind them, just as confused as Wright. What were we doing?

I adjusted my mask to clear my vision. Riley was gripping a length of rope. What the hell was going on?

"What the hell?" Mr. Wright echoed my thoughts, raising his hands as he backed away. Outside of class, he looked vulnerable—his frail body draped in a plaid robe and matching pajamas.

We stood in his living room, the TV humming softly with flickering shadows dancing on the walls from an old black-and-white show. A bowl of half-eaten popcorn and a can of diet Coke sat on the table.

"Sit down!" Diego ordered, pointing to the recliner.

Mr. Wright huffed an angry breath. "Now wait just a damn minute—"

Diego roughly grabbed Wright's arm and attempted to shove him into the chair, but Wright wriggled free. Wes moved in to help Diego, and together they forced Mr. Wright toward the seat, slamming him down. "Sit the fuck down," Diego repeated.

I stood frozen, watching everything unfold.

"You're not in charge anymore, *Simon*," Riley hissed as he circled Mr. Wright, snapping the rope.

Mr. Wright glared at Riley, clearly unafraid. His legs shifted to rise, but Diego and Wes pinned him down as

Riley wound the rope around his body. All three struggled, for Wright proved stronger than they expected.

Part of me wanted to laugh. What was their plan? Tie the guy up and then what?

Riley's patience wore thin. "Help us," he yelled back at me. I staggered forward and offered a hand to secure the knot.

Mr. Wright snickered and shook his head. "Look at you want-to-be tough guys. Pathetic."

Riley slapped him hard. "Shut up!"

I gasped—no one had said they were going to *hurt* Mr. Wright.

"This isn't your classroom," Wes said. "You're not in charge tonight, Simon."

Mr. Wright dipped his head, his shoulders bouncing as he laughed. "I try to do my job, and this is the thanks I get?"

I shifted nervously. Wright knew exactly who we were. "Guys?" I croaked, my voice muffled by the mask. "We should get out of here now."

Diego gripped Mr. Wright's hair and tugged his head back until he winced. "Didn't he tell you to shut up?"

In response, Mr. Wright's head collided with Diego's face, sending him sprawling backward in pain. Wright wriggled free, stumbled to his feet, the rope tangling around his legs.

"Don't let him get free," Riley shouted.

"Fuck," Diego muttered, clutching his head as he grabbed the end of the mask.

"Don't you dare show your fucking face," Riley warned.

This had spiraled out of control. What the hell were we still *doing* here?

Mr. Wright let out a hoarse cry, spun around, and brandished a baseball bat. "You think I don't recognize you, imbeciles? Diego. Riley. And, of course, the twins." He swung at me, cracking my shoulder.

Pain shot down my arm, numbing my fingers. "Ah!" I cried, stumbling back. As Wright raised the bat for another strike, Wes dodged and slammed into him, sending him crashing against a glass table, which shattered under his weight.

Time seemed to freeze as we all took in the sight. Wright lay in a mangled heap, his chin pressed to his chest and his head wedged under the broken table. Seconds stretched— then Wright gasped, his eyes flickering open, snapping us from our shock.

Mr. Wright made strange noises, pointing with a trembling finger.

"What the hell is he doing?" Riley murmured.

I turned to see an inhaler sitting on the mantel. Mr. Wright had asthma?

"Shit." Wes moved toward it.

"No!" Riley blocked him.

"What the fuck, dude?" Wes shoved him.

Riley shoved Wes back. I began toward the mantel, but Diego gripped my sore arm tightly, making me cry out in pain.

"We have to go," he urged me.

"No," I snapped. "We have to help him."

"We can't. Wright knows it's us," Riley argued, tugging Wes toward the hall. "Grab that rope and come on. We gotta go. *Run.*"

I stared at Mr. Wright. His chest heaved as if his lungs were about to burst. My stomach lurched.

Diego snatched the rope and shoved me from behind. "Go!"

We sprinted for the back door. Diego slammed it shut behind us as we dashed through the yard, our shoes crunching on dead leaves. We leaped over the fence and raced down the alley to the cars. The guys scrambled into Riley's station wagon, while I ran to Brooklyn's BMW.

"What the hell—?" she exclaimed, eyes wide.

I ripped off my sweat-soaked mask and immediately vomited.

11

EDDIE

NOW

It was the first day of school. Principal Marriott believed it was essential to begin with a meeting in the lecture hall.

"Everyone, please settle down. This isn't a hang-out session. I have an important announcement," Principal Marriott stated, standing confidently at the podium in a lavender pantsuit. Everything about her was crisp and on point—every curly salt-and-pepper strand was neatly in her bun, and her makeup was soft, elegant, and perfectly matched to her suit.

"First, welcome to Haywood High. I'm excited to see all of you again and look forward to a fulfilling year together. We are beginning this school year with the SAT test. I understand that a fellow student, Riley Donahue, is missing and that many of you were close to him.

"Please know that my door is open if any of you need to talk—no matter how embarrassing, personal, or touchy the subject may be. I'm here for you, and so is a grief counselor." Hushed whispers filled the hall. She cleared her throat and continued.

"As most of you know, we tragically lost one of our teachers last year, Mr. Simon Wright. For those who didn't know him, he was an outstanding individual with a passion for teaching. May his soul rest in peace." She paused briefly to scan the students.

Call me paranoid, but it seemed her eyes lingered on me just a beat too long.

I maintained my composure, hands clamped firmly to the sides of my legs. I didn't shift or make eye contact with anyone in my group. Ever since Diego's claim at the park, I'd been on edge. Wes remained unfazed, insisting that if I carried on as usual, no one would suspect a thing.

It was easier said than done, but I was determined to give it everything I had. My life depended on it. If I could just make it to the Nationals, I'd finally escape Haywood and its secrets.

"...I'd like you to welcome our new teacher, Miss Libby Harper," Principal Marriott announced, gesturing toward a short, petite blonde.

She had wide blue-green eyes that reminded me a bit of Margot Robbie's.

"Hello, everyone. I'm excited to be here." She spoke with a British accent, the complete opposite of Mr. Wright—young, friendly, and upbeat. Haywood High would tear her to shreds.

***

Later that evening, as we left the Japanese restaurant, Brooklyn sighed. "I'm sorry. I just wasn't that hungry."

I had convinced her to join me for dinner around six— early enough for her to be back home without her dad freaking out. She'd been moping all day, and I hoped dinner would cheer her up. Sushi was her favorite, yet she barely touched her plate.

"Is there something you want to talk about?" I asked for the hundredth time. "Is it about the Donahues?"

She sighed. "No. Yes. It's everything," she choked out before hurrying ahead.

I rushed to catch her, grasping her wrist. "Let's talk about it. What's on your mind?"

"I'm afraid, Eddie. I keep having these strange premonitions and dreams that something bad is going to happen to you."

"That's your problem?" I laughed. "You're not a psychic."

"Yes, I know, but it's still terrifying."

"It's all in your head. With everything going on, too much negative energy is weighing on you." I took both of her hands in mine. "Just let whatever happens happen. We're almost out of here. Julliard is just a short walk away. Try to focus for the sake of your grades." I managed a smile from her.

She then grabbed my face and kissed me. "You're right. All of this shouldn't be for nothing." Exactly my point. She bumped shoulders with me. "Let's go get ice cream."

I kissed her forehead, and that was when I saw a man standing a few feet behind her, his eyes fixed on us. There was something distinctly familiar about him—his scruffy beard, dark hair, and the long dark jacket, even though it was late summer. Yes, I recognized him: the creepy guy from the search party.

12

EDDIE

NOW

I grabbed Brooklyn's arm and pulled her along. "Let's get out of here."

"Hey, what's the matter?" she asked, frowning at my sudden mood change.

"Inspector Gadget," I muttered, casting my eyes over her shoulder to the figure behind her.

She laughed nervously. "Huh?" Then, checking over her shoulder, she gasped. "That guy from the search party? What is he doing here?"

"He's obviously following us. He must be a cop." I peeked back—and sure enough, he was heading our way. Shit. "Come on." I quickened my pace, bumping and parting through the crowd. I gripped Brooklyn's hand tighter as I sped along. I noticed the creepy asshole's pace quicken too. Breathlessly, we reached her car and scrambled inside, me at the wheel. I started the engine and sped away just as the guy stepped off the sidewalk in a mad dash.

"Who the hell *is* that?" Brooklyn cried.

"I have no idea. But he's definitely following us."

"Do you think he's trailing us now?" she asked, turning in her seat.

"No way he hopped in his car and chased us that fast." I sounded confident, though I kept glancing at the rearview mirror for reassurance.

"Eddie?" Brooklyn placed her hand over mine. If the steering wheel could feel, I'd have choking it by now.

"What are we going to do? If he's a cop, we can't keep running from him. It makes us look guilty."

I sighed, running my hand through my hair. "I know. It's bothering me that I have no clue what he wants. We didn't leave any evidence or anything...that I know of." I glanced at her.

"Maybe he just wants to question us about Riley. Isn't that his job—to ask his family and friends questions? No one said he had anything."

I shifted in my seat. "We need to keep our story straight. If someone comes around asking questions, we have to be consistent." She pressed her lips together and twirled a lock of hair. "Right?" I checked to see if she agreed.

"Or—we could follow through with that anonymous tip I mentioned. If the cops find Riley's car, it could at least steer them in a different direction. They wouldn't suspect foul play."

"Let's tell the others. I think it's the best solution too— the Donahues get closure, and it's a shut case."

If only things were that simple.

About an hour later, Brooklyn climbed into my lap as our kiss deepened. Her dad had called to say he was working a double shift and wouldn't be home until tomorrow afternoon. With her mom already away on a class trip with Brooklyn's little sister, we had the whole night to ourselves. Still, it was a school night and neither of us wanted to risk staying out late with the SAT on Friday looming. The news thrilled us so much that we stopped by a park to make out.

I tangled my fingers in her hair as we kissed passionately, our tongues wrestling. She pulled away to catch her breath, resting her face against mine. She smelled and tasted like peaches.

I licked my lips and stole a faint glance at her. She slipped off her top, and her hair cascaded in rivulets down her pale, bare shoulders.

"What are you doing? Somebody could *see* us," I said,

holding her shirt to her body.

She smiled slowly and shook her head. "No one's here but us, and this beautiful scenery," she whispered, leaning in carefully for another kiss. She tossed the shirt onto the passenger seat and pressed my hands into the small of her warm back, drawing me closer.

I shuddered and sighed into her mouth as we kissed again. She ran her fingers down my chest and abs, tugging at my belt. My eyes closed as she trailed kisses along my neck while unfastening my belt. Just as I relaxed, I heard a car door shut. My eyelids flew open. "Did you hear that?" I asked, catching her hands.

She stared, listening. "No…" she replied softly.

I slid her into the passenger seat and peered out the back window. "Is that someone's silhouette near that tree?" I whispered.

She sighed, glanced briefly, then ducked. "Maybe. I don't know." Quickly, she slipped her shirt back on.

I locked the doors and started the car. We weren't about to stick around and find out any more. Brooklyn remained silent for the entire ride back to my place. I could tell my paranoia was annoying her, but I couldn't help myself—we were in some pretty deep shit.

When I shut the engine, I took her hand. "I'm sorry about tonight."

She forced a smile. "It's okay, really."

"No—I wanted tonight to be special for you, to ease some of the tension. Instead, I made it worse by being so jumpy."

"It's not like I don't understand, Eddie. There's so much going on right now, I can't stay focused either. I feel like I'm losing it all the time."

I nodded, recalling my hallucination about killing Hank. "Yeah, I know what you mean. But you don't have to go through this alone. I'm always here for you."

She looked away, keeping her gaze low. "I know," she muttered. She wanted to say more but hesitated. Finally, with a gentle smile, she added, "You're sweet, Eddie." Then she hugged me. "Don't feel bad about tonight—I still had a great time. Hey…" She peered out at my house. "Since we're already here, why don't you show me your room?"

"Brooklyn, I don't think that's a—" I was cut off by the sound of glass shattering inside the house. *Hank.* Where was Wesley? "Brooklyn, go home," I said, fumbling with the door handle. I stumbled out from behind the wheel.

"What's wrong? Eddie?" she asked, grabbing my arm, but I broke free. Outside, the shouting and thudding grew louder—Hank was beating the hell out of Wes again.

"Brooklyn, I mean it. Go," I called over my shoulder as I stormed up the creaking deck.

"Why are you such a fuck-up?" Hank bellowed from inside.

I staggered into the hall. What was this about now? Wes getting fired? That was the only thing Hank seemed to keep tabs on. I found them in the kitchen—Hank's hands gripped around Wes's throat while Wes slumped, unconscious.

"Let him go, Hank!" I charged him, wrapping my arm around his neck and locking him in a chokehold. I tugged until he dropped Wes, whose body collapsed in a heap. "Hank, calm down, *please*." He reeked of booze and sweat.

Grunting, he thrashed violently, turning to slam me against the wall. His head crashed into mine—stars danced in my vision. My grip loosened, but I didn't let go.

"Hank, *stop*."

"You think you're a match for me?" he hissed, driving me against the counter and cabinets. Dishes clattered to the floor. He flung me like a ragdoll. Eventually, my arms fell limp. Before I could say another word, Hank turned and punched me in the stomach. I staggered away, gasping for breath, and caught a glimpse of orange. Brooklyn stood in the doorway, staring at Wes's body on the floor, then screamed as she rushed to his aid.

"No…go…home…" I sputtered between wheezes.

"Wesley, wake up," she sobbed, shaking him by the shoulders. "We have to help him."

"Why are you in my house?" Hank snapped at her.

Brooklyn gasped, slowly rising. "I'm sorry, but he *needs*

help." Her trembling finger pointed at Wes.

"That's not what I asked of you, you little bitch," he snarled, dodging toward her.

"Hank, don't—" I shouted, grabbing the nearest object—a metal toaster. With all my might, I hurled it at Hank's head. He staggered a shaky step forward and landed with a heavy thud in front of Brooklyn, his hand extended toward her feet. She jerked away with another scream. "Brooklyn, I told you to go home." I stooped, struggling to catch my breath.

"Why is this happening?" her voice broke. "I can call the police. I'm gonna go get my phone." She turned toward the door.

I hurriedly straightened. "No. *No*. Don't call anyone."

"But this isn't right. He could've killed Wesley."

I nodded, taking her hand. "Yes, I know. But Wesley's tough. Don't call the police, please."

"Why not?"

"Because he's still my dad." I drew in a sharp breath and rubbed my temples. "Look, Brook, you shouldn't be here." I pulled open the door. "Go home, okay?"

She crossed her arms. "*No*. Not unless you come with me. Let's leave together before Hank wakes up. Please?" Her lip trembled.

I shook my head. "I can't. I'll be fine, I promise." Leaning over, I kissed her forehead before gently ushering her out the door.

"Eddie, please…" she reached for me, but I shut the door. Her palm slapped against the other side. *"Eddie?"*

A lump swelled in my throat as I turned the lock.

13

BROOKLYN

NOW

With a hoarse groan, I slammed my algebra book shut. I could hardly concentrate on a single word without the Hawkins family invading my thoughts. I knew the twins had dubbed Hank a monster, but I hadn't grasped just how true that label was.

April was going to *kill* me. I had chewed and mangled my freshly manicured nails.

Once again, Eddie hadn't texted. I kept telling myself that I shouldn't have left him—or Wesley—for that matter. We should've forced him into the back seat and gotten him out of there.

And gone where? *Here?* Dad would have lost it if he

discovered both Hawkins boys sleeping in his house. There was the ratty cabin, but we couldn't go back there—we had sworn never to return after Riley's… accident. Besides, if our stalker was indeed who we suspected, trailing us to a crime scene was the last thing we needed.

I ran my ruined nails through my hair, unable to shake the image of Hank's enraged, hostile face as he pursued me. What the hell could drive someone to that extent? I could smell Hank's booze from a mile away—and it made sense—he didn't allow visitors because he was an abusive alcoholic.

Damn, the signs were everywhere, especially in Wesley, but we dismissed his beatings as random fights—like the incident at Mario's party. Could Hank have beaten him up after that as well?

I didn't notice I had started pacing until the steady patter of my bare feet reached my ears. I bit my lip as my brain screamed in protest, squeezing my eyes shut and covering my ears.

"Just calm down…" I murmured, steadying my breathing as my shoulders rose and fell. "That's it, girl. Now, focus and study for the test." I sank back into my desk chair and flipped open the book. I wasn't a math genius, but algebra had never really been a challenge.

Frustrated, I snapped my pencil. How could I hope to solve these equations when my entire life was one unsolvable mess?

I stared at the open pages, squinting at the droplets of water evaporating on the blurred words. When had the tears started streaming?

"That's it." I stood abruptly. Though I was home alone, I slid quietly over to my underwear drawer and fumbled for the pill bottle. Just as my fingertips grazed it, a knock at the window made me spin around. "Eddie." I slammed the drawer shut and rushed to let him in, wrapping him in a hug. "Where's Wes?"

"Diego picked him up. He even brought me here," Eddie replied.

"Diego?" I asked, frowning. Why hadn't I heard a car? I slowly turned away, caution rising—what if Dad came and caught me? I glanced at the drawer to confirm it was shut.

"You mean Diego knows about Hank?"

He turned to face me. "I never mentioned Hank or invited you over because it's embarrassing. Our worlds are so different. Look at this place," he said, glancing around my room. "My entire house is dwarfed by the size of this bedroom."

I stifled a laugh. "You're exaggerating now."

He smiled, cupping my chin gently. "You're my idea of perfection."

"Eddie…" I sighed. "No one is perfect—not even me…" Especially with all these secrets.

Eddie executed a perfect somersault in the pool. I sat at the edge, letting my feet splash in the water as I watched him—so serene, gliding freely beneath the surface. It was just as I'd imagined during my Jeux d'eau practice—minus that ominous red cloud, of course. He resembled a graceful underwater creature, each limb perfectly straight, slicing elegantly through the water.

After the day's turmoil, it felt good to unwind on this peaceful night. The sky was a deep indigo, dotted with bright stars. The air was warm, carrying a gentle, autumnal breeze. It was perfect until JoJo arrived, barking annoyingly at Eddie and me. That was the moment I realized Dad had trained him.

"Shoo," I spat, waving JoJo away. The dog cocked his head at me, then trotted off in the opposite direction. Stupid dog. I rolled my eyes, watching as Eddie performed another flip, diving so deep that he vanished from sight. I edged closer for a better view, and could just make out Eddie's form—a dark lump drifting near the bottom. Had he lost consciousness?

Instantly, I spotted Wes crumpled in the kitchen. "Eddie?" I croaked, pushing off into the pool. The shock of the cold water matched the panic mounting in my chest. "Eddie, are you okay?" When he still didn't surface, I dove under. I found him crouched low and motionless, his back turned to me, his arms hanging lifelessly. Oh no.

I swam forward and grabbed him. He spun around, startling me. Realizing it, he slipped past me and guided me to the surface, but I shoved him away. "You nearly gave me a heart attack," I panted.

"I'm sorry. I was just practicing my breathing techniques," he mumbled.

"Breathing techniques, my ass. You weren't even moving. I thought—" I groaned in a low scream, shoving him again. Eddie laughed and splashed me. "It's not funny." I splashed him in return, half-smiling as he dodged gracefully backward. Tilting my head, I studied him. "How do you hold your breath that long?"

"Blame Hank. When Wes and I were younger, he would hold our heads underwater—shoving our faces in like bathwater or dishwater. It was as if he contemplated drowning us and then suddenly changed his mind." He shrugged. "Our lung capacities grew, and eventually he got bored waiting for us to thrash for air."

I looked away and whispered, "That's horrible."

"Yeah. On the flip side, Hank inadvertently improved my swimming skills. Swimming is going to be my lifeline out of Haywood. And once I make it to the Olympics and you're at Juilliard, we can escape to somewhere warm for a break..." He moved closer, grinning. "Maybe Hawaii or someplace like that."

I heard him, though my mind was drifting. "Can I ask you something?" I said. He nodded, so I continued, "Where's your mom? Do you know where she went when she left?"

His smile faded. "Two men in jumpsuits took her."

"Took her?" My eyes widened. "But I thought she just left."

"No. I remember standing at the window, watching the van dump her. It was the hospital—AWA. I'll never forget those letters."

I gasped. "The Angel Wing Asylum? But that's a mental institution,"

"Yep. That's where my mom is."

"I'm sorry; I didn't know she was… ill."

"She wasn't—at least, not that I recall. Hank accused her of every possible lie, craziness being one of them." He shook his head. "I still hear him screaming about her having an affair. I didn't understand what that meant, but it must've been his ultimate transgression for him to slam her face against the wall."

I shifted, my gaze unfocused. I wondered if Eddie still felt the same about cheating now that he knew better. Guilt washed over me—I still hadn't told him about that kiss with Diego. Was it really cheating, though? I hadn't even kissed him back, yet I enjoyed it.

"Wes and I plan to visit her one day," he interjected. "But every time we consider it, Wes backs out. He hates her for leaving us with Hank. Even though Hank forced her hand, Wes remains bitter. She made us promise to take care of Hank, no matter what."

I scoffed. "She did? But why?"

"Love? I don't know—it beats me. That's why I wouldn't let you call the cops tonight. They wouldn't do anything anyway—they treat Hank like he's one of their own."

"Eddie, no offense, but your mom's been away for too long. Maybe it's time to drop that promise and start thinking about what's best for you. Hank could've killed Wesley tonight. And forgive me, but if that had been you— or if it ever comes close—you know I'd tell my dad. He'd know who to call if the cops wouldn't help."

He slowly grinned. "You'd actually call a rescue team for me?"

I nodded and motioned for him to come closer. As he inched over, I splashed him again. He laughed, boxing me in by grasping the edge of the pool on both sides. We were nose to nose. He gave a quick peck on my lips, but I took hold of his face and pressed my lips to his with longing. Eddie returned the kiss passionately, lifting me up as my legs wrapped around his waist while we caressed each other.

After a beat, he broke the kiss to catch his breath. I

continued kissing him—trailing from his broad face up toward his earlobe. He shuddered as I moaned softly into his ear.

"Babe?" I whispered, tickling his ear with my tongue.

He chuckled, shaking his head. "What are you doing?"

"How about we try again?"

"Try what exactly?"

"You know." I raised my eyebrows, and when he still didn't pick up on it, I slid my hand down from his abs to his shorts.

He pulled away so suddenly that my legs fell from around his waist.

"What is it?" I asked, stroking his face and meeting his eyes. "Don't you want to? I damn sure do." Eddie looked incredibly sexy—his body soaked, his hair damp and curly.

"Yes, but—we agreed to wait, and…"

"Sure, but haven't we waited long enough?" I clutched his face, attempting to kiss him once more, but he pulled away. I sighed.

"I'm sorry," he whispered.

I forced a smile. "It's fine. Let's just go watch a movie."

A few hours later, I sat up in bed. Eddie was sleeping on the floor, ready to hide under the bed if Dad showed up—but I didn't see Eddie himself. Only his sleeping bag, blankets, and pillows remained.

I coughed dryly as I padded to the window and pushed it open wide. The room was so hot that my shirt clung to my back. I peered down at the empty driveway—the coast was clear. But where was Eddie? Had he gone home?

It was unbelievable—we had the whole house to ourselves, and all we did was watch anime with a pillow between us. I didn't understand. Could it be that Eddie wasn't into me that way anymore?

My heart pounded anxiously as I coughed again. I couldn't bear to think about it then. If I didn't satiate my thirst soon, I might choke to death.

I opened my bedroom door, expecting the relief of cool air, but instead, I gasped in horror. Bloodstains dotted the floor alongside dark red drag marks. I clutched my mouth, wondering—what had happened?

My eyes followed the trail slowly, leading around the corner. Whoever was bleeding...or whatever had done this...was back there.

I stepped carefully over the stains, hearing low, repetitive murmurs—Eddie's voice, perhaps. "Eddie?" I called, staggering over swiftly.

There he was on the floor, back turned to me, arms hugging his knees as he rocked and muttered repeatedly, *"You can't hurt us now. You can't hurt us now."*

"Eddie, what are you doing, babe?" I asked shakily,

reaching for his shoulder. His eyes were glazed, still chanting that phrase. Something was terribly wrong. I shook him. "Eddie?" His head wobbled on his shoulders, and I closed my eyes before delivering a hard slap. When I opened my eyes again, he was blinking rapidly, having snapped out of his trance.

"What's happening?" he mumbled.

"I don't know. I found you here, mumbling and completely spaced out, and there's blood all over the..." I trailed off as I stared at the blood. Where had it come from?

"Eddie, are you hurt?"

"I don't feel anything," he said in a foggy tone. He tried to stand, letting out a sickening moan. "H-how did I get this?" He held up my letter opener—my sixteenth birthday present from Dad—its sterling silver blade now drenched in bright red blood. Eddie slowly rose, only to stumble into my arms. "Oh, no. *No*," his voice rising in panic.

"What the—" I paused and then screamed. JoJo lay in a mangled heap of blood and fur in the corner of the balcony. "JoJo!"

"I'm so sorry. I'm sorry," Eddie sobbed, clinging to me.

I looked back at him through teary eyes. "Eddie, how could you do this?"

His body trembled. "I—I don't know. I don't remember. Hank came into your room. He was after us."

"*Hank?*" I squinted. "Eddie, there's no one here but us.

Were you sleepwalking?" He gulped and broke into sobs again, burying his face in my nightshirt.

I cautiously reached out to comfort him while casting a glance at what remained of JoJo. Even though I hated that damn dog, he didn't deserve to end up like that.

14

BROOKLYN

NOW

I saw nothing like it. Eddie was a wreck—he wouldn't go anywhere near JoJo. He left the disposal of the dog to me while he did his best to scrub away the bloodstains. I still couldn't wrap my head around how he had done something so awful while sleepwalking. Poor JoJo.

As we drove out to the woods to get rid of JoJo, Eddie pressed his puffy, red face against the window, quietly shedding tears. If that weirdo stalker trailed us into the woods, he'd only confirm his suspicions when he found JoJo's remains. I didn't mention that to Eddie. It would have just upset and worried him more. Later, he insisted I take him home, saying he couldn't trust himself to be alone with me if he had another episode.

———————

I left for school early, unable to face my little sister after telling my parents that JoJo had run away.

"Parasomnia?" Mack called over my shoulder after the last bell rang.

I closed my Google search and quickly shoved my phone into my pocket. While stashing my things in my locker, I felt compelled to look up sleepwalking—the causes and dangers. Of course, stress could trigger it, but sleepwalking was also known to be hereditary. Perhaps Eddie got it from his mom? Could that be why Hank had her committed to an asylum?

It was probably best for Eddie to see a doctor. What he did was dangerous—if it happened again, it might be even worse.

I turned to Mack, whose hair hung to her shoulders in a single braid off to the side.

"Welcome to the club. I haven't gotten a wink of sleep in ages." I said nothing back, though I understood her frustration. "Anyway, it's nosey of me to pry. Well, considering what we're about to do..." She rolled her eyes. "Ready to go?"

"Um, soon. I just have to finish arranging my locker and, yeah...I'll be ready." I forced a smile. We were about to go on our first stakeout of Coach Donahue. Since he didn't leave the school until five, Mack wanted to show me around her house and see if I noticed anything unusual.

"Okay, I'll wait for you at the entrance." She turned and trotted off.

I exhaled, watching her leave. Unlike the rest of the gang, I thought it was the sickest idea we'd come up with—encouraging her to go against her father, an innocent man, when we knew the truth. We'd caused Riley's death, and I had played the most prominent role.

Keeping my emotions in check, I spun around, got my things, and shut my locker.

"Hey." April popped up. "Did something happen between you and Eddie? He wouldn't look your way the entire day, and we *all* know his world revolves around you."

God, I wished she'd stop with that. Just because Wes didn't love her didn't mean she had to tease Eddie. She grabbed my arm. "Wait, don't tell me—you two tried to…" Her doe eyes flicked around the hall. "…hook up and Eddie couldn't manage it?" She leaned in.

I shoved the horrifying JoJo moment to the back of my mind. "Will you come off that already? I should've never told you."

"Alright. Forgive me." She threw her hands up. "Hey, let's go have a post-birthday celebration. I'm starving. What do you want—sushi? We could study for the test, too, to pass the time."

I groaned. "I hate to turn down such a tempting offer, but Mack's waiting for me." I nodded in her direction.

April's grin faded. "Mack? Oh, well, don't let me keep you from your new bestie." She batted her lashes.

I shook my head in disappointment. "That's not fair—it was you guys' idea. You always make me do the dirty work."

She folded her arms. "Don't take it out on me. Maybe Diego suggested it because you're such a good actress." My jaw dropped, leaving me speechless. "I'm just saying." With a shrug, she turned and walked away.

Later, Mack said, "I have to charge my phone a bit. You can look around," after letting me inside her house. "Just keep it down, though—Mom's in the back taking a nap."

"How is she?" I whispered, muting my phone.

Mack sighed and shrugged. "You know how cancer goes."

I blinked, expecting more, but she just stared blankly. Not knowing what else to do, I nodded.

"I'll be back," she said, disappearing around the corner.

I shuffled over to the den—a small space with a loveseat, coffee table, and a small TV balanced on a pile of books. I glanced at the floral bedsheet serving as a curtain, recalling the rumors about the Donahues struggling with Mrs. Donahue's medical bills. I hadn't really given it much thought before.

"As you can see, my father removed all of Riley's photos," Mack said, appearing behind me.

I scanned the walls and realized she was right. There were pictures of Mrs. Donahue, the coach, and Mack during her Providence Academy days, but none of Riley.

"Weird, right?" Mack asked.

I licked my lips. "I don't know. Maybe…it's just too tough for Coach Donahue to see Riley."

"I thought that at first, too. But come, look at Riley's room." She waved me down, and at the end of the hallway she quietly creaked open the last door. The light flickered on, revealing what seemed like a storage room.

"He boxed Riley's stuff?" I blinked, taking in all the boxes and bins overflowing with familiar clothes, shoes, and Riley's fav baseball caps. Taking a breath, I was hit by Riley's scent—a mixture of vanilla and mint—until my throat began to ache.

Mack nodded. "How does he know Riley isn't coming back? Why would he do something like this? Unless he killed him."

"None of that is proof of such a heinous accusation, Mack. You're talking about your father," I whispered, gulping hard to keep down the bile rising in my throat. I staggered into the hall, gasping for air, my eyes blurring as I stooped and clutched my knees.

"Are you okay?" Mack appeared by my side.

"I'm sorry—I know..." I sucked in deep breaths. "...your mom is asleep in the next room..." my voice trembled.

Pull it together, Brook. Snap out of it.

I shut my eyes, haunted by Riley's last moments—his eyes wide with terror, grasping nothing but air.

I started sobbing.

"Hey—" Mack's voice was gentle as she placed a hand on my back. "I'm sorry. I had no idea you and Riley were that close. Come on, let's go to the kitchen. I'll make you some chamomile tea."

***

"You were right about this tea," I said after downing the last sip. "It really calms you." I placed her thermos in the cupholder. Mack and I were in my car, parked at the end of the block near school, with Coach Donahue's black Honda visible in the lot.

Mack waved her hand. "Luckily, we still had some left. It really helps my mom sleep." Then she turned to me. "Listen, if this is too much for you, I understand."

"No. It's just...why did you choose me to help you?"

She chuckled. "Well, I don't have a car. I couldn't

possibly do a stakeout in an Uber." I smiled, but then froze as Mack suddenly reached over and grabbed my hand. "You were the most honest, kind person I knew at Providence. No matter who was in trouble, you always tried to help. I never forgot that about you." Her words struck me like a knife.

"That's—sweet of you, Mack. Speaking of Providence Academy, why did you leave?" I blurted. She pulled away and shifted. "I'm sorry—if you don't want to talk about—"

"No, it's fine." Her chipped neon green nails twirled at the end of her braid. "What did people say?"

I hesitated. "They said Providence became too expensive." I decided not to mention Mrs. Donahue's mounting bills or the rumor about her being... inappropriate.

She cocked her head. "That's partly true. My parents could afford it, but then my mom got sick."

"Oh—I'm sorry."

"Do you remember Sandy?" she suddenly asked.

Immediately, her image flashed in my mind—tall Sandy with her athletic build and pixie-cut hair, probably a year older than us at Providence.

I smiled at the memory. "Yeah. I always wanted her on my team during competitions."

"She was amazing at everything she did," Mack said, her gaze distant. "She was my first crush. I told her how I felt and ended up grossing her out. She went to the teachers and spun some story about me feeling her up. Next thing I knew, Providence did my folks a favor by kicking me out."

I gasped. "*What?* I'm so sorry, Mackenzie."

She shrugged with a painful smile. "I'm sure people said I was a weirdo or some shit."

"No. I heard nothing like that. But hey, Sandy was a stuck-up bitch, anyway."

Mack stared at me, eyes wide. "OMG. The Disney Princess knows the b-word." She made me laugh. I playfully shoved her, about to retort, when she hushed me and pointed to her window. Coach Donahue hurried to his car and sat behind the wheel. I turned my key, preparing to follow him, but he didn't move. "What the hell is he doing?" Mack muttered after several minutes passed.

"Maybe he's on his phone?" I guessed, seeing him peering down at his lap.

"Hey—isn't that your boyfriend?" Mack nudged me.

"It's his brother," I said slowly, watching as Wes rapped on the coach's window before climbing into the passenger seat. Then, Coach Donahue's Honda started moving. I followed him, careful to keep my distance.

Mack and I stayed silent throughout the fourteen minutes we trailed her dad until suddenly he pulled into a motel lot. I shot a glance at Mack, whose forehead creased as she nibbled on her chipped nails.

Wes got out and jogged inside. After several minutes, he returned and hopped back into the car, and soon the Honda was on the move again. Eventually, I realized he was taking Wes home.

"What the hell was that about?" Mack asked as I dropped her back at her place.

"I don't know." What were a teacher and a student doing at a motel? Technically, Coach Donahue didn't go inside. But what if Wes had reserved the room for them…to return to later? I gasped.

"Are you thinking what I'm thinking?"

I turned to her. "What are you thinking?" We stared at each other in silence for a moment.

"If my dad is messing around with his student… That bastard."

"You don't know that for sure, Mack. We only know he dropped Wesley off at a motel."

She bit her lip. "You're right. I don't know. But I'm going to find out."

"Mack, just let the cops do their job, okay? We're driving around spying on your dad—it might not be the smartest idea." I didn't want to get involved anymore. If Coach Donahue and Wes were…hooking up…what was I to do? *Who* was I to tell? Eddie, maybe. But right then, it was only rumors. "Let's not jump to conclusions, okay?" I urged. She nodded, though her eyes were faraway. "What is it?" I touched her arm, and she blinked out of her trance.

"None of it makes any sense. Where would Riley go? It's not like he would've told me anyway—he doesn't give a shit about me."

My eyes lowered as I recalled the time Riley cracked a joke about Mack trying to steal his first girlfriend, calling her a freak in front of the whole cafeteria. And yet here was Mack, worrying her heart out about where that creep might be.

"All you can do right now is be there for your parents and let the cops handle the rest, alright?" She shrugged and glanced away, but I gripped her hand tighter. "Okay?"

"Fine. I will. It's just going to take some deep understanding of why my dad is erasing Riley's memory. He—I don't know. He's up to something. Mom's not all there most of the time." She tapped her temple. "Anyway, thanks. It's nice to have somebody to talk to." She pulled me into a tight hug then grabbed her thermos.

"Mack?" I called as she started to leave. "Why don't we hang out sometime?"

She smirked. "Well, I guess you owe me a cup of coffee, so why not?" Laughing, she hurried from the car.

I waited until she was inside before pulling off. Traffic caught me on my route home, giving me time to reconsider what had just happened. I couldn't decide what to make of Wes and Coach Donahue—I didn't want to believe they were involved, but what other explanation was there?

Nearly a half-hour later, I reached my driveway. As I walked up the pavement, the front door swung open.

Dad stepped out. "Where have you been? I've been calling and texting."

Damnit—I'd muted my phone back at Mack's place. "I'm sorry. A girlfriend really needed me."

"Well, you're needed in there. Someone's been waiting to talk to you."

I frowned. Who? I followed Dad inside and heard voices in the kitchen—Mom's voice and some deep baritone I didn't recognize. I entered and froze.

Sitting at the table, wearing his usual long coat, was our creepy stalker. He rose with a smug expression, probably because I couldn't run away.

"Hello, Brooklyn." He stopped in front of me and extended his hand. "I'm Detective Ron Brody."

15

EDDIE

THEN

"Welcome aboard, Edward!" Coach Donahue called, extending a hand to help me out of the pool. I wanted to smile, but everything felt so off—Simon Wright was dead, and we'd invaded his home and essentially murdered him. The rest of that weekend became a blur. Riley took over because we were too hysterical to think straight. He had disposed of anything that could serve as evidence—the masks, gloves, even that stupid rope. Wright's death was under investigation, and it had my nerves shot to the max.

Since Wes had been kicked off the team, Coach Donahue held swim tryouts again. Wes figured it was destined for me to make the team, even though Hank reminded him daily what a loser he was for being cut.

"You'll fit in with the team really well," Coach Donahue said. "I just hope you're not involved in any illegal substances. I have a strict no-drugs policy and test my boys every month—I'll kick anyone off the team if I catch them using."

"I don't take anything, sir," I vowed.

He stared at me for several seconds before nodding and ruffling his dark hair. "The opioid epidemic is sweeping through our youth. I wish parents and teachers would get more involved in stopping it. But then again, you kids never tell us everything, do you?" He arched an eyebrow.

My face flushed, and I struggled to force Wright out of my mind.

He gripped my shoulder. "Listen, you can come to me with anything, alright? Do you hear me?" His eyes burned into mine, hinting he had more to say—or maybe he already knew something. "I wish Riley could be more like you and Wes. You guys are driven. Riley only swims because I push him. Without me, he wouldn't apply himself to anything." I didn't know how to respond—no one prepared me for a Riley-onslaught. "Shit. I'm sorry," he chuckled nervously. "Riley and I had a huge blowup this morning, and I just..." His words trailed off. "Never mind that. Congrats on making the team."

"I'm ecstatic to be here, sir. You can count on me."

He smiled. "Well, this calls for a celebration, doesn't it?"

I wasn't in the mood, but Wes insisted we meet at the bowling alley, our usual hangout. "Yeah. We're heading over to Pin Palace tonight for pizza," I said halfheartedly, with a shrug.

"Awesome. But—don't forget about the team captain race. I secretly wanted to give you the title, but that wouldn't be fair to everyone else. So...may the fastest swimmer win." He winked.

That, without a doubt, was me.

I made my way to our usual booth in the back where Wes, Diego, and the girls sat, looking as gloomy as I felt. We couldn't pretend as if nothing had happened—someone was *dead* because of us. Life would never be the same. I slid in beside Brooklyn and held her hand under the table.

"We need to talk," Wes said. "I've been texting you all day."

"My battery died. What's the problem?"

"It's Riley," Diego replied.

"Riley?" I echoed, just noticing his absence. "What did he do?"

Diego slammed his palm on the table. "He crashed my fucking car."

"Shh," Wes hissed. "Keep your voice down."

I frowned. Diego never lets anyone else drive his baby.

"How did that happen?"

"Riley's blackmailing us," April answered.

Brooklyn shifted, releasing my hand.

"What?" I asked, turning to April. "What do you mean?"

"He claims he kept everything from that night," she whispered, eyes wide. "The masks, the rope, the gloves."

"But I thought he burned them. I don't understand. Why would he…?"

"The punk bitch lied," Wes snapped.

"But I don't get it. Why would Riley do that?"

Wes sighed, losing his patience. With his elbows on the table, he massaged his temples, leaving red finger marks. "He's threatening to go to the cops and pin everything on us unless we give him what he wants."

"Which is what, exactly?" I exploded.

Diego snarled, "He wanted my car for a date last night but couldn't drive it because it's a stick shift. Dumb fucker. Now it's going to cost me a fortune to fix."

"A date with whom?" April demanded. "Because he made me take photos of Jemma Hartley changing in the locker room." Jemma was captain of the cheer squad.

Brooklyn, who'd been quiet, gasped and spun toward April. "April, you didn't."

April nodded grimly. "That isn't even the worst part. I had to Photoshop them so it looks like Jemma is in his bedroom."

Brooklyn's jaw dropped. "But Jemma's dating the captain of the basketball team. You *can't* give those to him, A—you could get in serious trouble."

"We're already in trouble," April said in a lowered voice. "Don't you get it? Riley has our backs against the wall."

"We," Brooklyn said, wagging a finger at April, "did nothing. We never went inside you-know-who's house." Technically, she was right. How could Riley blackmail them if they weren't there?

"You can believe that bullshit if you want," Diego cut in. "We're all just as culpable as the next person. Every one of us wanted revenge on *you-know-who*."

"Wait. Is Riley using something else to blackmail you, April?" Wes asked, narrowing his eyes.

She nodded slowly. "Riley wrote my essay during midterms. I know it was wrong—especially now that I know he kept a copy. He said he'd tell people I stole it if I tried to deny it."

Wes's mouth opened, but he paused, staring out the window. "Shit. How'd he know we'd be here?"

I turned just in time to see Riley climbing out of his mother's car. My heart dropped. "I told Coach Donahue we were celebrating here." Everyone groaned.

"Thanks a lot," Diego muttered, rolling his eyes.

"I didn't know."

Within seconds, Riley strode back to our table.

"Everyone's here," he announced, spreading his arms in fake surprise. His face twisted into that famous James Franco smirk. Nudging me over, he slid in beside me.

I huffed, fighting the urge to punch him. "Riley, what the fuck? Why the hell are you doing this to us?"

"Me? My friends are gathering behind my back. What happened to my invitation? What's the occasion?" he taunted.

Wes crossed his arms. "Kick-Your-Ass Day."

Riley smirked again. "I highly doubt that."

I elbowed him in the ribs. "What is your bullshit about?"

"You know damn well what it's about. I'm sick of being pissed on by all of you," Riley hissed, slamming his fist on the table.

"But we never did anything to you," April whined.

Riley scoffed. "Oh please. *'Poor Riley, with the sick mother, outdated car, and hand-me-downs.'* And you two..." He turned on Wes and me. "If my dad compares me to you one more time..." He clenched his fist. "He only gave you team captain because he loves you that much," he spat at Wes.

"I got captain because I'm faster than you, shit-face," Wes snarled back.

Riley slapped his arm over my shoulder and pulled me close. "It doesn't matter this time because you're going to lose the team captain race on purpose." He jabbed me in the chest.

I glared at him. "You're kidding."

"I'm as serious as an *asthma* attack." He pretended to wheeze.

My heart sank. I had struggled like hell to get on the team—even taking my brother's spot—and here Riley was, depriving me of my chance to prove myself. He was lucky I didn't pound his face into dust.

"Why are you involving Jemma in this?" Brooklyn asked.

Riley scowled. "Because that stuck-up bitch said I wasn't good enough for her."

"So that's it," Diego finally said. "You're just going to go around wreaking havoc on everyone because your life is a mess?"

Riley cocked his head. "Yes, that's exactly what I'm doing. But you're missing the main point—I will come out on top in the end."

"You don't have a damn thing on me, Riley," Brooklyn declared. "And I will never do any twisted crap you ask."

Riley's stare was so cold that it sent shivers down *my* spine.

BROOKLYN

"Authorities have now determined that Simon Wright's death was accidental. It appears he fell, injured himself, and couldn't reach his inhaler. There were no signs of forced entry, and nothing was stolen from the home, according to Mrs. Wright."

Mom turned the TV down when she noticed I was there. "That is so awful. Brooklyn, you kids must be devastated. Wasn't he a class favorite?"

Where in the hell had she heard that? I forced a pained smile and bobbed my head.

She brought a hand to her chest and shook her head. "Truly awful."

I took a slow breath, making a conscious effort not to dwell on it. "I came to say goodnight. It's been a long day," I added, seeing the worry lines crease her face. "I'm okay— just tired."

"Alright. Have a good night, sweetie. Your father's working late, so it's just JoJo and me tonight." She patted the couch as our cocker spaniel trotted in.

The devil in disguise—I stifled a laugh. "K. Have fun." I bounded up the stairs, desperate to bury myself under the covers. The moment I approached my door, I knew something was wrong. The window was wide open. There was no way I'd done that and forgotten—I wasn't alone. I nudged the door open with my toe and scanned the dim room. I saw no one. After a moment, I stepped inside.

"Boo!" Riley jumped out and grabbed me.

A tiny yelp escaped my lips I prayed Mom hadn't heard. "What the hell are you doing in my room?" I demanded, jerking away from his grip.

"You weren't replying to my texts, so I came to check if you were still alive," he cackled.

"That's because I've got nothing to say to you." I shoved him, adding, "And keep your voice down—my sister's asleep in the next room."

"That's right. Little Janie. I bet she just adores her amazing big sister, doesn't she?" he teased, flashing a smile.

I shuddered, recalling a time when I once found him attractive. "Get to the point, Riley."

"What will she think when word gets around that you're cheating your way through school?"

I folded my arms. "What are you talking about?"

"Cut the bullshit, Brook. I saw you and Diego that day. I saw everything." He snatched one of my stuffed animals and smacked it with a loud kiss.

Dammit. I took a slow breath, trying to control my composure, though my knees wobbled. Luckily, he was too busy making out with my teddy—soon destined for the dumpster—to notice.

"I know all about your pill-popping business. But hey, your secret's safe with me, as long as…"

"You get what you want," I finished. He snapped his fingers and headed for the window. "Which is—?"

"For starters, you're going to convince Eddie to lose that race. I'll text you more details later, so don't even think about ignoring me." He climbed out the window the same way he had come in.

My eyes narrowed, and I wished I could push him off the ledge. "Damn it," I hissed under my breath. I fished my phone out of my pocket and quickly texted Diego two words:

Riley knows

16

EDDIE

NOW

"What did the cop want?" Diego demanded, his eyes narrowing until crow's feet appeared. "What the hell did you tell him?" He took a threatening step forward, his grip on Brooklyn so tight it made her wince.

"Hey," I snapped, stripping his hand from her arm. "Back off."

"I'm not in the mood for your damsel-in-distress act, Eddie. We need to know if this whiny bitch outed us," Diego continued.

"You'd better watch your mouth," I warned, grabbing him by the collar.

"Assholes—cut it out," Wes interjected, slipping between us.

It was Friday morning. Haywood High was prepping for the SAT when the bell rang next. But we gathered beneath the bleachers in the empty gym, edgy and ready to fight, because I was correct—that weirdo was a cop.

"Stop being such a dick, Diego," April said, tugging a stray braid behind her ear as it fell back into her face. "I'm sure you didn't say anything, right, B?" She nervously shot Brooklyn a look.

I trusted Brooklyn with my life, but even I had my doubts. She'd been toying with the idea of tipping the cops off for a while now.

Brooklyn licked her dry lips. "Of course I didn't. Don't you idiots think they'd be after us all by now? Or that you-know-who would be splashed all over the news?"

Diego folded his arms. "That's interesting. Why did he go to your house, first? How do we know you didn't ask to speak with him just to save your own ass?"

Brooklyn gasped. "Are you serious? How can you guys not trust me?"

I gently pulled her into my arms. "I don't doubt you," I murmured, smoothing her hair back into place.

Wes scoffed. "It's not about us trusting Brooklyn. Our worry should be whether that shithead Brody thinks you're telling the truth."

April let out a bitter laugh. "Haven't you seen Brooklyn's performance skills?"

"Really, April?" Brooklyn shot daggers at her as she pushed away from me.

"What?" April fired back. "I'm just saying we shouldn't have anything to worry about. I'm a million percent sure you were convincing. It's a compliment," she added, eyeing Brooklyn's clenched jaw.

It felt like they were discussing an entirely different topic. The bell blared above us, making Brooklyn jump.

I slid my arm around her shoulders in a comforting gesture. This nonsense had us all on edge.

"Well, what did he ask you about?" Wes placed Brooklyn back in the spotlight.

"The last time I saw Riley and what his state of mind was like," she answered. Diego cocked his head, waiting for more. Brooklyn shrugged. "I told him what we rehearsed. We didn't see Riley after he left Mario's party that Friday night."

I glared around. "Satisfied? Brooklyn didn't throw anyone under the bus. So what's your next move, Diego?"

"Not standing here looking like a bunch of dumbasses, I hope," April added. "We've got a test to take, remember? I can't afford to screw up." She turned to leave.

"She's right," I agreed. "We can talk later."

"Well, we're obviously good for now, so—" Wes looked at Diego. "What else can we do at this point?"

"You'd better not be lying," Diego hissed at Brooklyn.

Then he sneered at me before storming off with Wes.

I eased my hand into Brooklyn's. "Fuck Diego. Ready to ace the test?" She lifted her eyes to mine, rimmed red. "What is it? Don't tell me you care about what they think."

"No—it's something that happened when I was with Mack."

"Yeah?" I frowned.

She opened her mouth, hesitated, then closed her eyes and tucked her hair behind her ears. "What's the nature of Wesley and Coach Donahue's relationship?"

I frowned, confused. "Nature?"

She bit her lip. "Coach waited for Wes after school the other day. We followed them to…a motel…"

"Motel?" My voice climbed in pitch. "Did they get a room or something?"

"Well, that's just it. I can't say for sure. Wes went inside, but not the coach. But what if they met up again later?"

I backed away with a nervous laugh. "You're saying that the coach is sleeping with my brother?"

"I don't know, Eddie. Has Wes ever shown any signs of being gay?"

I wasn't sure. I could barely think straight. If what Brooklyn speculated was true, Coach Donahue would be in serious trouble. "Regardless, Wesley is underage. Coach Donahue has no right to…" I couldn't finish my thought. I needed to talk to Wes and hear his side.

"We should get to class," she mumbled, though I couldn't focus on the test with all this weighing on my mind.

A few minutes later, Miss Harper strode in to proctor the SAT. "There will be absolutely no talking." Dressed in a tight skirt and silk blouse, her blond hair pulled back into a sleek ponytail, she paced at the front.

"Your cell phones should be in your lockers. This test lasts three hours and fifteen minutes. The timer will signal breaks. Any questions before we start?" Silence. "We shall begin in three…two…one…" She began her timer. About an hour into the test, Wes suddenly rose and headed for the door.

"I'm sorry. What are you doing?" Miss Harper whispered, glancing up from her papers.

"I'm going to get a drink," Wes replied, reaching for the doorknob.

Miss Harper slid her chair back, stood quickly, and raised her voice. "Wesley, is it? I specifically said you could do that at break time. We're almost through. Take a seat." She indicated his chair.

But Wes didn't budge. He squared his chin and glared at her. "But I'm thirsty now. I can't wait. I've been stuck in this hot, cramped class sweating like a pig. I'm claustrophobic—I need air." He spun, grabbed the doorknob, and opened the door.

"Wesley, if you walk out of here…" Miss Harper began, only for the door to slam shut behind him. "…you automatically fail," she finished softly, her cheeks reddening as she glanced at the class. "Everyone else, carry on. There's nothing to see." She sank back into her seat, expression grim.

Wes had never left class like that before. Even when Mr. Wright gave him the toughest assignments, he always pulled through. I suspected it might have something to do with Detective Brody—or perhaps Coach Donahue. Three hours of testing felt impossible with everything else on our minds. Sweat even beaded on Brooklyn's forehead as she hovered over her test, double-checking her answers.

After what felt like two hours in what was actually only twenty minutes, the timer signaled a fifteen-minute break.

"Alright, everyone, pencils down," Miss Harper announced. "We'll have a fifteen-minute break."

I rushed to my locker to text Wes.

WTF?

I knew he was under pressure, but an automatic failure? Of course, he didn't reply. I scanned the boys' bathroom, the cafeteria, the gym—nothing. He must have gone home. By the time I finished searching, my break was nearly over. I returned to my locker to tuck my phone away and found

Brooklyn at hers, freaking out. She had dumped her backpack, with its entire contents strewn across the floor.

"Where is it?" she cried, dropping to her hands and knees as she scrambled through the mess. She searched inside her locker and on the floor. "No, *no*. It has to be here." She reappeared, hands in her hair.

I knelt beside her. "Brooklyn, calm down. What are you looking for?"

"None of your business," she snapped, spinning and shoving me aside. Between heavy breaths, she burst into sobs. "I—I must have brought the wrong bag," she wailed, covering her face.

"Is it your notes for the SAT?" I guessed.

She let out a small laugh as her hands fell. "Yeah." She took a deep breath, running her fingers through her hair.

"Well, I have some notes, and maybe April does too. I'll help you clean up and we can sort out the notes, okay? It'll be alright." I looked into her eyes, but she turned away.

"I'm so fucked," she muttered.

***

Later that night, I was home alone. Since Wes stormed out of class, I hadn't seen him, and Hank was probably getting kicked out of some bar.

It was so boring that I started doing laundry. After gathering my dirty clothes, I went to Wes's room to get his stuff. Hank never let us into his room—I never even dared to sneak a peek when he was out.

Wes had left his bed unmade and his clothes scattered on the floor. As I picked them up, I emptied the pockets of a pair of aqua-blue cargo shorts and found a receipt. "Sweet Haven Hotel…" I read it, my heart thumping as I noticed the timestamp: check-in at 4:52 PM and check-out at 5:38 PM. At least forty-five minutes.

I took a slow, shaky breath, rehearsing how to confront Wes when he interrupted.

"What are you doing?"

I turned to face him. His eyes widened when he saw the receipt. "Are you sleeping with Coach Donahue?" I asked bluntly.

His mouth opened, but no words came out. Instead, he snatched the receipt from my hand. "You had no right to go through my stuff." He crumpled the paper and tossed it aside.

"Wesley, seriously. If…if…God, I don't even know how to put it." I drew a sharp breath. "It's just wrong. He's a teacher. He could…"

"Where are you getting that from?" he interrupted.

"Brooklyn and Mack followed you two to a motel. Is that where you hook up?"

"Eddie—" he sighed. "Donahue knows about Monster. Sometimes he rents me a hotel room to get away from

Hank. If he could, he'd kick Hank's ass. But I always convince him not to. We've got to keep Mommy's promise, right?" He grinned smugly.

My shoulders fell. "I'm sorry, Wes. I shouldn't have—"

"No, you shouldn't," he snapped, tugging me toward the door. "Stay out of my room." He slammed the door in my face.

I stared at the closed door. Wes still hadn't answered my question: Was he sleeping with Coach Donahue or not?

17

EDDIE

"Happy birthday to me!" April belted that night at the Pin Palace, the local bowling alley known for its hot wings. The five of us gathered around a table overflowing with wings, onion rings, French fries, and milkshakes. Although everything looked enticing, my appetite was nowhere to be found. Wes was giving me the silent treatment, and Brooklyn was visibly tense. Of all nights, she chose April's birthday to bring up Riley. Brooklyn had promised to wait until after the cake was served, but after she and April got into a petty argument, she blurted it out.

"I think we should leave an anonymous tip about Riley."

April, licking her fingers, paused with eyes as wide as baseballs.

Diego nearly spat out his drink. "Are you fucking serious?"

Brooklyn shifted uncomfortably, stuttering, "Y-yeah."

Wes glared at me, asking, "And what do you say?"

I swallowed hard as Brooklyn shot me a withering look, prompting me to add, "I have to agree. Hear us out—" even as everyone scoffed and rolled their eyes. "With that Brody guy sniffing around, doesn't it make sense to throw him off our trail? I mean, we all know—" I lowered my voice. "We know the whole thing is staged to look like an accident. An anonymous tip wouldn't hurt. We could just say Riley always went to that lake." Brooklyn nodded as I continued.

Wes arched an eyebrow. "And let the cops trace our phone?"

"We could use a burner," Brooklyn replied.

"The point is, guys," I cut in, "this has dragged on long enough. We've got Mack—" I cleared my throat. Wes and I exchanged a look, but he broke eye contact, fidgeting with a fry. "She's following her dad around. A detective is tracking us down and even showing up at our houses. At first, I thought keeping quiet was best. But now—"

Wes waved a hand at Brooklyn. "She's getting in your head."

"It's not like that," I muttered.

Wes scooted closer, speaking just for my ears. "You know you've got the most to lose, right?"

I nodded. "I've thought about it, but if it all looks like an accident, how could what you're saying be true? No one should be in trouble if it's ruled an accident, right?" I searched his face. Wes sighed.

Diego pulled him away, jabbing a finger in my direction. "There's no way in hell anybody's saying anything." Wes reached to pull his hand down, but Diego snatched it free. "No, I'm done with this bullshit."

"You know what?" Brooklyn slammed a napkin onto the table. "This is crazy. What gives you the right to control our actions, Diego? You're acting no different from Riley."

He threw his hands up. "How? I'm doing the exact opposite—*I'm* the one trying to keep us all safe."

Wes exhaled. "Guys, let's just chill. The best thing that can happen is the cops stumble on this without a tip."

"But what if they never find him?" Brooklyn pressed.

After a moment, Wes said, "Once we leave Haywood after graduation, we can give your anonymous tip."

April nodded. "I like that idea. When I'm far away— maybe in Cambodia or somewhere, shooting photos for a project—I won't miss Haywood."

Wes scanned our table, lingering on Brooklyn and me a beat longer than the others. Diego and April agreed immediately. Though Brooklyn shook her head, she muttered a reluctant agreement.

"I don't have a choice, do I?" I finally grumbled, sliding

my seat back. "Excuse me, but I need some air."

"Eddie—" Wes called. I made my way to the front when a waitress nearly collided with me, carrying a tray of empty glasses. "Whoa." I reached out to steady her trembling tray.

"Thanks—hey, I know you." She pointed at me, and as I stared into her face, I stepped back in surprise. She was Brooklyn's lookalike. She giggled. "Well, I don't *really* know you, but…" Rolling her eyes, she added, "I'm Savannah."

"Eddie," I replied, shoving my hands into my back pockets as an awkward silence settled between us. It was uncanny—she and Brooklyn could be mirror images. Trying not to blush, I eyed her. "So, do you live around here?"

"Yeah. Just a few blocks away. My family just moved, and I'm starting school a week late because my transfer papers got screwed up."

"Oh—that sucks," I said, feeling lame. "Where are you going?"

"Haywood High."

"No way—I go there too."

She shifted the tray to the other hand. "It really is a small world."

"For real," I grinned, a bit too hard until my cheeks ached.

Then, rising on tiptoe to glance at our table, she

whispered, "Aren't those the assholes who were picking on me?" I rolled my eyes. "For what it's worth, they're not always like that."

She gripped my arm. "I'm just glad *you're* not. It's nice to know there are still good guys out there." I returned a sloppy grin, blinking at her magenta nails as my heart pounded. "Anyway, I better get back—the kid over there is driving me nuts."

She nodded toward a nearby table. "It was nice seeing you."

"Same here. See you at school," I added.

"For sure." With a curt nod and a smile, she hurried by. I watched her dark ponytail swinging behind her, and felt a flutter deep in my stomach.

WES

That night, April trailed her fingers down my chest as she, clad in nothing but lace panties, straddled me. We were at the Manor Inn, a shabby motel not too far from her place. The bed felt as solid as a concrete slab against my back and ass. She lowered her face toward mine and nibbled on my earlobe—her breath reeking of booze. I frowned and turned away.

"Thank you for the birthday present," she murmured,

kissing my neck.

I eased away from her lips. "What do you plan on doing with a thousand bucks, anyway?"

Her eyes flashed. "You'll find out soon enough."

Why had I even asked? I knew I didn't really care. It was almost torture lying so close—she could be such a pain.

"Who are you thinking about?" she pressed, squeezing my face with a sloppy grin.

I rolled my eyes. "Nobody." It was clear I'd rather be somewhere else. I hadn't touched her, even though it was her special day—she'd been a sport on my birthday. And even though I had been into her before, the least I could do was return the favor.

Her grip deepened around my jaw as her nails dug into my skin. "Liar."

"Stop," I snapped, shoving her aside. She squealed and fell next to me. I straightened until my back hit the cold headboard. "I can't do a damn thing on this cement mattress."

April slid up and dug into her purse, finally settling on a pack of cigarettes and a lighter. I glared at her sidewise. "Since when do you smoke? You know it's bad for you."

Ignoring me, she brought the cigarette to her lips, lighting it and drawing a long drag. Tilting her head back, she exhaled a funky puff. "Since when do you care?"

I snatched the cigarette just as her mouth puckered for

another drag. "Hey!" she protested as I extinguished it in my palm. Licking her lips, she narrowed her eyes. "Okay. That was sexy."

"Oh, you like that?" I replied, keeping my gaze on her as I flicked the cigarette to the floor. Leaning in, I kissed her deeply. She cupped my face and climbed back on top. I pushed aside the memory of her reeking of a bar as I gripped her ass, our kiss intensifying. I wanted to be into it—I really did. My dick certainly was. But my heart was somewhere else, lost in thoughts of Brooklyn. Why was she suddenly trying to change Eddie's mind? Had that detective said something Brooklyn wasn't telling us? Was it possible she was feeding information to the cops behind our backs?

"Ow." April's face came into focus as she pulled away from my lips. "You bit my tongue."

"You used to like it rough," I teased, playfully nibbling her chin, shoulder, and the top of her right boob. She rested her arms on my shoulders, giggling as I nibbled from one side to the next just as my phone beeped. "I gotta check that," I said, easing her off my lap. She sighed in exasperation. "Calm down. I'll get to you in a sec." I grabbed my cell from the nightstand.

Have you talked 2 Eddie?

"It's Diego," I said as I typed back.

Eddie's not the prob, Brook is

April scoffed. "Of course it's Diego. I swear he wants to fuck you." She rolled onto her side, back toward me—missing the death stare I shot her.

Diego texted again:

I know how 2 shut her up.

I'm heading 2 her house now

My brow arched. What the hell did that mean? How was he going to shut her up?

Another text came:

U need 2 handle Eddie

I glanced at April and noticed she'd slipped off her panties. Grinning, I set my phone aside. Eddie would have to wait. I stood and scooped April up in my arms, backing her against the front door.

Twenty minutes later, we were settled on the rock-hard bed, both panting for breath. "That—was the *best*—birthday present ever," April gasped.

My bare chest rose and fell as I lay back, hands outstretched over my head. "You took all my energy," I sputtered. She giggled, kissing me as she prepared for round two. I yawned. "No, I'm exhausted."

She pouted and batted her lashes. "Please?"

I used to love those big eyes in another lifetime. Rolling over, I murmured, "Maybe later."

"I'll hold you to it," she said, edging toward the bed's perimeter as I heard her pad off to the bathroom.

My phone pinged again. "What now?" I sighed, slapping my palm on the nightstand while fumbling for it. The message read simply:

I WANT YOU

My breaths grew shallow as I reread the words.

"Diego again?" April guessed as she reappeared beside the bed.

"Uh—yeah. He really needs my help." I scrambled to my feet and grabbed my clothes.

"But—"

"I know. I'll make it up to you later," I said half-heartedly. April sank back onto the bed, toying with a braid. I leaned in and kissed her cautiously. "I promise," I added, backing away. A Cheshire cat grin spread across my face as I left the motel room. I guess there was room for round two after all.

18

BROOKLYN

NOW

I stood on the balcony, clutching the railing with a clammy hand, relieved that Mom had finally managed to get Janie to sleep. When I got home from the Pin's Palace, she'd spent all night bawling about JoJo. I'd suggested a million times to Mom and Dad that we get her a new puppy, but they disagreed, convinced that JoJo would come home—though JoJo was in a bag in the woods.

I pictured the bloody clump of fur that was left of him, and my throat ached. I tried swallowing, but it felt like sucking through a straw jammed in a frozen drink, and the thought only made me thirstier.

I took the stairs two at a time but slowed when I caught sight of a silhouette on the porch, tapping softly at the door.

Through the slim crystal windowpane, I could just make out a red baseball cap. Diego? What the hell did he want? I checked to ensure Dad wasn't around before quickly cracking open the door. "What are you doing here?" I hissed, sticking my head out.

"Why the hostility?" he asked, surprised. "Aren't you going to invite me in?"

"Like hell I will. My dad is here."

"So, let's go for a ride."

My eyes widened. "Right now?"

"No—next week. Of course now."

I squinted, trying to gauge his seriousness. Diego glared at me, his boyish face twisting into a smirk as he extended his hand.

I sighed. Oh, what the hell. I stepped out onto the porch and shut the door behind me. The breezy air smelled of rain, with a storm clearly brewing in the distance, and all I wore was a thin eggshell T-shirt over white leggings. I wrapped my arms around myself and shivered.

Diego slid his arm across my shoulder as he led me to his Charger. It was too chilly to shrug him off—or maybe I just didn't want to.

I sank into the passenger seat as he hurried around to the driver's side. "What is this about?" I asked once he was behind the wheel.

"Can't a friend just check in on you?"

I scoffed. "Since when did we become friends?"

He stayed quiet and shifted his gaze out the windshield as he drove. After a while, he pulled over at the park across the street from the school. Raindrops splattered on the windshield. "So, I hear Eddie's got a dysfunction problem."

I whipped around quickly. "What? Did April tell you that? You really need to mind your own business."

"You're right," he shrugged. "I mean, you and Eddie cherish your V cards. That's what makes him so special, right?"

I rolled my eyes. "I'm not about to discuss our relationship with you. Now you've got two seconds to tell me what the hell you want."

He took a deep breath, brushing a hand through his hair. "I—I just wanted to see how you're doing." My eyes narrowed as he raised a hand. "Honestly, you must be under a lot of pressure with that major recital you've got tomorrow."

"What do you care?"

"Can you drop the bitch shield for one second? I'm being serious. I know how hard you try, B, and I know the lengths you'll go to achieve."

My shoulders slumped as I tentatively rubbed my neck. My throat swelled. I gulped hard and lifted my gaze to Diego's. His greenish-brown eyes searched mine, genuinely waiting for a response, but my aching throat wouldn't allow even the tiniest peep. I shrugged, blinking back tears. "I'm not so sure about my SAT score," I finally croaked.

He frowned. "What does that mean?"

"I didn't have my…help."

He stared blankly for a moment before catching on and then gasped. "Are you out already?"

"No. Well, yes, but I had it then. I just forgot the bag. I'm going to need more for the recital, though." My voice was barely audible. "I can pay you."

He glanced away. "I don't want your money. But you *know* how I feel about supplying you, B. We were supposed to have stopped that ages ago."

I shoved him gently. "Do you think I like it, Diego? I can't fucking focus without it." Rain now thudded heavily on the roof. "If my dad or Eddie or anyone from school found out I'm getting it illegally…" I dropped my head, my hair shielding my tears. "Everyone expects me to be perfect, but I'm just a loser."

Diego gripped my shoulder. "Hey. Look at me." He cupped my chin. "That is not true. You're smart and talented, and you know it, B. But you're not perfect— you're human. Anyone who can't accept that, fuck them." He looked at me steadily, and I shivered as goosebumps prickled my skin. "Are you cold?" he asked.

I nodded, trembling into a full sob. He clicked on the heat and inched closer, enveloping me in a warm embrace.

"It's okay," he whispered as I kept my forehead pressed against his collarbone and cried. His soothing voice brushed away my tears. "Why are you crying? You're almost at the finish line. Once you cross it, you never have to look back. Hey—" He pulled away slightly to meet my gaze. "You can check into a hospital any time to detox. I can go with you."

I met his eyes. "Do you mean that?"

"Just tell me when you're ready, okay?" he said, sincere and earnest. I slowly nodded and squeezed him tighter, pressing my face against his. He eased his hand into mine, turning until his lips grazed my cheek and trailed soft kisses toward my mouth.

Even though I turned away, my heart leaped into my throat in anticipation. "I can't, Diego," I whispered.

He toyed with a lock of my hair. "You can't, but you want to," he murmured, his eyes studying every inch of my face as a dimple deepened in his right cheek.

I couldn't look away. I leaned closer—especially to his lips—hesitantly.

He kissed me, pulling me by the waist and drawing me even nearer, but I climbed into his lap and straddled him. The rain fell in heavy sheets, its soothing sound setting the mood. I let my fingers trail through the tiny curls at the back of his neck as our kiss deepened and our tongues began to wrestle.

Thunder crackled overhead, momentarily pulling us apart.

I pressed my forehead against his and clutched his face. "I'm ready to ditch my V card."

His eyes widened. "Are you sure?" he whispered.

I kissed him, replying, "I'm positive."

<hr>

An hour later, Diego pulled onto my block and shut off the engine. The rain had stopped. "Are you okay?" he asked.

I'd been chewing my lip so hard I might have bitten it off. "I don't know what to say," I admitted.

"Was it that bad?" he teased, making me laugh. I playfully shoved him, though deep down I knew it had been mind-blowing. He shifted closer. "You don't have to say anything. I enjoy being here with you—like this," he said, taking my hand for what felt like the umpteenth time that hour.

I rested against his shoulder, though something gnawed at me. I truly enjoyed being there, but I knew we couldn't stay—someone might see us. My dad. Abruptly, I straightened. "I've gotta go, Diego."

"Hey, wait." He stopped my hand as I reached for the door handle. "I know you're under a lot of pressure right now, but can you just remember why we did what we did?"

"You mean…Riley?" I croaked his name.

Diego nodded. My brows dipped. "Is that why you really came over? To shut me up about Riley?" I turned away. "God, I am such an idiot."

"It's not like that," he insisted. "I wanted to talk about Riley—to remind you that every wrong thing we did was for a better tomorrow. If we break our pact, it'll all be for nothing."

I glared at him. "You are fucking unbelievable, you know that?" I reached for the door again, but he pulled me into a long, lingering kiss that I didn't want to end. Yet we were in dangerous territory—far from the privacy of the park.

Just as I broke free, he slipped a small baggie of pills into my palm.

"This has to be the last time, B."

I gripped the baggie tightly. "But that's not your decision to make."

His brow arched. "It is if I care about y—"

My heart stopped, and the car fell into silence. I blinked at him before shifting to the door. "I have to go," I whispered, then dashed out of the car.

"Where are you coming from?" Dad asked when I burst into the house.

"Daddy!" My eyes widened as I clutched the baggie even tighter. Shit. I tucked my arms behind my back and came up on tiptoes to appear innocent. Dad stood in the center of the staircase, and he came all the way down, stopping right in front of me with worry etched into his usually handsome face. Apparently, the JoJo business wasn't just affecting Janie. JoJo—I mentally gasped, a new idea forming. "I just stepped out onto the porch for a second. I thought I heard JoJo barking, so I went to check, but it turned out to be a false alarm."

He sighed and ran a hand through his dark, bushy hair. "Yeah, at the rate Janie's going, we're going to have to get her JoJo's brother."

My nose scrunched. "I didn't know you were in touch with the breeder."

"I'm not. But Janie doesn't need to know that."

I slowly nodded, offering him a weak smile. "So she'll love this dog just as much if she thinks JoJo sent his brother to meet her, too. Real clever, Dad. I wonder what you lied to me about when I was that age," I teased, instantly regretting it as the weight of the pills in my palm pressed down on me.

Laughing, he slid an arm around my shoulders and kissed my forehead. My body tensed, scared he might smell Diego's husky cologne on me. "I could never fool you. You were always one step ahead," he murmured. I hoped my face didn't betray how sick I felt. When Dad pulled away, he eyed me carefully as if reading my mind. "Are you okay?" His expression was grim. I broke eye contact. "I know you miss JoJo, too, but don't stress. Everyone will be happy once another fluffy tail's wagging around here," he said with a smile. Yeah. Not really. "Now try to get some last-minute practice in before you go to bed."

I stifled a yawn. "Now? But what if I wake Janie?"

"She's out cold. You should be fine. Besides, tomorrow is a hit-or-miss situation. Mrs. Keeler is going to be in the front row listening. You want to be as crisp and on-the-ball as possible."

"I know, Dad. You've been reminding me of this day ever since I could talk," I replied, unable to resist a hint of sarcasm as I stepped away, keeping my hands behind my back.

"What's that supposed to mean?" he asked, blinking at me in confusion.

"Dad, come on. All you ever preach is how perfect I need to be. We were having a moment, and you had to ruin it."

His frown deepened. "A moment? No one said you needed to be perfect. I just really want you to do well—to get into Juilliard. Isn't that what you want too?"

I sighed. "Forget it, Dad. I'm going to go put on some sleeves and get back to practice." I left him baffled as I folded my arms and stomped up the plush steps, slamming the door behind me and forgetting about Janie.

Oh, well. Putting her back to sleep was hardly payback. I paced the room, clutching the baggie to my chest as

Diego's words echoed in my mind. Everything we had done was supposed to be for a better tomorrow, yet two people were dead because of us—just so we could have a do-over after our mistakes. Who were we to decide if we deserved a second chance?

Damnit. I needed to clear my head for the recital.

I crushed two pills beneath the base of my lamp and, using a rolled slip of paper, snorted the powder. I dropped onto the mattress, my eyes blurry as I stared up at the ceiling.

How had I let myself get to this point—relying on illegal prescriptions to keep going? It was all Mr. Wright's fault. If he hadn't given me that unrealistic time frame, I wouldn't have taken speed in the first place. If we hadn't broken into his house, Riley wouldn't have been able to blackmail us.

I buried my face in my hands and took a deep breath as the pills began to kick in.

19

BROOKLYN

NOW

I paced outside the auditorium, nervously chewing my lip. In moments, I'd be called on stage to perform, and my nerves were through the roof. I couldn't understand why— I'd practiced so much that I could play the piece blindfolded, with my hands tied behind my back. It should have been a breeze, so why wasn't I confident?

"Hey! Psst," someone hissed behind me. I spun around and saw Diego's head peeking out of the supply closet. "Come here," he beckoned.

I hurried over and closed the door behind me. "Diego, what the hell? Aren't you supposed to be at swim practice?"

"I'm on my way. I just wanted to see you first. You didn't return my call." His eyes searched mine, silently asking for an explanation.

I couldn't deal with this right now—not before the most important moment of my life. "Diego, I have to go." I turned for the door, but he grabbed my wrist.

"Will we talk later?"

I wriggled free. "There's nothing to talk about. Last night shouldn't have happened."

His brows knitted together. "You're not mad at me, are you?"

"Yes. No. Look, I don't want to think about it right now. I just can't." I closed my eyes, trying to calm my racing heart as I focused on my breathing.

Diego placed his hands on my shoulders. "I didn't mean to distract you."

"Yeah, well…" I shrugged, a silent "obviously" in my gesture. He sighed. "Diego… last night was a mistake. We really shouldn't have done that."

He glanced away. "Well, I don't regret it at all, and I don't think you do either."

I jutted out my chin. "Fine—maybe I don't. But it can never happen again."

Diego smirked. "So you say."

"Diego, I mean it. I love Eddie."

"Again, so you say." He kissed the corner of my mouth before leaving.

I cracked my knuckles and dove into my piece several

minutes later. Despite everything, I closed my eyes and pictured a waterfall—its soothing, gushing waters and the white mist spritzing the air. Tucking my lip between my teeth, I even imagined its salty taste. As Dad had insisted during my pep talk at breakfast, I brought my A-game.

I caught sight of Mrs. Keeler at the front. I was certain it was her—no one would wear such a sexy bodycon dress to a high school event. The slim brunette sat with her long legs crossed while a sparkly stiletto tapped in time with the music.

Dad flashed me a proud smile from the seat behind her. I was about to return it when I noticed a silhouette standing at the back of the room. I recognized the coat immediately. Detective Brody. What did he want?

The notes began to pour out rapidly. Had I skipped a beat? I couldn't tell. I licked my lips and shifted, attempting to focus on the keys, but Brody was moving through the audience. It wasn't like it was a sold-out concert—I could count the heads on my fingers and toes. Who was he here for?

Eddie wasn't there—he had swim practice. It was better that way since Dad watched me like a hawk. Of course, Wes didn't show up either. Mack, however, was in the back row, her feet lazily propped on the empty seat in front of her. The overhead light was blinding me. I blinked, scanning toward Brody as his footsteps and the swish of his coat fell in perfect time. Sweat trickled down my face.

Then the black and white keys came into focus. I tried to steady my concentration, but my eyes flicked to the seats again. Squinting, I watched Brody approach April as she shakily rose to follow him out. What did he want with her? What was so urgent it couldn't wait until after my recital? How did he even know where to find April? Was he following us all? Did he see me dump JoJo in the woods? Had he been watching me—and Diego—last night?

My brain filled with questions, and I lost track of what my fingertips were doing. One thing was clear: I'd missed the glissando long ago.

"Don't you think this looks suspicious—meeting every time Brody questions one of us?" April asked with an exasperated sigh. "I have to get home. It's urgent."

About a half-hour after school, we all met at the Busy Bean Café.

"That's exactly why we need to stay in tune and not mess anything up," Diego said. "Riley knew everyone at Haywood High. So why is Brody only questioning us?" He glanced around at each of us.

"He believes we know something," Wes added.

Eddie reached under the table and grabbed my hand. "Are you okay?" he whispered. "I'm really sorry I couldn't make the recital."

The recital. My heart ached. As the others' voices droned on, I gazed sadly out the window, remembering the look of disappointment on Dad's face when my recital ended.

"You have potential but..." Mrs. Keeler had said afterward, followed by criticism:

"With more practice,"

"Takes precision,"

"Not a good fit."

Her words tumbled out in clusters—an obvious sign that I was never headed to Julliard.

"It's over, Eddie," I whispered.

"It couldn't have been that bad, Brook."

I shook my head slowly. "It's over. I fucked up. When I saw Brody, my mind just...I panicked. I couldn't concentrate." I sighed. "It's over."

"He can question us until he's blue in the face," Diego insisted. "He'll keep getting the same answer— we know nothing, right?" His green eyes lingered on me for a moment longer.

"Anyway," April brightened, "guess who's going to the Institute of Arts?" She bounced in her seat.

I had to clench my teeth to keep my chin from hitting my chest. Everyone congratulated her—except me. "How? We haven't even gotten the SAT scores back yet." It would be another fifteen minutes before we could officially check.

April scowled, flipping her braids over one shoulder. "Don't you mean, congratulations or I'm happy for you, too?"

I laughed nervously, shifting away from Eddie's cold touch. "Well, of course I'm happy for you. I'm just…curious."

"Well, since you're *wondering*, I received my acceptance letter today. My mom just texted me the news."

I bit the inside of my jaw. "That's…that's great." Still, jealousy stabbed at my chest—I'd been preparing for Julliard my entire life. And because of the mess they all dragged me into, I couldn't concentrate when it mattered most. I jumped to my feet. "Excuse me, I have to use the restroom." I caught Diego's worried gaze, but I pressed on, silently praying no one else noticed. Maneuvering around the table, I scurried to the women's room. Barely had I closed the stall door when I broke into sobs, sliding against the door into a pathetic heap on the floor.

My phone pinged. Trembling, I pulled it from my pocket. It was a text from Diego:

R U OKAY

I shut my eyes. It wasn't fair. None of it was fair. All that shit was supposed to lead to a better future—the secrets, the lies, the *murders*—all in service of our goals. And yet, we still failed. *I* failed. But what was I to do now? What else could I do?

I muffled my sobs as I held a hand over my mouth.

"Hey, Brooklyn?" I heard Eddie tapping on the main door several minutes later. "What's going on in there?"

I stood by the sink, splashing cold water on my face. "Nothing. I'll be there in a sec." I kept my voice steady as I dried my face with a handful of napkins and forced a phony smile while opening the door. Eddie waited with his hands buried in his pockets, his expression grim. "Sorry. I think my latte came with whole milk instead of soy. My stomach's upset." I fiddled with my phone.

He smiled, though it was strained—he knew I was lying. "Brooklyn, it's not the end of the world. Maybe you could redo the recital. I'm sure your music teacher could arrange a do-over."

There it was again—do-over. Was I destined to keep repeating the same mistakes until I finally succeeded?

I nodded. "Maybe. I'll see about that. Thanks, Eddie."

He hooked his arm through mine. "Come on, we're about to check our test scores."

He guided me back to the table, where April and Diego were already tapping on their phones. Wes didn't have a score to check, so he sat back, sipping his frappé with a bored expression.

Diego went first. "1220. Not bad." He shrugged. He'd barely made it, but hey, it was better than nothing.

I shifted, lowering my gaze as I cautiously entered my details.

Suddenly, April's triumphant shout: "1510! Yes!" She pumped her fist. 1510? I glanced up quickly.

Eddie leaned over quietly to show me his score: an even 1300.

I half-smiled as the loading bar on my screen slowly filled. Finally, the black numbers appeared: 1190.

I blinked uncontrollably, willing the numbers to change, but they stayed the same. 1190 stared back at me mockingly. I hadn't passed. I'd expected a poor score, but not even breaking 1200? That couldn't be right. Someone *must* have done that on purpose—it just couldn't be.

I stood abruptly, my chair clattering to the floor behind me. A nearby table gasped, but I didn't give a shit.

"What's the matter?" Eddie asked, appalled. I said nothing, shoulders tense as I stormed out of the coffee shop.

I slowly drove across the street to a downtown hotel. It was a little after nine when I got an urgent text from Mack telling me to meet her there ASAP. Without hesitation, I jumped in the car and hurried over. I wasn't doing much at home anyway—hiding in my room, unable to face Dad. Luckily, he had just left for his office, so I slipped out.

I peered through the window, clutching the steering wheel even though the car was off. What was going on? Was Mack inside?

I licked my dry lips. The silence was deafening. Maybe I should text her. I reached for my phone when the passenger door swung open, and Mack dashed into the seat. "What the hell?" I choked out, raising a hand to my heaving chest. "What are you doing?" Mack slumped further into the seat, staring past me at the hotel. She panted for breath, wearing dark leggings and an oversized black hoodie with the hood up.

"You look like you're on a stakeout," I remarked, then gasped as I realized we were.

She nodded. "My dad's in there with somebody."

"Is it Wesley? Wait—how do you know?" I asked.

She closed her eyes and sighed. "It's a long story. I overheard my dad on a phone call, and he said, 'I'll meet you there' and yada yada. Anyway, I hopped in the back of the car and hid on the floor. We drove here, and I saw him go into Room 34. A woman answered the door."

My eyes widened. "You hid in the back of your dad's car? Are you insane? What if he saw you?"

"I don't give a damn," she snapped, folding her arms stubbornly. "He owes some explanations."

I rolled my eyes. "Well, so do you."

"Look. My father is clearly cheating on my dying mother, and I can't bring myself to tell her."

My brows furrowed. "What do you mean, dying?"

Mack wiped her face with the back of her sleeve and sniffled. "The doctors can't say exactly how long my mom's got left. They suggested we spend as much time with her as we can." Her voice broke as she buried her face in her hands and sobbed.

"I'm so sorry, Mackenzie," I whispered.

"What for? Sorry doesn't cure cancer. It's just a waste of a word."

I glanced at the hotel. Spying on Coach Donahue wasn't helping anything. I started the car and drove as far away as possible.

A short while later, Mack gripped her coffee cup in both hands as we sat in a local diner, sipping hot cocoa. She shook her head as she removed her hood, though her hair still clung to her forehead. "This is all so fucked up," she said, her voice trembling as if she might fall apart at any moment. "How can he do something like this? My mom needs him now, and he's in a hotel with some random slut." She slammed her cup down, splattering a few brown drops on the table.

I didn't know what to say. Thankfully, my parents had never gone through something like this. Yet my heart sank at the thought of Eddie. What about me and Diego?

Mack whipped around so quickly it was as if she read my mind. "He couldn't even wait for her to die?" she frowned.

I placed my hand over hers. "Mack, I know this might sound silly, but what if that's his way of coping? I mean, we don't really know what he's doing in that hotel room—maybe he's finding comfort in some other way. Massage therapy really relieves stress, you know."

Mack blinked at me. "Nobody's that naïve, Brook. Not even you."

I sighed, nodding in agreement—it was a long shot. "At least now you know Coach Donahue isn't guilty of what you suspected about killing Riley."

Mack rested her face in her hands. "I don't even know which is worse. The news of this would kill my mom, and the blood would still be on his hands." She drew a sharp breath, eyes locking onto mine. "My mom can't die before the cops find Riley. *She just can't*," she cried.

Oh my gosh—I struggled to hold my composure. That poor family. I handed her a napkin. "She won't, Mackenzie. I'm certain the cops are on the case twenty-four-seven. Something's bound to come up soon. Besides, the doctor didn't give a specific timeframe. You just have to have hope, if nothing else, okay?"

She pulled away to blow her nose. "You mean like

miracles or some shit? Someone praying over my mom?"

I pressed my lips together and nodded. I knew it sounded far-fetched, but I had no other comfort to offer. Besides, the idea wasn't entirely unappealing.

But Mack laughed bitterly, tears staining her cheeks. "Just stop, Brooklyn. I appreciate what you're trying to do, but just stop. My family is all screwed up."

I took a long sip of cocoa, burning my tongue in the process. It was a brief distraction. I continued fanning my mouth with a napkin.

"I'm sorry," Mack blurted. "I'm such a mess."

I shrugged. "It's okay. I understand."

"No. Let's talk about you. Tell me how great your life is." Demanding a change of subject, she prodded. Reluctantly, I mentioned Julliard and my failing SAT.

"Wow." Her lips formed an "o" as I finished. "That's too bad. What are you gonna do now?"

I brushed my hair behind my ears. "I don't know, Mack. My dad hasn't heard about the SAT scores yet. He's so pissed about the recital that I don't even know how to tell him."

Mack drummed her fingertips on the table. "Well, it isn't the worst thing, you know. So, what? You didn't get into Julliard? You can always study something else."

"I thought about that, too, but music is my life. I don't know what I'd be without it."

She clicked her tongue. "Maybe it's time you figure that out. But don't beat yourself up over it." Leaning closer, she lowered her voice. "If I could afford it, I'd have bought a cheat sheet from Mario like some people did—but he was charging a grand a pop."

She said something else I didn't catch as the room started to tilt around me. Now I knew how April could've gotten such a high test score.

WES

"Oh—you're such a naughty boy, Wesley." Her British accent enunciated my name seductively as Libby's warm tongue nibbled on my earlobe while I marked a hickey on her neck, moaning into her skin. Her elegant, light rosy perfume was nothing like the cheap cologne April wore. She pulled her naked body from mine and dropped onto the plush covers beneath us in our usual room at Sweet Haven. Miss Libby Harper certainly put the *sweet* in the hotel's name.

I glanced at her perky breasts rising and falling as she caught her breath. A few blond strands clung to her perspiration-damp forehead. Her eyes closed peacefully, her plush pink mouth forming a subtle heart-shaped pout.

I smiled slowly, my heart leaping in my chest. I'd never felt this way about anyone before—and to know that Libby genuinely felt the same was incredible. I exhaled deeply. How did *I* get so lucky?

It was just last week when she asked me to stay after class. She'd noticed I was struggling with history. I didn't give a damn about how society came to be—everything still felt fucked up—but when she explained how the past shapes the present and future, all while her perfect boobs spilled from her blouse, I decided a journey through history could be worth it.

Then during our first tutoring session, I impulsively suggested we make our own history. Libby looked confused. Without a second thought, I kissed her. She shoved me away, but I couldn't help noticing the pause— the slow beats that passed before she responded. The next day, she slipped me a note asking me to wait after school so we could discuss what had just happened. That night, we had sex in her car parked near a river just outside Haywood.

I gently brushed the wet strands from her forehead. "Thank you for getting me the makeup test for the SAT," I murmured.

Her eyes fluttered open as she turned to face me. "That was ballsy of you to leave."

"It was your fault—strolling around in that tight skirt. I wanted to toss my desk and pin you against the chalkboard."

She smiled slowly. "Maybe I'll wear a nun's habit next

time."

I traced her cheek with a single finger. "You'd still be beautiful. Hey—" I sat up, remembering I had something for her. Digging through my bag, I finally found the tiny box.

She gasped when I presented it. "Oh, Wesley, you shouldn't have."

"Open it."

She shifted against the headboard and looked inside. "It's beautiful. Wesley, I can't accept this," she said, shaking her head as she held out the necklace—two diamond-encrusted, intertwined hearts. She brought a hand to her mouth in surprise. "These are genuine diamonds. How did you afford that?"

"You're really special to me, Libby. Besides, you deserve that and so much more."

Her mouth fell open, leaving her speechless. I removed the necklace from its box and carefully fastened it around her neck.

She adjusted her hair as I secured it at the back, then tentatively touched the heart pendants. "This is too much," she whispered.

I slid closer to her, wrapping an arm around her slim waist. "I won't surprise you anymore if you don't like it."

She turned, cupped my face, and kissed me slowly and passionately. As our lips parted, our faces nestled together.

"Promise me something," she murmured.

I closed my eyes, eager to melt into her warmth. "Anything," I whispered.

"Promise you'll do your best on the SAT," she said, her gaze earnest. I pulled back and looked carefully at her as she nodded. "I mean it. I'll help you prepare if you need it. But you must pass that test. You'll have a better chance of getting into college."

I shrugged. "I don't want to be saddled with student loans if I can't get a scholarship. It all feels pointless now." I straightened up, turning a little away from her.

"You mean because you're not on the swim team?"

"Do we have to talk about this now? All I want is to be with you after high school."

Her cheeks flushed. "Wesley, our relationship can't be public. We both know the consequences of what we have."

"Not if you leave Haywood with me. You could get another teaching job in a city that doesn't know our secret. We could live the life we want."

She smiled sadly. "It sounds so nice, but it isn't that simple."

I gripped her hand. "We could try."

She gently stroked my hair. "Let's just focus on the test for now, okay?" My shoulders slumped. "Oh, cheer up, baby." She kissed my cheek. "We'll talk about this later— *after* your SAT results. For now..." With a playful peck on my nose, she eased down onto the bed. "I must properly thank you for my present." With a devilish grin, she disappeared beneath the covers.

20

EDDIE

TWO WEEKS AGO

"It was an accident. I only meant to stop Riley from—" I faltered, glancing toward Brooklyn in an appeal for help explaining what Riley was doing to her, but she remained silent. My eyes, wet and glistening, fell again on Riley, his dark pupils locked in time as we hovered over his motionless body.

"Can someone please close his eyes?" April murmured, turning away with a shudder.

Diego cautiously reached over and did so, then jerked his hand back. "That was seriously creepy."

"What are we going to do?" Brooklyn whispered.

I sniffled, wiping my tears away with the back of my arm. "We're calling the cops and telling them everything."

I looked at Brooklyn, silently begging her to meet my gaze and speak, but she still wouldn't.

"What happened?" April demanded.

"It doesn't matter now," Wes interrupted sharply. "And we're *not* going to the police."

I thought of Simon Wright. "Wesley, no. We can't do this again. I can't keep another secret. Riley was—" My voice caught, and I stole another glance at Brooklyn. She turned away. I sighed deeply. "It was an accident. I have to tell the police that. They'll understand."

Wes waved me off, patting Diego's shoulder. "Come on. Let's get rid of him."

Brooklyn gasped and took a step back.

"Wesley, please." A choked sob burst out of me as I grabbed his arm.

"Stop it. *Stop*," Wes ordered, breaking free and shoving me aside. "You're not going to jail for a piece of shit like Riley. You've got your whole life ahead of you."

"We all do," April snapped, spinning around as her dark braids swung. "Riley was trying to tear us apart. It's over now."

"No, it'll never be over, A," Brooklyn murmured. "Every day, we're one step closer to our graves."

"Everybody—shut the fuck up," Wes bellowed, frustrated. "Damnit, I can barely hear myself think." Everyone fell into silence. After a long beat, Wes proposed,

"All in favor of going to the cops, raise your hand."

Mine shot up immediately, but my heart sank when Brooklyn's hand stayed down. "Brook?" I managed, my lips trembling.

"I'm sorry, Eddie," she whispered, shaking her head. Several dark strands of hair clung to her face. "But I don't think you should take the fall for this either."

"It's wrong," I protested, my chest tightening. I turned away, gasping for air. I needed to escape. My legs buckled beneath me as I tried to run.

Then someone appeared behind me, looping an arm around my waist. It was Wesley. "Just breathe…" he urged. I shoved him away and collapsed to the ground, desperately drawing in deep, ragged breaths. Slowly, he lowered himself beside me. "Living with the fact that you've killed someone—it's never going to get easier."

He was referring to Mr. Wright. I sniffled, gazing up at him. "Riley was hurting Brooklyn," I whispered.

Wesley nodded. "When Wright came after you with that bat, I stepped in to defend you too. That doesn't make us monsters, Eddie. You shouldn't be punished for protecting someone you love." We sat for a long moment in silence— Wes cross-legged and me curled up on my side. "We can make this all look like the accident it was, just like with Wright," Wes suggested.

I forced myself to stand, my head spinning like a storm.

"What do you mean?"

"Just trust me, okay?" He extended his hand. I placed my palm in his.

———

Wes and Diego hoisted Riley's body into the backseat of his station wagon. We gathered our belongings from the cabin, dismantled the tent setups and food, and loaded everything back into Brooklyn's and Diego's cars.

"Let's make a truce," Diego said as we congregated near the vehicles.

Wes nodded. "That's right. We all agree never to return to this cabin or mention it to anyone. Not a single person. Promise?" We all nodded. "Good. Now let's get this over with."

Wes and Diego hopped into Riley's car. April took the wheel of Diego's Charger, and I rode in Brooklyn's car. She composed herself a bit, gathering her hair into a topknot, and kept her focus on the road as we drove into the night.

After twenty long minutes of silence, I finally broke it. "Why didn't you tell anyone what happened, what Riley was doing?"

"I don't want to talk about it, Eddie."

"But—"

Her intense eyes flashed at me. "I said I don't want to talk about it."

I sank back in my seat, staring out the windshield. Brooklyn wasn't being fair. It wasn't easy for me to discuss either, but my reaction had ended with someone dead. I licked my lips. "I understand. But when you're ready to talk, I'll be here, okay?"

Her thumbs drummed on the steering wheel as she carefully navigated the bumpy road. "Yep," she replied quietly, her expression remaining guarded. A lump formed in my throat as we resumed our silent journey.

It felt as though we'd driven to the edge of the world before we finally stopped near a body of water. Everyone piled out. The full moon loomed huge and low in the pitch-black sky, almost within reach. Thousands of stars shimmered above, silent witnesses to the secret we were trying to bury. We used our phone lights to find our way around.

Wes and Diego, grunting and straining, propped Riley against the steering wheel of his car. His head thumped against the back of the seat, causing his lips to part slightly.

I gasped, my nerves overwhelming me. What if Riley was still alive?

They buckled his seatbelt securely. Was his eyelid twitching at all?

"Wait," I cried out, startling everyone. I staggered over to Wes. "Are you sure he's—?"

"What? Dead?" Diego interjected. I nodded frantically.

"Want to check his stiff skin and see for yourself?"

"Fuck off, Diego," Wes snapped, gently shoving me aside. "He's gone, Eddie," he murmured before returning to work. They started Riley's car, propped a foot on the accelerator, and closed the door. Then they moved to the back of the station wagon and began pushing it, as it barely budged on its own. "We need your help, Eddie," Wes called, his face taut with effort. The old car was stubborn, moving like a boat in the current.

With a deep swallow of bile, I leaned against the trunk and dug my heels into the dirt. Together, with one hard shove, we set the car rolling toward the water. We watched, transfixed, as the station wagon sank until only bubbles and ripples remained on the surface.

21

EDDIE

NOW

"Happy birthday," I whispered into Brooklyn's ear as I approached her locker on Tuesday morning.

She glanced over her shoulder with a half-smile. "You remembered?"

"Well, how could I forget the most special day in the world?" I laughed, though even I knew that was too corny. "Have you made a wish yet?"

She chewed on her lip and nodded. "I just hope it comes true."

"Me too." I kissed her and took her hand. "This is for you." I slid a promise ring into her palm—a silver ring set with a sapphire, her birthstone, engraved inside with **ED & BROOK 4EVER.**

Her mystic eyes read the inscription over and over, her expression blank and detached. Then she blinked several times as tears pooled in her gaze.

"Hey, what's wrong?" I asked, squinting at her teary face. What the hell was happening?

"Brooklyn, what is it?" I wrapped her in my arms as her body trembled.

Through sniffles, she confessed, "I did something bad, and I really hope you can forgive me."

"Of course, I will. You never have to worry about that."

But she shook her head. "You have no idea how awful it is," she whispered, large teardrops trailing down her cheeks.

I pulled her into a tight hug. "Whatever it is, we can get through it. Okay?"

She pulled back slightly. "Do you promise?"

"Yes, Brooklyn. Now, please calm down—it's your fucking birthday." I managed a laugh.

She dried her face and slipped on the ring. "Eddie, no matter what, I hope our feelings for each other never change."

I kissed her gently. "We're going to be just fine."

The bell rang for first period. We made plans for dinner later and hurried to homeroom, where Miss Harper stood at the front alongside Principal Marriot, both wearing grim expressions. Something was clearly wrong, but what?

"May I have your attention, please?" Principal Marriot said in a stern tone. A few beats of heavy silence followed before he continued. What was going on?

Taking a deep breath, she announced, "I am heartbroken to confirm that Riley Donahue is deceased. Authorities found his body early this morning. We have postponed first period for a mandatory grief counseling session. We will call students individually in alphabetical order; when you hear your name, please report to the guidance counselor's office immediately."

My ears rang as cold sweat broke out. Riley had been found? But how? I wanted to scream—the only way someone could have found him was if one of us had told...

I slowly turned to Brooklyn, thinking of our conversation just moments ago. I stared at her—although her back was turned and her gaze fixed ahead, her foot tapped nervously under the desk.

At lunch, I growled, "We're not doing this right now, Diego," as he attempted to rally the gang to meet up at the park across the street.

Wes wasn't there today, and he hadn't responded to any of my texts. I knew Diego intended to get away and pin the blame on Brooklyn. We all suspected her guilt—from her nervous ticks to her lack of eye contact, her very expression practically shouted confession. But why would she commit the act and not tell any of us? Especially me—I would have understood.

"Eddie's right, Diego," April agreed, whispering, "we can't keep sneaking off for private chats every time something new comes up," her wide eyes darting around cautiously. They landed on Brooklyn, prompting April to scowl. "But I can't *believe* you."

Brooklyn shook her head softly. "You guys don't understand…"

"Save it, Brook," Diego snapped, leaping to his feet. "I can't stand looking at you." With that, he stalked away, and without a word, April left as well.

Taking a deep breath, I began, "Brooklyn…"

"Don't look at me like that, Eddie, please…" her voice broke as she pleaded.

"Like what?" I asked gently.

"Like you hate me." She buried her face in her hands and sobbed.

I reached over carefully to free her fingers. "I just need to know why you did it, Brook. I could never hate you."

She hesitated, hiccupping, then murmured, "You don't know what it's like…"

I scooted closer to console her. "So, tell me—what's going on?"

After a long pause, she took a deep breath. "Mrs.

Donahue's dying. Mack told me so. She can't bear to die without knowing what happened to Riley, and I just couldn't live with myself, Eddie…" She squeezed her eyes shut. "Please, try to make the others understand for me."

A gnawing pit formed in my stomach. Mrs. Donahue was dying? Could the whole ordeal with Riley have worsened her condition? And now Mack was accusing Coach Donahue of murdering Riley—we'd shattered the Donahue family piece by piece.

I took her trembling hands in mine. "I understand. It was the right thing to do." Finally, someone did something correctly. We owed the Donahues at least that much.

Brooklyn blinked through her tears. "You're not upset?"

"No," I replied, kissing her hand. "I love you even more for being so compassionate and selfless."

She laughed through the tears as she hugged me tighter. "I love you, too, Eddie."

"Everything's going to work out," I whispered, fingers gently threading through her curls.

A car horn blasted as I walked home from school, the counseling session weighing heavily on me—it all felt like my fault.

"Check it out," Wes called from behind the wheel of a small white Toyota as he stuck his head out of the driver's window.

I frowned. "What's this?"

"Come on—hop in," he insisted, swinging the passenger door wide.

I hurriedly circled around the hood and climbed into the seat. Once the door shut and we pulled away from the school grounds, I turned to him. "Brooklyn tipped off the cops about Riley. They found his body." I waited for his reaction, but he kept his gaze fixed on the windshield, his grip tightening. "I tried texting you."

"I was retaking the SAT—I passed," he replied, nonchalantly.

My mouth dropped open. "Well, that's great. I didn't think you cared, but I'm glad you changed your mind."

He shrugged. "Anyway, wasn't finding Riley what you and Brooklyn wanted? Aren't you two satisfied now?"

Under the circumstances, I suppose I was relieved. Not only was a heavy burden lifted from my shoulders, but the Donahues finally had answers. I quickly updated him about Mrs. Donahue's condition and Mack's suspicions.

"I'm sure that pissed off Diego and April, right?" he said.

I scoffed. "'Pissed' is an understatement."

Wes waved a hand dismissively. "They'll have to get over it. Now we just stick to our story. Brooklyn isn't planning on changing it, is she?"

"Not that I know of," I answered, uncertainty knotting

my stomach. I'd need to talk to Brooklyn later. I glanced at Wes, noting his rigid posture and a spark in his eye. "What's with you? You barely reacted to Riley's discovery— you're so...calm. And where are we headed? You missed our turn."

A grin tugged at his lips. "We're going for a long drive, so buckle up."

"A long drive? Wes, what are you talking about?"

"You're going to see Mom. That's why I saved up for this car—well, I kinda put it together myself, fixing it and everything."

He rambled on, while I fixated on the thought of Mom. "Wait...what?"

Wes blinked at me. "Yeah. Isn't it about time?"

I shrugged. "I don't know—you always put it off, so I assumed you didn't want to."

"Oh—*I'm* not going in. I'm making sure you get there, though."

I almost asked him why he harbored such resentment toward her, but I decided not to ruin the moment—and make him turn the car around. I took a deep breath as I settled into my seat.

Wes snickered, as if reading my mind. "Just relax. You'll be fine."

"How can you say that? We haven't seen her in nearly ten years. What if she doesn't recognize me?"

"That would be her fault, wouldn't it?"

"Wes—?"

"You know what? Let's test out these speakers." He cranked the radio up to full blast. I rolled my eyes. I'd never seen him act like such a big baby.

After an hour, we arrived at the Angel Wing Asylum. The stone building loomed like a gloomy mansion, its many windows gazing like empty eye sockets.

"Here we are…" Wes intoned ominously as he shut off the engine.

I stared at the imposing building. "Are you sure you're not coming in?"

"A hundred percent," he replied, leaning back with his arms behind his head. "Go on…"

I climbed out, my legs feeling like jelly as I hobbled up the rocky pavement. In just a few moments, I'd see my mom. *My mom.*

I stepped through the entrance when suddenly someone grabbed me roughly by the shoulders. "Hey!" I cried, jerking free.

A security guard standing by the door clasped my shoulder again—this time more gently—and said, in a gruff tone, "Gotta search you." His beefy hand waved a metal detector over my outstretched arms.

Why was he searching me for metal? Was there danger here? I scanned the foyer and spotted a friendly-faced woman behind the desk, offering an apologetic smile for his brusqueness. Realizing I had nothing, he stepped aside and motioned for me to proceed. What an asshole. I straightened my shirt.

The receptionist waved me over. "Hi there."

Clearing my throat, I said, "I'm here to see Kira Hawkins."

She handed me a pen to sign in and directed me to the third floor with a visitor's pass. The elevator dropped me into another lobby where a male orderly, leaning against a desk and in animated conversation, paused at my approach.

He wore the same uniform as the guards who had taken Mom. I searched his face but hadn't seen him before—it seemed he couldn't have been much older than me.

"Can I help you?" he asked.

Holding up the visitor's pass, I replied, "I'm here to see Kira Hawkins."

He exchanged surprised glances with the receptionist. "Interesting. No one has visited Kira in quite some time," she observed. The orderly, who appeared to be in his fifties, simply nodded.

Had Hank not visited her, too? The thought of Mom being alone there made my skin crawl. Why had it taken me so long to summon some courage?

"Well, she's right this way," the orderly said, gesturing me onward. Her room was the first door on the left. I had noticed her name alongside the steel door, which gave me pause—why steel?

The lock clicked as the door slowly swung open, snapping me from my thoughts. My breathing quickened as a soft beam of sunlight flooded the room.

"She loves the outdoors," the orderly remarked. "Kira, there's someone here to see you. Isn't that great?" Glancing over his shoulder at me, he added, "Come on."

I dried my moist palms on the back of my jeans and cautiously advanced. The drawn shades let in a golden glow that made me squint. As my eyes adjusted, I detected a thin figure standing by the largest window. Gradually, I made out Mom's thick, curly hair.

The orderly approached her, speaking in a gentle tone, "Kira, he's here." He carefully grabbed her shoulder and guided her along.

My heart pounded as I took in the sight: Mom's features had not changed since the day they brought her to the asylum. Her sharp, dark eyes still held that spark Hank had tried so hard to extinguish. Dressed in a pale green scrub uniform—a color close to her favorite—she appeared almost timeless.

"Who is that?" she asked, squinting at me. Taking a step forward, her beautiful, youthful face emerged against her soft brown skin.

"It's me, Mom. Eddie," I said, clearing my throat and clenching my fists to steady my nervousness.

Her head tilted upward as she murmured my name under her breath. Then, she gasped from deep within.

"Edward? My beautiful boy? Christ, look at you." She staggered forward.

The orderly moved to stop her, but I motioned that it was alright. She stopped just inches away, tears streaking her face. I was taller now, and she peered up at me, arms outstretched. "May I?"

"Of course." My voice came out dry and hoarse as I closed my eyes while she wrapped both arms around me, drenching me in her warm floral scent. I enfolded her fragile frame in my arms, noting how little remained beneath her clothes.

I'd waited all my life for that moment, yet I felt only an empty void.

Mom rested her head against my shoulder and inhaled my scent, her grip tightening. "I never thought I'd see you again. And yet here you are, as handsome as ever." She pulled back and chuckled wildly. "Look at you—all that hair." She playfully tugged at my ponytail. "So, how's… life?" Her voice dipped, turning serious.

I stepped away from her embrace. "It's been going," I shrugged, stuffing my hands into my pockets and fumbling for words. I told her about Brooklyn, my SAT score, the championships, and my dream of making it to the Olympics.

Her eyes brightened with every detail, as if confirming I really did have the perfect life I described. "I'm so proud of you," she whispered. "I always knew you'd grow up to be something greater than your father and me—" Her voice choked off just before she could finish.

I frowned. "Mom?"

She stared past me, eyes wide. "Wesley?" I spun around to see Wes surveying the room. "Wesley, you came too?" She reached out to stroke his face, but he ducked away.

"Yeah, I just thought, since I'm here, why not say hey? So, hey." He forced a sarcastic smile.

Mom covered her mouth with both hands and giggled like a little girl. "It feels like Christmas—both of my beautiful boys are here." She grinned before reaching for Wes again, climbing on tiptoes to hook an arm around his neck. "What amazing stories do you have for me?"

"Amazing stories?" Wes repeated, frowning.

"Yes." Mom spun to face me. "Edward's been telling me such wonderful things."

"Is that so?" Wes arched a brow and folded his arms.

Mom clucked her tongue at his stubbornness. She brushed her hand through his hair and gasped as she inspected the scars on his face. "Oh no," she whispered. "He's—he's doing it to you, too?"

Wes jerked away angrily. "What the hell do you care? You're the one who left us with him."

Mom's lower lip trembled as she backed away, eyes filling with tears. "I never thought he would hurt you too. You were just kids…" Her voice broke.

Wes scoffed, his face contorting. "Oh, look at those crocodile tears." I nudged his arm in protest. "I'll be outside." With that, he stormed away.

Mom covered her face, shoulders shaking.

"Mom—it's okay. It's not as bad as it looks," I tried, "Wes is a big boy now. We can handle ourselves." I glanced at her, wondering why she was still there when nothing about her seemed insane.

"Hey, Mom?" I gently removed her hands from her face. "When are you leaving?"

"This is my home now, Edward. Thanks to Hank, I can't ever leave. I've tried so many times." Her eyes widened as her words tumbled out in agitation. "If I'm good, they'll let me go. But I just keep saying the wrong things." She banged her forehead with her fist.

"Kira…" the orderly called sternly.

"They want me to admit I attempted suicide, but I never did. It was all Hank's doing—Hank fabricated everything." Her voice rose. "Now, I'm never leaving this place." She pounded her forehead with both fists repeatedly.

"Kira!" The orderly grabbed her again, and she bounced in his hold, struggling to break free. "Can I get some help here?" he shouted.

"But it's my fault!" Mom sobbed. "Understand—it's *my* fault, not Hank's. Hank never meant to hurt us. Tell Wesley that, please."

"Sir, I'm going to have to ask you to leave now, okay?" a woman said from behind me. Before I could respond, she ushered me down the hall and slammed the door in my face, leaving Mom's hoarse screams echoing in my ears.

Wes and I barely spoke during the ride back. I decided not to mention Mom's final words—even after all these years, she still took Hank's side. None of her ranting made any sense. What suicide? What was her fault? Maybe the asylum was where she belonged after all.

"The silence is driving me nuts," Wes finally said, switching on the radio.

"*…the autopsy report confirms that Riley Donahue died from a drug overdose. Traces of OxyContin were found in his stomach. Authorities dragged Lake Tallahawa yesterday and discovered Shannon Donahue's vehicle with Riley still inside. The car was reported missing around the time he vanished and apparently sank into the lake while Riley was driving under the influence. Here's a statement from Sheriff Owens, and I quote…*"

Wes abruptly switched the radio off.

I blinked, my heart pounding. "What are they saying?

When did Riley start taking drugs?"

He gripped the wheel with both hands, shifting uneasily. "Who knows what that fucker did?"

"*I* know," I yelled suddenly. "I *know* Riley didn't do drugs. We had a swim meet the following week—we were going to be tested! Why would he risk that? Cheating his way to team captain? Nationals meant as much to him as they do to me."

Wes's eyes flicked my way. "Then what are you suggesting? How else do we explain the drugs in his system?"

I couldn't bring myself to say it aloud—the only logical explanation was that someone else had drugged Riley long before I shoved him out the window. I gasped.

Brooklyn.

She'd been alone with Riley in the cabin long before I returned. Could *she* have done it?

22

BROOKLYN

NOW

"One thousand one hundred and ninety? You *must* be joking, Brooklyn!" Dad barked, spinning me around from my vanity mirror.

I was still wrestling with my hair, all because Eddie was determined to go ahead with my birthday plans—even though all Haywood could discuss was Riley's dead body. All because of me.

I stared at Dad, mouth agape. How did he even find out about my SAT score?

I bit my bottom lip, scrambling for words.

"Principal Marriot called this afternoon, worried about you. Seems I should be concerned too. What's going on? First, you ruin your chances at Juilliard. Now these lousy test scores? You'll be lucky to hit community college." He slammed his fist onto my dresser.

Taking a deep breath, I felt tears welling up. "It's been really tough, Dad."

"How? All I expect is for you to focus on your grades. And where exactly do you think you're heading?" he snapped, glowering at my lavender blouse.

"Out with Eddie."

"Like hell you are—"

Before he could continue, Mom forced her way into the room, glancing between us. Hadn't Dad told her? Damn it. I hid my face behind my hand.

"Brooklyn failed her SAT test."

Mom gasped and spun toward me. "That must be a mistake, right Brooklyn? You could ace that test in your sleep."

"I just felt overwhelmed, Mom. It wasn't my fault—I was worried about the Donahue family. I—"

"That isn't your concern," Dad cut in harshly. "The kid overdosed. Haven't I warned you about the company you keep?"

Riley wasn't the pill popper, Dad. I was. Just tell him already, you coward. Admit everything you've done. My jaw tightened; no—I shook my head and squeezed my eyes shut. "*No.* Just shut the fuck up!"

"*Brooklyn?*" Mom whipped around. "What the hell?"

My eyes widened in shock. Had I really said that? "I'm—I'm sorry. I didn't mean it. I—"

Dad puffed out his chest. "Just save it, Brooklyn. I'm grounding you."

"But I didn't mean it," I protested, my voice rising. "It's my birthday, Dad, please…"

"Dana—" Mom started, softening, "That's harsh."

"I don't give a damn. Do I have to list every misstep you've made? I barely recognize who you are anymore," Dad raged, his glare heavy with disappointment.

Mom laid a hand on his shoulder. "Let's take a breath and talk this through calmly—no shouting, no swearing," she urged, nodding at me, "and canceling her birthday isn't an option, Dana."

"It's not just about my birthday, Mom. Riley is dead. I need to be with my friends."

"Being with your friends is exactly why you're turning out this way," Dad argued.

Mom shook her head. "You're not being fair."

"Look," Dad said, placing a hand over his heart. "My condolences to the Donahues—I mean that sincerely. But they should've done a better job raising their children. Robert's a coach. Why didn't he notice his own kid was using?"

My eyes narrowed. A valid point, Dad. Why don't you?

Mom sighed. "How the Donahues run their home isn't

our business. We have our own issues to work through."
She fixed her gaze on me. "Brooklyn, something's off. Now,
what is it?"

I hesitated. Would confessing all of it help? Starting at
the beginning with Mr. Wright... I met Mom's look—a
mix of genuine concern and a desperate need for the truth.
If I came clean, they could help me. But Dad was a lawyer—
and just the thought of that made my stomach flip. They
found Riley's body. I could go to jail. So could Eddie and
everyone else.

I closed my eyes as my mind raced.

"Honey?" Dad's gentle grip on my shoulder made me
shudder as I began to sob. He guided me over to the bed
where I sat.

I looked him in the eyes. "I'm...so...sorry..." I choked
on the words, overwhelmed with grief.

"Listen to me," Dad said quietly. "Whatever it is, we can
help you."

"That's right," Mom added. "We're always here for you."

But would that still be true after what I needed to
confess? Of course not. They'd shun me for sure. I wrapped
my arms around myself and rocked back and forth.

"How about this? Take tonight to collect yourself, and
tomorrow morning we'll talk it out," Mom suggested.

I nodded. I had the night to work through what I had to
say. "Okay," I whispered, my throat sore and swollen. I

wiped my tears away with the back of my hand. "I'll tell Eddie we need to postpone our plans."

"I'll call him. You should rest," Dad said. I didn't argue—I just agreed.

"Good," Mom sighed in relief. "Maybe I'll make that strawberry French toast you love tomorrow morning." She leaned in and kissed my forehead. "Sleep well, Brook."

I watched as she left, with Dad following close behind. He fixed me with a long look before silently closing the door.

I collapsed back onto the bed with a heavy exhale, trying to figure out the best way to be honest. The truth was the only answer.

***

"Brooklyn? I brought you cookies and a glass of milk," Mom called through my bathroom door half an hour later.

As if I were Santa Claus. I rolled my eyes. "Thanks, Mom!" Her footsteps echoed as the door closed behind her. I stepped out of the shower and wrapped a towel around my hair.

Soon, I padded back into my room in a bathrobe. The snack sat invitingly on my nightstand, its snickerdoodle aroma making my mouth water. I reached for a cookie when a tap at the window made me spin.

"April?" I whispered. "What are you doing here?"

"Trying to figure out what the hell is going on," she replied from the windowsill, clutching her side as if winded. "Your dad called Eddie and told him not to meet you. So Eddie called, but you didn't answer—which now makes sense." She gestured at my robe. "Eddie sent me to get the straight story, but your dad said to scram. So I sneaked up here to hear it straight from you."

I shrugged. "Nothing. I'm just grounded—can't get into Juilliard and I bombed my SAT. Dad's livid. He even canceled my birthday." I stalked over to the drawer for my pajamas.

April scoffed. "People make mistakes. Why doesn't he just take the stick out of his ass already?"

I met her eyes in the mirror, a slow smile tugging at my lips. We locked eyes briefly, but she quickly diverted her gaze and answered the question I had on my mind. "I'm sorry about Riley," I said instead.

She shrugged again. "Yeah, Eddie mentioned that too. I just—" She closed her eyes for a moment and then fixed her stare on my reflection. "I don't get why you care so much about the Donahues. Everyone's got problems. What makes them any different?"

"It was the right thing to do, April. It's not like I threw you all under the bus or anything."

"Well, the autopsy shows someone fed him drugs."

I whirled around. "No one said that."

"It doesn't take Einstein to figure it out. Riley was clean. Don't you think Brody will come back to question us? Do you even care?"

I sunk onto the edge of the bed with a heavy sigh. "It's overwhelming, living this lie. That's why tomorrow morning I'm going to tell my parents everything."

She narrowed her eyes. "You're telling them what exactly?"

"Everything. I have to come clean eventually."

Her eyes squinted in disbelief. "Is this because things didn't work out for you? You're just going to give up because you couldn't pass the SAT? It's not the end of the world—you can retake it. Hell, you can even buy the answers from Mario."

"Like you did?" I challenged.

Her face hardened. "Yeah, so what? I did what I had to do. I'm leaving Haywood. Don't expect me to do it the Little Miss Perfect way. Besides, you're not perfect anymore, not with your little drug problem." She tilted her head. "I know what you and Diego have been up to."

I shifted uncomfortably. It was déjà vu, just like when Riley confronted me that night. I couldn't deny it any longer. "I'm not perfect, April. Diego tried to help me at first, but it turned into something more." I immediately wished I could take back my words—they came out completely wrong.

April's jaw dropped. "You fucked him, didn't you?" Her mouth hung open as she turned away, laughing bitterly. "You slut. I thought Diego was *gay*—I honestly believed he was into Wes. No wonder he wouldn't give me a chance. He wants *you*." She recoiled in disgust.

My eyes flashed with anger. "Damnit, April. Are you trying to sleep with the entire school? Is that why you mock Eddie all the time—because you can't have him?"

She clenched her fist. "Do you even deserve Eddie, though? You're not as loyal to him as he is to you. You're such a hypocrite."

"You've overstayed your welcome, April."

Her eyes welled up, blinking rapidly. "I'm just saying— if you're going to come clean to your parents, when will you tell Eddie the truth? Why keep stringing him along with your fake angel act?"

"Get. Out." I pointed at the window, my lips trembling. I struggled to rein in my emotions—she was right. I had to tell Eddie the truth—about the drugs, Diego, Riley, everything.

With a quick swipe at her tear, April dashed to the window and disappeared.

After pacing for a moment, I opened my underwear drawer for my pills and downed a couple. Then, I finished Mom's snack and wept.

23

EDDIE

"I still haven't heard from Brooklyn," I told Wes as we packed our things for school the next day. I'd spent the night restless, with too many questions tumbling through my mind—questions for Hank about Mom and that suicide she mentioned, questions for Brooklyn about what happened at the cabin with Riley, and even questions about Brooklyn's dad, Mr. Dimitri. What was his deal?

Hank was gone at dawn, mumbling about a job interview while reeking of booze—a sure sign of its inevitable disaster. "What did April say?" Wes asked, hopping on one leg as he pulled on his sneaker.

"April said Brooklyn could go to hell. She's really pissed about Riley."

Wes rolled his eyes. "Well, the cat's out of the bag now. April just needs to get over it."

"Yeah. I was wondering…" I paused, clenching my textbooks as I stuffed them into my backpack. "What happened at the cabin before I pushed Riley? How did he get his hands on oxy? Somebody must've given it to him—someone like Brooklyn, right?"

Wes shrugged. "I don't know. Why are you so sure that Riley couldn't have gotten it himself? That was enough oxy to kill him if taken alone. If Brooklyn did it, did she really intend to kill him? And where the hell would she find oxy? Eddie, you're not thinking straight. But you can go ask her your questions. We've still got some time before class."

I nodded, a chill crawling up my back as I imagined Brooklyn's answers. The more I thought about it, the more things didn't add up. Brooklyn had been so cold on the ride to the lake, and right after Riley fell, she made sure no one else knew what had happened.

"It's weird she bailed on her birthday," I said as we climbed into Wes's compact car. "Her dad was a real asshole about it too. He said Brooklyn wanted to sort out her life without my distractions. That didn't sound like her at all."

Wes snorted behind the wheel. "Maybe we should teach the dickhead a lesson and key his car."

"Wesley—" I started.

He threw up his hands. "I'm just kidding." We pulled up to Brooklyn's block, where chaos reigned: an ambulance and a couple of police cars parked outside her house. "What the…?" Wes stopped the car.

I sprang from the seat, heart pounding in my throat. On the lawn stood Mr. and Mrs. Dimitri, while paramedics raced from the house carrying a stretcher—with Brooklyn on it.

"Brooklyn? *Brooklyn*!" I dashed forward, but an officer grabbed my arm.

"Son, stay back," he ordered.

"What's happening?" I demanded, twisting to free myself.

"By the looks of it, she overdosed."

Overdosed? I felt lightheaded, my vision swirling. Brooklyn didn't do drugs. What the fuck was going on?

Mrs. Dimitri wailed for Brooklyn as the paramedics hoisted the stretcher into the ambulance. "This is *your* fault!" she screamed, smacking Mr. Dimitri.

"Hey. Someone get those two apart," a man called out. "Edward Hawkins?" I turned to see Detective Brody, who introduced himself as part of the homicide unit.

I stared, speechless. My mind couldn't wrap around what I'd just heard about Brooklyn. How could it be? Brooklyn didn't do drugs. Brooklyn *didn't* do drugs.

Wes came over and draped an arm protectively across

my shoulders, jolting me from my shock. "How do you know my brother?"

"I know both of you, Wesley. You were five or six years old when I last saw you."

"What?" Wes and I blurted out simultaneously.

Brody grinned. "I was your father's partner a long time ago."

I blinked, picturing his face without the beard and mustache. I remembered seeing that very face in the car with Hank in kindergarten. I gasped. "I remember you now."

Wes didn't. He eyed Brody skeptically. "So you became a homicide detective and left Hank and Haywood behind?"

Brody casually rocked his hand. "You could say that."

"Then why come back here?" Wes demanded.

Brody sighed as he looked at Brooklyn's parents. "I was here today to speak to Brooklyn—and I discovered this…" His voice trailed off as we watched the ambulance speed away.

"Will she be alright?" I asked.

"I can't really say." His eyes locked onto mine. "Do you think this was an attempted suicide?"

I furrowed my brows. "What do you mean?"

"Perhaps Brooklyn was feeling guilty."

"How would we know what she's feeling?" Wes cut in. "Her folks are right there. Shouldn't you be questioning them?"

Brody nodded. "I did. They had some pretty interesting things to say."

"Like what?" I pressed.

"How about you come back to the station with me? I've got a couple of questions for you too."

"Sounds lovely, but we've got school," Wes protested, tugging at me lightly.

I hesitated—was he serious? I couldn't head to school with Brooklyn in the hospital—I needed to be with her. "No, I'm going to the hospital," I insisted.

Brody forced a smile. "The questions will be brief. By the time we're done, the doctors should be finished with your friend."

I glared at him. "Brooklyn's my girlfriend."

"Got it. Sorry, but you don't want to be stuck in a waiting room, dying for answers, right? Come spend some time with me at the station—it's a win-win. Plus, I can write you a note for school explaining your absence."

"Okay." Wes nodded. "But you can't split us up. Technically both of us should have a guardian present. I'm responsible for my brother."

"I respect that. And for the record, no one's in trouble. This is just a brief interview." Brody added with a smile that made my insides churn.

Wes returned a sarcastic grin. "Guess we'll follow you in

our car." He ushered me back into the passenger seat, then sank into the driver's seat with an exasperated sigh. "That guy was Hank's old partner? You really think he's lying?"

"I remember him. He was nice to Mom and us. Remember how he once picked us up from school when Mom and Hank were at the hospital?" I recalled, remembering Mom's story about tripping on the basement stairs—when in reality Hank had slammed her head against the wall, leaving a hole in the plaster.

Wes's jaw dropped. "Wait—the guy with long hair? Did *he* age?" He laughed, but then quieted when I didn't join in. Wes gripped my knee. "Did you even know Brooklyn was taking anything?"

"No. It just makes no sense. Brooklyn is too smart—" My words caught in my throat as my breaths came in short, hoarse pants. "Wesley—I can't—breathe—need air—" I fumbled with the door handle.

Wes grabbed me firmly. "No, take it easy. Calm down, you're hyperventilating." He rummaged through his backpack, dumped out his lunch onto the car floor, and handed me a brown paper bag. I buried my face in its peanut butter scent and took deep, shaky breaths. Wes patted my back. "Everything's going to be fine. *Brooklyn* will be fine."

"Can I get you a soda or some water?" Brody offered, beckoning Wes and me to sit across from him. We were now at the police station—the same one they'd taken us to after the fight at Mario's.

The interview room was bathed in harsh overhead lights as we sat around a large steel table in mismatched chairs. I settled into a desk chair while Wes flopped into a folding seat.

Wes scoffed. "What, so you can get our DNA? I know how you cops work—I'd rather swallow spit."

Brody dropped into the seat across from us. "Suit yourselves," he said, tapping his pen on the tabletop. "Eddie—when I saw you and Brooklyn on the street that day, why did you run?"

My mind blanked. When?

"He did what anyone would do if they thought some weirdo was following him. Didn't you identify yourself as a detective?" Wes demanded. "I don't think you did."

Brody gave Wes a smile. "I would've, if given the chance." He scribbled on his notepad. "I'd also like to know about the last time you saw Riley."

I licked my lips. Riley—what had Brooklyn's parents said about him? That was what I needed to know. "It was that Friday night, at Mario's birthday party. Everyone was there."

"Did Riley seem…off?" Brody pressed.

Wes sneezed.

"Bless you," Brody said automatically.

I glanced sideways at Wes, who kept his gaze fixed ahead. His sneeze was forced—a silent cue for me to agree. But why?

"Uh—maybe," I mumbled.

"How so?" Brody leaned forward, pen poised.

I shrugged. "I don't know. Just—"

"Being a pain in the ass," Wes interrupted. "Getting under everyone's skin, picking fights, and flirting with girls he knew were off-limits. Stupid, reckless shit."

I struggled to keep a straight face. Riley never acted like that at Mario's party. Still, when Brody looked at me, I nodded in quiet agreement with Wes.

Brody jotted down another note. "I understand Riley was captain of the swim team. You fell short of that role, right, Eddie?"

How did he know that? I clenched my fist under the table but kept my face stoic. "I didn't want to be team captain."

His eyes widened. "Really? But weren't you the one finishing your meters in almost half the average time for someone your age? I'd say that title suited you, wouldn't you?"

I shook my head and shrugged. "It wasn't a big deal. Riley swam just as well."

"But now that Riley's, well...dead, you get another shot at that title, right?"

Wes's irritation was palpable. "What exactly are you getting at?"

Brody shrugged. "Maybe it's nothing. But when you look at recent events, it seems that nothing goes your way until someone is removed from the picture. Take Simon Wright, for example." He leaned back, as though he'd struck gold.

My right cheek twitched. Was he linking us to Mr. Wright?

Wes inched forward, covering my hand under the table. "Or maybe some people are just luckier. Either way, what does all this have to do with us? Why are we here? Are we under arrest?"

I wondered at how calm Wes remained. The detective wasn't stupid—he'd brought us in because he thought we were connected.

"No, you're not under arrest. This is just a friendly chat, as I promised." Brody raised his hands defensively.

"Well, I've got a question for you," Wes said. "If Riley overdosed or whatever happened, why is a homicide detective so obsessed with this case?"

"It's funny you should ask. The autopsy found skull fractures on Riley's head—clear evidence of foul play."

My heart pounded like a bass drum. Everything was

falling apart. After Riley's accident, his death was meant to be ruled an accidental drowning. But then the oxy incident surfaced, shifting it toward an overdose—and now, the cops might discover that I pushed him out the window?

Wes frowned. "You pulled his car out of a lake. Isn't some bodily harm bound to happen?"

Brody shook his head. "The car sank underwater—it didn't slam into a brick wall. The Donahue case and Simon Wright's case are still open. I wanted to question you briefly since you knew them both."

"Most of Haywood knew Wright and Riley," I pointed out.

"True," Brody agreed. "But not as well as you two. I also heard Mr. Wright had it out for you boys."

Wes rolled his eyes. "Most of Haywood High was his enemy. Mr. Wright treated everyone like shit."

"Wait a minute," I cut in. "What exactly did Mr. and Mrs. Dimitri say about Brooklyn?"

"Right." Brody's gaze drifted back as he recalled. "Brooklyn had a fight with her parents last night. They figured it was due to some ongoing problem she'd been dealing with. She promised to tell them everything this morning, but when they went into her room, they found her unconscious in her own vomit. There was also an empty bottle of Adderall under her bed."

"The study drug?" My voice wavered high. "Was it

prescribed?"

Brody pressed his lips together, pausing. "No."

My stomach lurched. I leaned forward, clutching my knees as vision blurred through emerging tears. Why hadn't Brooklyn told me? Worse, why hadn't I noticed?

Fragments of memory returned—the day of the SAT exam. She wasn't rummaging through her locker for notes—she was searching for pills.

Tears streamed down as I met Brody's eyes. "I have to go to her. I need to be with her when she wakes up."

"I'll take you," Wes declared, shooting Brody a meaningful glare. "Are we done here?"

Brody nodded as our chairs scraped the floor while we stood. "One more thing," he said, gripping Wes's shoulder. "Where'd you get that shiner?" he asked, nodding toward Wes's partially healed eye.

Wes tightened his jaw. "You were Hank's partner—tell me, then."

Brody's expression softened. "Wait, here's my card." He slipped it into my palm. "Call me anytime if you ever need help. You too," he told Wes. Sincerity shone in his eyes, so I thanked him.

At the car, Wes half-joked, "You're not planning on keeping that card, are you?"

I slipped it into my back pocket.

When we reached the hospital, Mr. and Mrs. Dimitri waited with a guard stationed between them. Where once Mr. Dimitri's face was set in a perpetual scowl, worry-lines now marred it.

Mrs. Dimitri glared hard as she spotted us, storming over like a raging bull. "Where did my daughter get drugs? Was it you?" she shouted, jabbing a finger in my face nearly to my eye.

Wes moved between us and calmly pushed her arm down. "Get out of his face, woman."

"Don't you talk to my wife like that!" Mr. Dimitri snapped, moving to grab Wes, but the security guard intercepted him.

"If you don't all stop, I'll toss you out of here," the guard warned, glaring at us. He allowed Mr. Dimitri to join his wife, their anger united against Wes and me.

I crossed a hand over my chest. "Mrs. Dimitri, I had no idea Brooklyn was taking anything," I said as earnestly as I could. "I really care about her." I shot a pleading look at Mr. Dimitri, who glared back, breathing heavily.

Mrs. Dimitri's shoulders slumped. "I'm sorry. I just don't understand what's happening..." Her voice broke into soft sobs. "When Brooklyn went to bed last night, she was perfectly fine. I even left her milk and cookies for her birthday."

Mr. Dimitri nodded. "Here comes the doctor now. Maybe she'll wake up. Doctor?" He and Mrs. Dimitri rushed toward a middle-aged woman standing nearby—a tall, thin woman with wiry red curls pulled back into a ponytail and black square glasses. After a heavy pause, she said quietly, "I'm very sorry. Your daughter didn't make it."

24

WES

NOW

"Wesley?" Libby said softly, squeezing my shoulder lightly. I lifted my face from my hands only after noticing how long I'd been staring—my eyes finally catching up to the fluorescent lights above each satin-covered table.

We were at some Moroccan restaurant with a name I couldn't even pronounce, chosen by Libby. It was a couple of miles from Sweet Haven, and she mentioned that it was popular with the college crowd, making our meeting look like just another tutoring session.

I grabbed her hand tightly. I longed to kiss her, but the risk was too great.

Not even the spicy hints of turmeric and coriander could completely cover the sickening reek of a hospital.

Clenching my teeth and shutting my eyes, I recalled Eddie's animalistic wail as he crumpled after hearing the news. I feared a nervous breakdown was imminent for him.

Libby sighed, releasing my grip, and dropped her bag on the floor as she slid into the seat across from me. Wearing a mauve tracksuit with her hair pulled up in a high ponytail, she shrugged when she caught me watching her. "I still had to go on my late-night run."

Lowering my voice, I said, "You look as beautiful as ever. I'm just…glad you're here. You have no idea what it means to be surrounded by anything other than grief."

Clicking her tongue, she replied, "My heart goes out to that poor family. And your brother…" She stretched her arm across the table. "…he must be falling apart."

I didn't want to dwell on it. My head already throbbed from trying to figure out what the hell Brooklyn was doing with an illegal dose of Adderall—and who the hell gave it to her.

"Good evening. Can I start you off with some drinks?" asked a dorky server. With his unkempt, mousey curls, bad acne, and a gap between his front teeth, he double-took at Libby, his face reddening like a tomato.

Clearly, he hadn't been this close to an attractive woman before. I clamped my hands in front of me and pressed the bridge of my nose against my knuckles as Libby ordered spiced Moroccan coffee.

Just as the server was about to leave, I halted him. "While you're at it, why not grab a cold glass of something and douse yourself in it?"

"Excuse me?" he finally retorted, turning toward me.

Tilting my head, I replied, "Your temperature's shot up, hasn't it? Because you think my tutor's hot?" He whirled around, stumbling nervously.

"Wesley…" Libby frowned.

"You're just stealing the spotlight."

She pulled back, eyes wide. "Speaking of which, I swear someone was tailing me."

"What?" I responded, sitting up straighter and scanning the restaurant.

"No, not now. I'm probably just paranoid."

"Well, did you bring the—uh, stuff with you?"

"Of course." She rummaged through her bag and pulled out a file folder containing the day's schoolwork I'd missed. Opening it, she showed me my homework.

Aside from an elderly Middle Eastern couple and a woman with two small kids, Libby and I practically had the place to ourselves—it was a slow night.

"You can never be too careful. What happened? What spooked you?"

"Just some asshole on the freeway tailing me. Every time I changed lanes, he did the same. I took an exit, and so did he. I didn't lose him until I was almost here."

I leaned back. "Probably just some idiot, completely wasted."

She blinked thoughtfully. "Maybe. But when I was in the lot, I distinctly heard rushing footsteps, and yet when I looked, no one was there."

"Would you feel better if I went to check it out?" I asked in a monotone, reminiscent of a detective from an old black-and-white series.

She whipped her head back and burst into laughter. "Yes. But wait until my coffee comes—maybe you can splash him in the face while you're at it."

I laughed. "Ooh...good one."

Her expression then grew serious. "Alright, we better get moving." She gestured toward my homework, and for the next few minutes, we pored over math equations. Tomato Head reappeared with Libby's drink and menus, then vanished as quickly as he'd arrived. Keeping her focus on my paper, she said, "I must ask you something, but first I need your word that you'll be honest." I nodded, waiting for her to continue, only for her eyes to narrow at my answer. "That's incorrect."

I flipped my pencil to erase the mistake. "I knew that," I fibbed. "I was just testing if you were paying attention. You're not yourself tonight."

She squinted. "What do you mean?"

"You're going on about some stalker who isn't even

here…"

Covering her mouth to stifle her laughter, she said, "Will you cut it out already?"

"Well, shit, what if it was Tomato Head?"

"Tomato?" she whispered in confusion, then giggled until her eyes watered. "Wesley, please—this is supposed to be serious." She pointed at my paper. I scribbled what I thought was right and shot her a sidelong glance for confirmation. She nodded and then, pausing to clear her throat, asked, "So, are you involved with drugs?"

"Are you asking if I take drugs?" I replied, arching an eyebrow.

"Yes."

Meeting her gaze squarely, I said, "Nope. I don't do drugs."

"But?" She studied me intently, searching for any sign of deceit. It reminded me of… Mom.

"Nothing," I fibbed. She didn't need to know all of my secrets.

"Alright then. I'm not here to police you, just please be careful—especially with what's been going on with Brooklyn and the Donahue kid…" She sighed. "It's like a pandemic. I just couldn't bear it if—" I stared at her, and in that silence, we both understood. Still, I shuddered at the thought of being in Eddie's shoes. I'd just found a taste of happiness with Libby, and I wouldn't trade it for anything.

She smirked. "Eyes back on your work," she muttered through clenched teeth.

I glanced at my equations before shifting my gaze back to her. "I say we settle the bill and head to the Haven for room service," I whispered.

She leaned back. "Sounds like a plan."

I blinked awake, shuddering from the cold. Even though it was late September, the hotel's air conditioning was still blasting. The moon shone as brightly as a streetlamp through the curtain. Pushing myself up on an elbow, I realized we'd tossed the covers onto the floor—no wonder it was freezing. There lay Libby, nude and curled in a fetal position, her butt pressed against my hip.

Sighing, I swung my feet out of bed and headed to fetch the blankets. The clock read 2:08 A.M., and I couldn't help but picture Eddie, alone and grieving his beloved girlfriend.

"Fuck," I muttered into the cool, dark room. Why had I listened when Eddie told me to leave him alone? I thumped my forehead in frustration before quietly slipping back into my jeans and shirt.

Libby stirred, shifting on her stomach as her gentle snores filled the quiet room like a kitten's purr.

My shoulders slumped as I ran a hand through my hair.

As much as I wanted to stay, I couldn't. I carefully draped the blanket over her, kissed her cheek, and slipped out before she could notice.

But what could I do for Eddie? Nothing could bring Brooklyn back. Even if I had something to offer, it wouldn't matter. It was easy to spout empty condolences to a stranger, but Eddie was my twin brother.

A blinking billboard caught my eye: HOT GLAZED DONUTS.

I raised an eyebrow. Nothing compares to comfort food, right? Especially when paired with a cup of coffee.

"Yeah, turn him into a cop."

I pulled over anyway and grabbed the food—after all, A, it's the thought that counts, and B, I was starving and needed to get home fast. Hank's truck was gone and the porch light was off—Eddie was the only Hawkins who ever remembered to turn it on.

Stepping into the dim hallway, I noticed Eddie's bedroom door was ajar. A quick glance inside confirmed he wasn't there. That meant he must be in the basement. I sighed and headed in that direction.

Pausing at the unlocked basement door, I strained to hear the shuffling below. Were those voices? I edged closer. I could clearly hear Eddie, but who was he talking to? Monster? I highly doubted it.

"Hey, Eddie, you okay? I'm coming down," I called out,

deliberately stomping to ensure he heard me.

Eddie stood in the middle of the room with his back turned. "We'll go tomorrow," I heard him murmur.

Who was he referring to? "Yo, Eddie?" I called, setting the coffee and donuts atop the drying machine while never taking my eyes off him. "Eddie," I repeated, snapping my fingers for his attention. Catching up to him, I asked, "Hey—who are you talking to?" as I grabbed his shoulder.

Eddie met my gaze with glazed, distant eyes before simply saying, "Brooklyn."

25

EDDIE

NOW

"What you're experiencing is classic somnambulism—sleepwalking," explained Dr. Kenneth. "Are you at all familiar with sleepwalking?"

I shot a glance at Wes, who sat to my left, tapping his foot nervously. I couldn't fathom why he'd arranged this appointment, but whatever it was had clearly terrified him.

Wes had confided in the doctor about the 'murdering Hank' situation, conveniently leaving out the part where I believed I had killed him. The doctor appeared to be aware of something else as well—he and Wes had kept that a secret. None of that mattered to me now. How could I care about anything when Brooklyn was gone for good?

Dr. Kenneth leaned closer, and I scowled.

"How hard can it be to figure out? It's simply walking while asleep."

Dr. Kenneth nodded. "Exactly. But the term encompasses more than just walking. When sleepwalking, the body can execute various complex activities—even ones as challenging as driving. And when you wake up, you won't recall any of it."

"Did I drive a car the other day?" I asked, turning to Wes. But he pressed his lips together, arms crossed tightly, eyes fixed on the doctor.

Tapping his pen on the desk, Dr. Kenneth continued, "Here's what we're going to do, Edward." They both ignored my question. "I'm starting you on a mild antidepressant. Your parents need to monitor you..."

"I will monitor him," Wes interrupted.

Antidepressants? I wasn't eager to gulp down any pills. Was Wes doing this because Brooklyn had died? I hesitated, glancing between Wes and the doctor while biting my tongue.

"Mmhmm. Wesley will keep an eye on you for the next four weeks. I plan to run a couple more tests in a week," Dr. Kenneth said, scribbling a note, "and I'd like you to schedule an appointment with a mental health counselor."

I abruptly stood up. "I'm *not* crazy. Sleepwalking is harmless. Why are you making such a big deal of it,

Wesley?" I snapped at him.

He grabbed my wrist and pulled me back into the seat. "Act like you've got some sense. The doctor was talking," he muttered through clenched teeth.

I wrenched my arm free. "Why did you bring me here? Do you think I'm losing it?"

Dr. Kenneth cleared his throat nervously. "If you two need the room, I'd be happy to—"

"Nope. Carry on," Wes said curtly. "We'll set up that mental whatever appointment." It took every ounce of self-control not to lean over and smack him upside the head.

Dr. Kenneth nodded and asked, "What sorts of physical activities do you engage in, Eddie? Sports, swimming, biking, etc.?"

"Well, I'm—"

Wes sneezed. I glared at him. Did he really want me to lie right now? He was becoming a pain in the ass.

Forcing a nervous chuckle, I said, "Nothing more than the usual PE stuff at school," as Dr. Kenneth's cheesy grin lingered. I couldn't help but wonder if he slept with that grin on his face.

"Alright. Until your body adjusts to the prescription, I'd like you to refrain from strenuous activities and operating any motor vehicle—side effects can vary widely. So, to be safe, take it easy." His lips twitched above his teeth.

Whatever. Could I leave now?

"Certainly, doctor." Wesley shook his hand. As they discussed where to pick up my prescription, I rose and stalked out of the room. Wes caught up with me by the elevator. "Hey—I know you're pissed, but…"

"What the fuck?" I shoved him as forcefully as I could. For a split second, hurt flashed in his eyes, but quickly his bad-boy scowl returned, exactly as I expected.

"Why did you bring me here? Do you realize how much of a waste of time that was? I could've been with Mr. and Mrs. Dimitri."

His eyes narrowed. "For what?"

"Anything. Helping with funeral arrangements. I wouldn't know because we're busy messing around here. And you're too much of a jackass," I swung at him, "to even explain why I'm here." Wes grabbed my arm and twisted it behind my back. "Let me go." I struggled to break free.

"Listen. You were talking to Brooklyn when I got home the other night."

"What?" I tried to peek over my shoulder.

He released my arm and shoved me away. "You thought Brooklyn was in the basement making plans with you. It was totally weird. I had to whoop your ass to snap you out of it—and I could do it again if you don't cut this crap out."

"I was talking to Brook? H-how?" I stared at him, expecting a joke. But he just threw up his hands and shrugged.

"That's why we're here, Eddie—because I'm worried about you. I know what Brooklyn meant to you. It'll do you good to talk to someone—that counselor Dr. Giggles suggested."

I wanted to laugh, but dread coiled in my stomach. *Was* I losing my mind? I hadn't even noticed until he mentioned it. Why couldn't I remember certain things?

My breath caught. Would I rather believe Brooklyn was still alive than face this bleak reality? I let the questions go—the answers terrified me.

Wes gripped my shoulder. "Trust me, everything will be fine. Just follow what the doctor says, and you can…"

"How can you *say* that? Brooklyn is gone forever. My life is over, Wes."

"I didn't mean it like that, bro. I was talking about the sleepwalking crap. That's why I didn't want you to admit you're a swimmer—I know how much swimming means to you. The last thing you need is losing that too. You have to stay focused on the Nationals so you can get out of here, right?"

"Are you really thinking about the Nationals now?" I shrugged him off.

"Well, no. I mean—I don't know. I'm trying, Eddie."

"And you've done enough. But right now, I need you to leave me the hell alone. I'll find my own way home." And before he could reply, I stormed off.

"Do you need a moment alone, Eddie?" Miss Harper asked the next day.

I blinked up at her, waiting for her face to come into focus. Everything seemed unnaturally bright that day—or maybe that was just a side effect of my new medication. "I'm fine, Miss Harper." My voice was so gruff and hoarse it forced a cough out of me.

She smiled apologetically. "Would you like a drink of water?" I nodded. "Savannah, could you accompany Eddie to the water fountain, and please discuss with him what we've talked about?" Miss Harper requested.

Savannah? I spun around just as she rose from the back row. Squinting against the harsh lights that hurt my eyes, I saw her smooth the fabric of her flowery dress and wave at me. I ignored the gesture, climbing to my feet and heading for the door. The water fountains were near the gym entrance at the hallway's end, and I practically jogged to put distance between me and Savannah. "I don't need anyone to hold my hand for a drink of water," I muttered, keeping my back turned to her.

"Of course not." She chuckled—a small, high-pitched laugh like that of a child.

Nothing like Brooklyn's laughter. That thought made me straighten and finally meet her eyes. I needed to double-check something. She didn't resemble Brooklyn nearly as much as I'd imagined. For one, she didn't have Brooklyn's enigmatic eyes—hers were just…flat. How had I ever associated her with Brooklyn before? She smiled, and I responded with a frown.

"What do you want?" I asked sharply.

"Right. Miss Harper and Principal Marriot thought it'd be a good idea for us to partner for after-school study sessions."

"Why?" I couldn't hide the hostility in my tone. Why were Miss Harper and Principal Marriot concerned about me? I hadn't done anything wrong.

"Well…" she hesitated, tugging at a lock of her black hair. "You're going through a rough patch. They're worried you might need some help—"

My voice shot up so loud it ricocheted off the lockers, startling her. "Going through a rough patch? My girlfriend OD'd. Calling it a rough patch is an understatement."

"I'm sorry. I didn't mean—"

"Why can't you just mind your own damn business? I'll handle Miss Harper and Principal Marriot myself and let them know I don't need any of that."

She nodded, clearly understanding. "Eddie—I'm sorry." I turned back to the fountain, my lip quivering. "I'll see you around," she added.

"Yeah." I closed my eyes briefly as a tear trailed down

my cheek while her footsteps retreated. I didn't want anyone to pity me. Miss Harper and Principal Marriot had no right dragging Savannah into this—she knew nothing about me. And yet, I'd been an asshole just now.

I swiped at my face quickly, about to apologize, but the hallway was empty. My throat tightened, so I bent forward for another drink of water.

"How are you holding up, Edward?"

Brody? I bolted upright, wiping my chin with the back of my hand. "I'm in school, aren't I?"

"True. Physically, you're here, but your mind could be anywhere."

Was he speaking with Dr. Kenneth? I wanted to scowl, but instead I merely shrugged. "Why did your mind bring *you* here?"

Brody's lips curled into a slow smile. "Something you all mentioned during our chat." He pulled out his notepad and flipped through the pages. "Wesley mentioned it, actually. At Mario's party, Riley was being obnoxious— flirting with girls who were off-limits and all that."

"Yeah?"

He closed his pad. "No one else seems to recall that. Except Wes, Diego, and April—but of course, you all roll in the same clique. It confuses me, though—if Riley was really flirting with someone else's girlfriend, shouldn't they remember it? So, what were those kids' names?"

I threw up my hands. "I don't remember. Maybe they didn't attend Haywood High."

He nodded toward me with his pad. "That just reminded me of something else. The anonymous caller led us to Riley's body, and only his closest friends would know he liked that lake. If you all were truly best friends, then the caller must be someone within your group." My chest sank. Brody stared at me silently for a moment before adding, "You know, Edward, I can tell you're not like Wesley."

I swallowed hard. What was he implying?

As if reading my thoughts, he continued, "I think that if it came down to saving yourself or doing the right thing, you'd choose the latter. You were always a lot like Kira."

My shoulders slumped as memories of Brooklyn surfaced. Before she died, she had tried to give the Donahues some closure. All along, *she'd* been the one striving to set things right.

"Tell me the truth, Edward. Did Riley take the drugs as part of some dare? Did things spiral out of control—maybe he fell down the stairs and died? Did you all freak out and toss him in the lake?"

I nearly lost it—he was painfully accurate. Except I couldn't help but note that I hadn't been involved with the drugs at all. I had no idea what had happened before our fight. I was so fed up with lies. And at that moment, did anything even matter? Brooklyn was gone. I had originally planned to leave Haywood with her—she would have been in New York while I headed for the Olympic trials. But she overdosed, and I never even suspected she was using. Could it be that Riley had been on drugs too, and I'd simply missed it? Yet how had he managed to pass his monthly drug tests?

I locked eyes with Brody, ready to answer truthfully, when Coach Donahue interrupted.

"Detective?" Coach squinted at him.

"Mr. Donahue," Brody replied, his gaze shifting back to me.

"What are you doing here? I hope you're not up to something without an adult present or Principal Marriot's permission." Coach Donahue folded his burly arms and eyed Brody suspiciously.

Brody forced a smile. "Edward and I were just having a friendly chat. Right, pal?" He nudged me lightly.

Coach Donahue then looked at me, and when I didn't respond, he said, "I'm sorry, but you have to go, Detective."

"Very well." Brody gave a curt nod to Coach Donahue. "We'll speak soon, Edward."

"Following proper procedures, I hope," Coach Donahue called after him. Once Brody had left, he turned to face me. "Did I hear him asking you about Riley?"

"He, uh—" It pained me to use that excuse. "No. Brooklyn." My eyes closed as I forced down the bile churning in my throat. When I opened them, the room was spinning.

Coach Donahue's expression softened with sympathy. "I'm sorry about what happened." He patted my shoulder, and his touch jolted me like a shock as I inadvertently pictured him and Wes together in a motel.

Should I confront him about that?

Maybe not. They had *just* discovered his son's body a few days ago. The proper thing would be to offer condolences as well.

I glared at him. He returned my look, confused. Clearing my throat nervously, I managed, "I must say the same."

"Excuse me?" His brows furrowed.

"About Riley…I'm sorry for your loss."

He fell silent for a moment before checking his watch. "You'd better get back to your history class, bud."

I watched him leave, utterly baffled. Why wasn't he more affected by Riley's death?

26

WES

NOW

I hoisted the machine and yanked it around. What the hell was wrong with it? For sixty bucks, the damn thing should at least work.

"What are you doing?" Eddie called out as he entered the kitchen.

I spun around, caught off guard by his early arrival. Eddie was wearing the outfit I'd chosen—black slacks paired with a button-down dress shirt and a gray necktie. His thick, curly hair wasn't pulled back in a ponytail for once—instead, it rained in a full, curly fro.

"You got a coffee maker?" he observed, his eyes landing on it.

I sighed. "Yeah. I didn't think you'd be up for breakfast,

but I figured you needed something in your system to get you through this."

Eddie nodded, glancing down at himself. "Thanks for the outfit."

"You almost look half as good as me," I grinned. He returned a smile briefly before his gaze grew distant. "Hey—" I caught his attention. "If you can't do this, I understand. Mr. and Mrs. Dimitri will too."

He drew in a sharp breath, as if even breathing hurt. "I can't miss her funeral. That's the last time I'll ever see her," he said, his voice trembling.

I hadn't looked at it that way, though we were about to view the body. I shuddered. Was *I* even up for this? Hell no, but Eddie needed my support. "It'll be like your last goodbye?"

He pressed his lips together in silence for a moment before frowning. "Were you…trying to make coffee just now?" he asked, pointing at the maker.

"Yeah, but this machine isn't working," I replied, giving it another hit.

Eddie burst into a maniacal laugh.

I eyed him warily. "What's so funny?"

"You haven't even plugged it in, Wes."

I blinked in disbelief. "Motherfucker—" I muttered, gathering the cord and shoving it into the socket. Instantly, the orange light flickered on.

Eddie laughed so hard he clutched his stomach. "You're getting old, bro."

"Old? I've got your old," I retorted with a laugh, grabbing the coffee maker's box and unleashing a handful of foam puffs over his head.

"Oh—you're going to pay for that," Eddie declared, scooping up an armful and flinging them back in my face.

I staggered away, still laughing, only to collide with Monster.

He clamped his hand on the back of my neck and squeezed. "What is this—comedy hour? Do you realize how much ruckus you're causing at this hour?"

Droplets of spit splattered on my face between his words. Disgusting bastard. I swiped at my cheek so forcefully I might have torn the skin. Besides, any normal parent would be at work by now, you good-for-nothing piece of shit.

As if in response to my swearing, he shoved me against Eddie and then turned his scornful glare on him. "You have a job interview?" he sneered, eyeing Eddie's clothes in distaste.

Neither of us replied. Hank was oblivious to anything outside the realm of liquor. The news of both Riley and Brooklyn had dominated every reporter and newspaper— there was no way he hadn't seen it on TV.

"Now you've got nothing to say," he said with self-

satisfaction. "Clean up this mess and let me get some sleep."
As he stalked out of the kitchen, I glared at the back of his
glossy brown head.

One day, Hank, I'm going to fuck you up.

———

I wiped my forehead with an already soaked napkin. Hell
couldn't possibly be hotter than this. I tugged at the collar
of my dark, Polo-style T-shirt, wishing the Dimitris had
held the ceremony outdoors instead of in that cramped
church.

The place was packed wall to wall with every relative of
the Dimitri family and nearly every student at Haywood
High. I hadn't realized Brooklyn was that popular.

I stayed close to the door, hoping each time someone
entered I could catch a bit of fresh air. Eddie sat in the front
pew with Brooklyn's parents. Mr. Dimitri—such a dick—
probably wouldn't have allowed it, but as soon as we
stepped in, Mrs. Dimitri grabbed Eddie's arm and led him
away. She had even offered me a seat at the front, but I
passed. It seemed Mack Donahue had taken the spot next
to Eddie.

My brow furrowed. When exactly was Riley's pathetic
funeral? I wasn't going. I refused to sit through a pastor
wasting ten hours raving about what a good Samaritan
Riley was supposed to be.

Then April and Diego breezed in, accompanied by a gust of wind. April immediately wrapped her arms around me, looking utterly disheveled. If I didn't know better, I'd have thought she had pink eye, given how bloodshot her eyes were. The skin beneath her nose was red, raw, and flaky, and her navy, flowy dress looked as though it hadn't seen an iron in ages.

I leaned in, wrapping one arm around her, and stole a glance at Diego—his face was turned away—but was he crying?

I frowned. I understood that grief was expected here, but *Diego*? He actually hated Brooklyn. Brooklyn was April's best friend, and in my case, losing her would be like losing Eddie. I couldn't imagine keeping myself composed enough to even dress if something happened to him.

April's slight frame trembled under my arm as fresh tears streamed down her face. "I just don't know what to say," she whispered.

I, too, had nothing to say, so I nodded. "You should probably take your seat now. It's about to start," I whispered. I almost slapped myself for sounding like we were at the movies. April was too out of it to argue. After giving her one more gentle squeeze, I watched her make her way down the crowded pews.

"You holding up alright?" I asked Diego, not turning to meet his eyes. It felt awkward, knowing Brooklyn hadn't exactly been his favorite person.

He hesitated. "It...it's weird. I keep thinking I'll wake up and find that this was all just a nightmare."

I couldn't help it—my frown deepened. "What brought on this sudden change of heart about Brooklyn? You used to think she was just a stuck-up bitch."

"Dammit, Wesley. The girl's dead. Does any of that even matter now?"

What the *hell*? I tilted my head. "I didn't mean it like that. You're just...so broken up about it. It's surprising, that's all."

He shrugged. "Yeah, well, people change. Brooklyn was okay."

I slowly nodded, watching him intently. What was really going on with him? We both squinted simultaneously—me looking at him and him focusing on something ahead— when the commotion grew louder, as if someone had cranked up the volume.

"What are you doing in that seat? *I* was Brooklyn's best friend, not you!" April stood over Mack, shouting at the top of her lungs, looking every bit the madwoman. Everyone watched until April grabbed Mack by the collar and tried to drag her out of the pew.

Mr. Dimitri and a few others stepped in to break it up. Mrs. Dimitri kindly offered April a seat next to her, though it looked like a tight squeeze. I certainly wouldn't want to be shoulder-to-shoulder with anyone for the next four hours, sweating as if I were in a sauna. Nevertheless, April accepted happily.

"April's a hot mess today," I muttered.

Diego shook his head. "I'm going out for a smoke," he said quietly, slipping outside before I could comment.

Someone followed him in, greeting him politely as they passed. It was Libby's sweet, flowery perfume that gave her away. I didn't need to be told—but my eyes took her in. She looked gorgeous in an ash skirt and matching jacket. Libby could make even a plastic bag look sexy.

I wanted to grin, but I pulled myself together. This wasn't the time or the place. Libby seemed to sense it too, as she slipped past me and took a seat in the far corner. Damn.

It was nerve-wracking trying to focus on what the pastor and the Dimitris had to say about Brooklyn while avoiding Libby. Twenty minutes passed, and she hadn't looked in my direction, making my brain scream her name. I had been sneaking glances at her when the pastor announced the front row could move closer to the casket.

Oh no. My eyes flicked ahead as weeping began to rise. I couldn't tell if it was Mrs. Dimitri or April—the shoulders of both trembled.

When Eddie's turn finally came, I slowly started down the aisle. I watched as his knees buckled slightly when he hesitantly peeked inside. He took a deep breath, leaned in for a full view, and then crumpled in a heap on the floor.

27

APRIL

I kept my eyes fixed on Brooklyn's photo as I took a long swig of vodka, the clear liquid trickling down the corners of my mouth. I swallowed hard.

Why couldn't you have just left things alone? Now look what's happened. I shut my eyes and wept quietly.

No one else was meant to die. We were supposed to leave Haywood together. Go off to college. Marry our twins. But you ruined everything. You ruined it *all*.

"You dumb bitch," I whispered, splashing vodka onto the picture frame, catching a glimpse of my reflection through the wet glass as eyeliner streaked down my cheeks.

"April?" Mom tapped gently at my door. What was she

doing home so early? Her shift wasn't supposed to end until ten tonight.

I quickly scanned the room for somewhere to hide the vodka bottle. I stashed it between my pillows just in time as Mom entered.

"Oh, honey—" she began, coming to me with open arms, still dressed in her black chef uniform and hat from her job at the bar and grill.

"I'm so sorry I couldn't be at the funeral with you. I know how much Brooklyn meant to you." She hugged me tightly. "I tried to leave earlier, but my asshole manager needed me to cover a call-in."

I buried my face in her shoulder, inhaling her smoky scent. Normally, I'd complain about her needing a shower, but I was relieved she was there. I didn't want to be alone. I'd bombed Wes with texts, asking if he'd stay with me for a while, but hadn't received a response yet. We'd always had our on-again-off-again thing, always gravitating back to each other, but lately Wes had been giving me the cold shoulder—and I had no idea why.

Mom pulled away to look into my face. "How was the wake?"

I shook my head, tears welling up again. "There wasn't one. They canceled it because Eddie—" I swallowed. "Eddie fainted. Everyone was so freaked out by it. I guess the Dimitris just wanted the burial to be a private affair."

"Oh, poor kid. He must've really loved her."

My eyes flashed, a sudden heat surging through me. I was *sick* of everyone fawning over how much Eddie loved Brooklyn. Their relationship was far from perfect.

"What do you think?" Mom interrupted my thoughts.

I blinked at her. "About what?"

"I was saying maybe we should invite the guys over so you can have your own private memorial for Brooklyn since you had to miss the wake. I wouldn't want Eddie blaming himself for something like that. Is that a good idea?"

I managed a smile. At least then, Wes couldn't ignore me. "That's perfect, Mom."

She kissed my forehead. "Alright. I'm going to order us a pizza, take a shower, and then we can go through some of your favorite photos of Brooklyn and make a collage."

I closed my eyes as she gave me one last tight squeeze. Once she was gone, I grabbed my phone to text Wes.

WES

My phone beeped, catching my attention. I hurriedly reached into my pocket to lower the volume before it could wake Eddie. But when had I fallen asleep? It was only five in the evening. I sat up and scanned Eddie's bedroom.

I rose from my sprawled position at the foot of his bed. Eddie lay near the headboard. We hadn't slept like this since we were kids.

After I got Eddie some fresh air (I knew that church was too damn hot), he came around, and I took him home. He had argued with me about being there for Brooklyn's burial, but I'd had enough. If he couldn't stand seeing her in a casket, there was no way he'd tolerate them throwing dirt on her. I'd called Dr. Kenneth, who agreed with my decision.

The moment Eddie's head hit his pillow, he was out cold. I kept watch for any sleepwalking episodes, but must have dozed off from boredom myself.

I checked my phone. April had sent *eighteen* texts. What the actual fuck?

Then my phone vibrated again—a text from my unknown contact, Libby.

> Can you meet me? I'm at school

I quickly typed back:

> Yep

After sending my response, I realized I hadn't considered Eddie. What if he woke up while I was gone and had an episode? If that were possible, wouldn't he have already done it? It had been quiet for hours now. Eddie was exhausted. Hopefully, he would sleep through my absence.

I slipped from the bed, careful not to disturb him. He didn't budge. I promised myself to keep my meeting with Libby brief. Besides, she was at school, and we couldn't do too much anyway. Without overthinking, I slipped into my shoes and quietly crept out of the room.

Only a few cars were in the school's lot—probably a couple of students and teachers lingering for advanced classes or something. The hall was empty, though. I found Libby at her desk, wearing the same skirt from the funeral but paired with a white spaghetti-strap tank. I tapped on the door. She glanced up and waved me in. Once inside, I closed the door and drew the shade.

She stood, fidgeting with her fingers. "How's Edward doing?"

"He's asleep. I have to get back before he wakes, so…" Damn, did I sound impatient? But part of me was. What did she need at school?

She bobbed her head. "Sure. Of course. I could've texted, but I—I just wanted to see you." She edged closer. "I'm sorry for avoiding you at the funeral." She paused right in front of me.

My eyes drifted to her lips. "I understood."

She tentatively trailed a finger along my jawline. "So, am I forgiven?"

I nodded before shutting my eyes as she kissed me.

When she pulled away, I blinked. "Isn't that risky?"

Her lips curled into a smirk as she looked at me teasingly. "It's rather exotic, don't you think?" She draped her arms over my shoulders and kissed me again.

As our kiss deepened, I gently pulled her hands away. "Eddie, remember?" I whispered.

"Yeah." She breathed, resting her forehead against mine.

"We can get together tomorrow night if you're free," I suggested.

"If I can stay away from you that long…" She tapped my nose playfully. "I'll hold you to it, then." She sauntered over to her desk as if she were on a runway, practically daring me to notice what I was missing. I bit my lip—Libby was such a tease. "Tell your brother I wish him well," she added while rifling through a stack of papers.

"For sure." I slipped out, determined to keep it short. It took everything not to turn around and sit her on that desk. I grinned at the thought.

"Wesley?" Coach Donahue called just as I'd gotten a few feet from the homeroom.

I spun around. "Coach?"

He eyed Libby's door then returned his gaze to me. "She's something, ain't she?"

I frowned inwardly. What was he hinting at? I shoved my hands into my pockets. "Harper's a hardass, making me bring a paper on a Saturday. And on the day of a funeral,"

I added quickly—feeling a small win for that one.

He crossed his arms. "Do you know why a detective is questioning Eddie about Riley?"

"What are you talking about?" I asked, my shoulders dropping.

"There was a guy here the other day. I swear I heard him asking Eddie what he knew about Riley. Eddie looked like he was about to spill something, but I stepped in. A detective shouldn't be on school grounds questioning a minor without an adult, so I shut it down. But seriously, Wesley, do you know what that was about?" His eyes searched mine.

My mouth hung open in bafflement. "This is the first I'm hearing about it. And you couldn't have heard right— we don't know what happened to your son, Coach." I said as sincerely as I could. "Besides, Eddie's been a little off recently. I have to check on him now." I turned away.

Damn. What the fuck was Brody doing, questioning Eddie without me? I'd warned him about that before. Did we need to get a lawyer or something?

"Wesley?" Coach Donahue stopped me at the doors. "You boys better be careful. I wouldn't trust that detective."

I nodded. Donahue wasn't wrong about that.

28

EDDIE

"Come on in, you guys. I'm thrilled you're here," April's mom said as she ushered Wes and me into their modest home. Her gaze lingered on me a moment too long as she patted my shoulder, and I quickly broke our eye contact.

"We appreciate you doing something like this," Wes said, offering a polite smile.

Wes clearly admired Ms. Sutherland—and I did too. The hardworking divorcee had always treated us kindly and welcomed us in. Though I suspected Wes harbored a bit of a crush on her, her genuine warmth never faltered.

"I made kebabs, and there are chips, salad, and non-alcoholic drinks," she added, "You know the drill—help yourselves," before heading out the front door.

At the clack of the door shutting behind her, April met us in the hallway and rushed over to Wes with open arms. His hug, however, lacked sincerity as he half-heartedly returned it, and April clung tightly until Wes practically had to peel her away. "Come on. Diego's already here," she said, heading for the den.

Catching up with me, Wes asked, "Are you sure you're up for this?"

I had to be—I'd spent far too long moping in bed, unable to function, and Brooklyn certainly wouldn't have wanted that for me. "I'm alright now. You don't have to worry about me, Wes."

Grinning, he replied, "Then what will I live for?"

Rolling my eyes, I playfully nudged him. "I'm actually pretty hungry," I admitted, my stomach rumbling on cue— I hadn't eaten in days.

"I'm happy to hear you've got an appetite. But if Diego's here, he's probably already demolished everything," Wes laughed as he hurried off to check.

I stepped into the living room and stopped dead in my tracks. On the mantel, next to a bouquet of white roses, hung a large portrait of Brooklyn—a photo I'd never seen before. Though in black and white, her piercing blue eyes provided the only hint of color, lending the image an almost mystical quality.

April came up beside me as I admired it. "That's still my

best design so far," she said.

I gaped in disbelief. "You photographed that?"

Tilting her head to examine her work, she replied, "Yep. Brooklyn hated that picture, but it perfectly captures her eyes—exactly what I intended. Beautiful, isn't it?" I nodded, my throat suddenly tight with emotion. April clapped her hands. "Let's get this thing started."

"Remember the time I dared Brooklyn to walk across the stage backward for her valedictorian speech?" April recalled a couple of hours later, giggling drunkenly as she passed a bottle of gin to Wes.

Diego, sprawled on a reclining chair, laughed until his eyes watered. "I was sure Marriot would slap the hell out of her."

Wes belched loudly, drawing hoots and laughter from the rest of us. Settling on the couch with April at his feet, he raised his glass. "To Brooklyn." His red eyes briefly met mine. "I know she meant the world to you—I only hope I find someone as special someday."

April fluttered her lashes and teased, "But haven't you already?"

He continued with a wry smile, "I'm not talking about puppy love, April—I mean something *real*. Someone I want for a lifetime, who makes me a better person when we're together." Playfully wagging a finger at her, he added, "You sure don't do that for me."

Was it the alcohol making him so lyrical, or was he hinting at something deeper—perhaps even the way Coach Donahue made him feel?

April pursed her lips and turned to me. "And did Brooklyn do that for you, Eddie?"

I managed a half-smile. "Of course. Brooklyn was an amazing person."

"I'll drink to that," Wes said, taking a thoughtful sip of his drink.

Staggering to her feet, April suddenly shouted, "Okay, this is bullshit," swaying on unsteady legs.

"Sit down, April—you're drunk," Diego remarked.

She spun on him, retorting. "Not too drunk to admit what a conniving bitch Brooklyn was. And you all know it, too. Except…" Slowly turning to me and pointing, before breaking into tears. "You, Eddie. Poor, poor Eddie."

What the hell? I slid to the edge of my seat as she sank to her knees right in front of me.

"You're so sweet, Eddie. Brooklyn didn't deserve you," she whispered, clutching my face and trying to kiss me.

"Whoa—*whoa*!" Wes jumped up. "Clearly someone's had too much to drink." He scooped April up by the waist. "Come on, April, let's get you to bed."

"No, I'm not done," April protested, wrestling with

him. In that instant, her tears vanished. "I *said* I'm not done. Take your hands off me." She scratched Wes's arm.

"Ow! You—" he started, stumbling over his words. "What the fuck, April?"

"I'm tired, okay?" she shouted back. "I'm so sick and tired of hearing about what a sweet little angel that sneaky bitch was."

Diego shook his head and eyed me. "Are you just going to let her trash-talk Brooklyn?"

I couldn't comprehend what was happening—April had just come on to me in front of Wes, while accusing the guys of keeping secrets about Brooklyn from me. "What are you talking about, April? What did Brooklyn ever do to you?"

"Don't feed into what she's saying," Wes argued. "She's drunk."

I reached out to her gently. "What do you know?"

She giggled again. "I know a secret," she said, beaming with mischief.

"This is crazy. I'm out of here," Diego announced as he too stood up. "You need to stay off the bottle, April."

"And you, Diego, ought to stay to hear my secret," she countered, reaching into her pocket for her cell phone. "Brooklyn was cheating on you, Eddie."

"Wait—what?" I squinted in disbelief.

She held up her phone, flashing a photo of Brooklyn kissing Mack. "She doesn't look so innocent there, does she?"

I quickly turned away, though the image burned into my memory. How could Brooklyn do that? First the Adderall, and now this? Had I even known her at all?

"Put that shit away, April," Wes barked over the clamor.

Still taunting, April maintained her laughing gaze on me as she wobbled on unsteady feet. "I followed them once, on their little stakeout. I guess they needed to pass the time somehow."

Wes swatted the phone from her hand. "Put it away."

Taking a slow, controlled breath, I realized I couldn't cry in front of them, no matter how much it hurt. With Wes and April yelling at each other until my head split, I couldn't take it anymore. "Wes, let's just go." I spun around, noticing Diego standing in shock with his hand over his mouth.

"Come on, Eddie," Wes urged, brushing past me toward the door.

"But don't you want to know the rest, Eddie?" April pressed.

"We're out, April," Wes called over his shoulder.

"Diego was her dealer!" the words tumbled from her lips.

We froze. Wes spun around, confronting Diego. "You gave Brooklyn the Adderall?" Diego struggled for words as Wes lunged at him—the two collapsing near an end chair.

Wes punched Diego, splitting his lip.

April screamed. "No. *Stop*!"

Diego's shoe thudded against Wes's midsection, knocking him off balance. "What the fuck, dude?" he exclaimed, clutching his bleeding face.

I moved in quickly to restrain Wes as he geared up to attack Diego again. "Stop it," I commanded.

"But he knew Brooklyn was off-limits!" Wes shouted, throwing another punch.

"*Wesley*!" I tightened my grip on him.

"Fine," he grumbled before tearing away. "Let's just get the hell out of here."

April reached for him, pleading, "Wes, wait, please."

He stormed ahead, and I hurried after him. Outside, Wes fumed as he sat at the steering wheel. Once I buckled in, he turned to me. "I'm sorry about Brooklyn."

"Did you know?" I asked sharply.

His eyes widened. "Of course, I didn't know."

"It seems I'm the only one left in the dark. What the hell did you mean by Brooklyn was off-limits?"

His gaze dropped to the windshield as he started the car. "Nothing."

"Wesley, what aren't you telling me?"

He licked his lips, hesitating. "You promise you won't get mad?"

My heart hammered in my chest—could it really get

worse than Brooklyn cheating on me?

"Eddie?" Wes prompted.

I blinked. "Yeah. Just tell me."

"Diego broke the rules."

"The rules?" I echoed.

"Diego and I sell drugs. I know—" He glanced at me apologetically. "I lied to you, and I'm sorry. But it's been going on for a long while now. Even Riley was in on it."

"*Riley*? But the coach made us swear never to get involved with any illegal substances. I don't understand."

"You're not that naïve, Eddie. Riley had nothing but the shirt on his back—just like us. Coach Donahue couldn't provide a damn thing, so we did what we had to. When Riley started blackmailing us, he became greedy and unfair with our shares.

"But Diego—he broke the rules. We were never to give anything to anyone in our circle. Shit like Mario's party were supposed to be harmless."

That wasn't acceptable. I arched an eyebrow.

He rolled his eyes, as if reading my mind. "What pisses me off is that it all happened right under my nose and I didn't catch it. Diego never mentioned anything."

"Neither did Brooklyn." I realized there was so much she hadn't told me. I glanced toward the window, seeing the image of her with Mack in my mind. I bit my jaw and clenched a fist. How long had this been going on? Diego supplying her, her interest in Mack—what else had Brooklyn hidden from me?

Detective Brody

Mrs. Dimitri shook my hand warmly. "The flowers you sent were lovely. Thank you," she said, offering a tight-lipped smile.

"My pleasure," I replied.

She gestured for me to sit across from Mr. Dimitri, who stared blankly at the wall—a faraway look I recognized all too well in grieving parents.

"Dana—the detective's here. Dana?" Mrs. Dimitri called out, her voice rising.

Mr. Dimitri blinked—his wife nodded in my direction. Pretending nothing was amiss, I fumbled in my jacket for my pad and pen.

"Oh—" Mr. Dimitri laughed heartily. "How nice of you to stop by."

"Would you like some tea or perhaps some cheese and crackers?" Mrs. Dimitri offered, her hands poised as if playing a piano.

The mention of the piano caught my attention for a moment, but I quickly refocused. "Oh, no—I'm fine. I only wanted to ask a few more questions about Brooklyn, if that's all right," I added, noting their quizzical glances.

"Sure, but I don't understand. I thought Brooklyn's case was closed," Mrs. Dimitri remarked.

I forced a nod and maintained a straight face. "I'm just tying up a few loose ends. Once more, I'd like to revisit what Brooklyn was like in the days before—" I gestured toward the piano, "I understand she had a recital?"

Mr. Dimitri squinted at the piano, as if noticing it for the first time. "Yes. Brooklyn wanted to go to Julliard next year, but she didn't qualify."

"It wasn't like her to be so distracted," Mrs. Dimitri sighed sadly. "But I suppose that's what the pill business was all about…" she waved a dismissive hand.

I nodded slowly. "I'm trying to determine whether it was an accident or suicide."

"Suicide?" Mrs. Dimitri turned toward me slowly.

I slid to the edge of my seat. "There were traces of two drugs in Brooklyn's system—amphetamine and methamphetamine."

"Meth?" Mrs. Dimitri echoed, glancing at her husband, who looked equally bewildered.

Clearing my throat, I continued, "Yes. So, if Brooklyn talked about the future and made plans for tomorrow, it was most likely an accident." They exchanged another loaded glance.

"Well, the three of us had planned to speak the following morning about what troubled her," Mr. Dimitri recalled. "But we never got that chance."

"You don't know what might have been wrong?" I asked.

Mr. Dimitri's shoulders slumped. "It had something to do with that boy, Edward. I just know it."

My heart skipped a beat. "What makes you say that?"

As Mr. Dimitri began to explain, his wife abruptly cut him off. "Just stop it, Dana. You can't assign blame to anyone but us. We were too late—we spent so much time expecting the best of her that we couldn't see the pressure she was under. If anything, Edward was her relief." Mrs. Dimitri rolled her eyes and buried her face in her hands.

But Mr. Dimitri shook his head. "She changed after that boy came into her life…"

"She grew up," Mrs. Dimitri snapped, glaring at him. "That's what teenagers do."

"On the night you last saw her, you grounded her, correct?" I asked.

"Yes. Dana forced her to cancel her birthday plans. She was seventeen, not twelve," Mrs. Dimitri hissed at her husband.

"She failed her SAT exam and didn't even tell us," Mr. Dimitri countered. "I was just doing what I normally would. Had I known she might…"

"Is it okay if I look in Brooklyn's room?" I interrupted.

Mrs. Dimitri nodded. "Sure. Everything is just as she left

it." She rose to accompany me, but I told her I was fine. "It's the first door on the right," she called after me.

I ascended the stairs straight to Brooklyn's room and flipped on the light. The bed had been made up with oversized teddy bears. I nudged one aside to search beneath the pillows—there had to be a journal or something.

"Who are you?" a tiny voice piped from behind me.

I spun around and straightened up. "Janie, right?" Her head bobbed—she looked like a pint-sized Brooklyn with the same mystical blue eyes and waist-length hair. I flashed my badge. "I'm a detective."

"Like a police officer?" she asked, scrunching her nose.

"Smart girl," I replied.

"What are you looking for?"

"Well," I said, tucking my badge away, "a secret."

Her eyes lit up as she rushed over. "I know a secret," she whispered loudly enough to catch my attention.

"Really?"

She nodded. "Brooklyn had a friend over after Mom left her a snack." Her wide eyes blinked up at me.

"Are you sure? Your mom and dad said they grounded her."

"Uh-uh. I heard them fighting," she confided, waving me closer. Leaning in as she cupped a hand to my ear, she whispered, "They called Brooklyn a slut."

Intrigued, I said, "That's a big secret, Janie. Think you

can get your mom to pour me a glass of juice?"

"I can pour it!" she declared, spinning on her heel and darting down the hall.

I quickly dialed my partner. "Do you have anything for me?"

"Unfortunately, not yet."

I nodded. "Someone knows more than they're letting on. I just found out a friend of Brooklyn's was here the night she died."

"You think it's the boy?" my partner asked.

Did Eddie have something to do with Brooklyn's death? I slowly took in the room, my gaze landing on the window where a huge oak tree stood just outside. "I don't know yet. But keep at it—someone's bound to slip soon."

29

EDDIE

"So, for the social studies lecture, I've assigned your partners," Miss Harper announced on Friday. "When you hear your new teammate, sit with them and take notes together." She then called off a list of names, and naturally, she paired Savannah and me together.

I shifted in my seat as she quietly moved to place hers beside mine.

"…and finally, Diego and Wesley…" Miss Harper finished, setting down her slip of paper.

"Like hell we are," Wes grumbled loud enough for everyone to hear.

"I don't want a piece of shit partner anyway," Diego fired back.

"Ooh!" someone jeered.

Wes leapt from his seat and stormed over. "Fuck you, Diego." He shoved Diego out of his chair, and gasps erupted among the students as a fight broke out.

Diego staggered, regained his balance, then lunged at Wes. Soon, the two sprawled across the floor, wrestling and exchanging punches.

"*Hey*!" Miss Harper shouted as she dashed from behind her desk. I moved too, trying to rein Wes in. I reached under his armpit and dragged him away while he thrashed and kicked in Diego's direction.

"Get to the principal's office!" Miss Harper ordered, pointing at the door, her voice seething as she glared at Wes. If I hadn't intervened, she might've taken his head off.

"But—"

"I don't care," she snapped, stepping forward threateningly. "Go!"

Wes bumped her shoulder as he stormed past. Both she and I stared in disbelief. What the hell was he thinking? He knew the penalty for fighting in class.

I sank back in my seat until I caught sight of Diego. Wes had only fought him in defense of Brooklyn—after all, Diego was the one who sold her the drugs that killed her. Diego shot me a glare as he settled back into his chair with his arms crossed. I gripped the desk's edge and began to rise when Savannah suddenly clamped her hand over mine.

"Don't…" she whispered, her voice warm and gentle.

My shoulders heaved as I fought for control of my breathing. I shrugged off her hand and sank back into my seat.

"You're not off the hook either, Diego," Miss Harper warned fiercely. "Come with me."

Diego snickered as he passed by. Fists clenched, I kept my gaze fixed ahead.

"Hey." I caught up with Savannah as school ended. She slipped out the door just as I slammed my locker shut.

Glancing at me as she continued on, she said, "Sup."

I hurried to match her pace. "I just wanted to say thanks for earlier." She gave me a sideways look. "For stopping me from kicking Diego's ass."

She nodded. "Oh yeah. There was no point in you getting detention, too. Besides, that guy was hardly worth it."

"Oh, he kinda is." She paused, blinking expectantly. "Diego killed my girlfriend."

"What?"

I shook my head. "Sorry. I should be clear—I mean, he gave her the drugs she overdosed on."

Her mouth opened in shock, and she fumbled for words. Adjusting her backpack, she murmured, "Maybe I should've stayed out of it then. That sucks. Have you told anyone? Can we hold him accountable somehow?"

I hesitated. If I turned on Diego about that, he'd surely rat us out—the lake incident with Riley, Wes's involvement, and his drug connections would all come crashing down.

"I—I don't know if it'll do any good. The case is closed, or something."

She shrugged. "Maybe it isn't too late. I bet her parents would still want to know where she got it from."

Realizing I shouldn't have mentioned it at all, I quickly switched topics. "What's that necklace?" I asked, noticing it looked like an animal's tooth.

She glanced at it and laughed. "You'll think it's silly."

"Try me."

"It's—" She hesitated and then shook her head. "It's nothing." Quickly, she tucked it beneath her shirt.

I half-smiled. "Hey, I'm really sorry about earlier. I wasn't myself."

She waved it off. "No need to explain. I'm just glad we got paired anyway. And that's why I didn't want you to get detention too—Saturdays are the only time I have free for that project." She winked, and I laughed.

"And here I thought you cared about me," I teased, placing my hand over my heart in mock hurt.

She giggled. "No shit. My folks would kill me if I got

anything less than an A."

My pace slowed as thoughts of Brooklyn crept in— her grades were just one of the many pressures weighing on her.

"Well, if you ever need help with anything, don't hesitate. I'm no Einstein, but together we can figure it out."

Her gaze softened. "Thank you. That's really kind." At the corner, she pointed, "I'm that way."

"See you tomorrow then?"

She grinned. "Yeah, so long as you stay out of trouble."

WES

I glared at Libby. "I can't believe you sent me to detention. Why couldn't you have my back?"

"What did you expect me to do? Let my students think they can get away with anything? What were you thinking, Wesley?" Libby demanded, giving me her infamous evil eye for what felt like the umpteenth time. We were at the Sweet Haven Hotel, but this was not our usual meeting.

"If you'd given me just five more seconds, you'd have known what I was thinking."

She rolled her eyes. "Yeah, and I suppose your petty beef is worth being expelled? Why bother studying for the SAT if you're just going to throw it all away? And why are you so pissed at Diego? I thought you two were best mates."

"Fuck him. You wouldn't understand it anyway." Just then, my phone pinged—it was April.

I REALLY NEED 2 C U

Ever since Brooklyn's funeral, her calls wouldn't stop.

See me? I'm not hooking up with her anymore.

"Who are you talking to?" Libby asked, a trace of jealousy in her voice.

Really? I could have rolled my eyes, but I played along. "Just some girl," I shrugged nonchalantly. "Anyway, what's it to you?" She took a deep breath, her lips forming a thin line.

April pinged again:

PLEASE

Libby crossed her arms as I scrolled through the texts. "Anyway," she sighed, "you left me no choice but to give you detention. Act like a child in my classroom, and I'll treat you just like one."

I looked up from my phone. "Yes, ma'am, Miss Harper."

"Fuck you, Wesley." She spun around, gathering her things to leave.

"Wait, wait—" I sprang to my feet, shoving my phone into my pocket. "I'm sorry, alright? I'm an idiot, but I promise to be better. In your class, you're the boss—I'd even get that tattooed on my ass if it'd make you happy."

She frowned briefly, then broke into that boisterous laugh of hers. "You need help."

I pouted. "So help me…" I leaned in for a kiss. In that instant, my phone beeped again—it was April. Why was she going psycho on me after all that time?

I pecked Libby on the lips and checked my phone again.

I'm in trouble Wes
come over ASAP

A chill ran down my spine.

"You can go if it's urgent," Libby said, settling on the edge of the bed. "But you know what's waiting when you're done." A slow grin spread across her face.

"Then I won't keep you long," I said, giving a small salute before heading to my car. "This had better be worth it, A," I muttered.

I parked across the street from April's house a short while later. There she sat on the bottom stoop, a cigarette dangling between her fingertips. Draped in an oversized cardigan with short shorts, a nightshirt sporting an owl, and a dark silk scarf covering her braids, she looked disheveled.

Taking a long drag, she exhaled in the opposite direction as I approached. I almost took the cigarette away, but she seemed desperate.

"What's so goddamn urgent?" I asked, raising my arms as I stopped in front of her.

She lifted her gaze, revealing a tear-streaked face. "Let's go inside." She stood and led me to the door. Sighing, I followed. Once in the kitchen, she rifled through the fridge. "Want something to drink?"

Was she serious? "Sure. I'll have a bottle of what the fuck is going on."

Spinning to face me, she slammed the fridge door. "I messed up, Wes. Big time." Tears fell in heavy drops as she pressed a hand over her mouth to stifle her sobs.

I'd never seen her like that. On impulse, I hurried to her side. "Hey—just breathe, okay?" I guided her to a stool. She slumped down, defeated. I nuzzled her shoulders gently. "What's going on?"

She swallowed hard and wiped her face with her wrist before, with blank emotion, blinking up at me, she said, "I killed Brooklyn."

The words hit me like a bolt of lightning. My legs wobbled—I gripped the counter, fearing I'd collapse. "What do you mean, April?"

She lowered her head. "Brooklyn was a drug addict, and I only wanted her parents to notice she was high—not to kill her. It was an accident."

"What did you do, April?" I asked, clenching the counter as my knees threatened to give out.

April clutched a fistful of her braids, her gaze distant. "I crept into her room that night and dropped pills into her glass—enough to get her high. I don't understand how it ended like this. I didn't mean for her to die. You have to believe me." She searched my face desperately, but I could barely speak. It felt like a 300-pound man was sitting on my chest.

I dashed to the sink, fumbling to turn on the tap. I pressed my lips beneath the running water, gulping mouthfuls. Gasping, I straightened up, water dripping down my chin as tears streamed unchecked.

She groaned, stomping a foot. "Brooklyn was going to tell her parents the truth the next morning. I wanted them to find her high and send her to rehab or wherever. She was going to spill the truth about Riley—what we really did to him.

"She was going to ruin our lives, and she did it out of jealousy. She failed her SAT, blew her chance with Juilliard, and now she's making *us* pay." She sniffled. "And that detective—he knows something."

"Knows what?" I finally croaked.

"I—I don't know. He asked me today if I'd met Brooklyn the night she died."

"Mr. Dimitri grounded Brooklyn. Brody can't prove you were there."

She laughed bitterly. "That's what I thought, until I fucked up and dropped the pill bottle under her bed. It's only a matter of time before they find my prints on it." Her enormous eyes searched mine. "I'm fucked," she whispered.

I bit my lip, tempted to grab her shoulders and shake her, but instead, I closed my eyes and took a deep breath. "Okay. So what if your prints are on the bottle? If anyone asks, just say you and Brooklyn took the Adderall together. Brody can't prove a damn thing."

She slowly nodded as she mulled it over. "Yeah—I could say we were both under pressure because of the SAT." I didn't care what excuse she used, as long as she had one. A sad smile of relief broke over her. "I'm glad you came, Wes. You always know how to fix things."

I wanted to smile back, but I felt like vomiting.

She stood to embrace me and then suddenly gasped. "Since I'm being honest, there's one more thing."

Could it get any worse? Judging by the flush of embarrassment on her face, apparently, yes.

"That picture of Mack and Brooklyn isn't real. It's Photoshopped."

My fist clenched. "Why the fuck would you do that?"

"It was stupid, I know… but I just wanted Eddie to see

Brooklyn as the slut she was."

"No, just stop, April. You have no idea how ignorant that was. You've only deepened Eddie's pain. I could slap you." I turned and punched the side of the fridge instead.

She jerked. "But it's true. Brooklyn and Diego were hooking up."

"What?" I glared. "I don't believe—" Wait. Why was Diego so broken up at Brooklyn's funeral? I'd assumed his guilt over the Adderall was to blame, but now I wondered—had he been in love with her?

I jabbed my finger at April. "You will tell my brother the truth."

Her eyes widened in panic. "Everything?"

"No. Only about the picture." But was it really better for Eddie to believe Brooklyn overdosed, causing him self-loathing for not being there?

"I'm so sorry, Wes," April interjected softly. She stepped forward, taking my face in both hands. "Please tell me it's okay." Pressing her cheek against mine, she laced her fingers through my hair.

"Please?" Her lips pressed against mine. "Say you'll forgive me. Please." Her head drooped as she wailed.

I gently pulled her into an embrace. "It'll be okay," I murmured, though deep down I knew I could never truly forgive her.

EDDIE

I peered out the back door. It was after midnight when April showed up, insisting it was urgent—obviously, it couldn't wait until tomorrow.

Hank and I had raked leaves earlier, but with the trees shedding so heavily, it felt like we'd barely made a dent. Hank was so wasted he wouldn't even remember our first try.

April appeared at the back gate. I opened the screen door as she scurried across the yard in the freezing cold. She dashed inside, shivering. "Brrr…" she mumbled, her body trembling.

"Careful," I warned, gesturing toward the rakes and garbage bags piled by the door.

"I haven't helped my mom with this crap yet," she sighed. "Time is really flying."

I nodded, unsure what to say. I hadn't seen April since our last get-together at her place, and her arrival only stirred my anger. All this while, I'd believed she was Brooklyn's best friend, but in truth, she hated her guts. Did Brooklyn know?

April settled at our new table. I glared at the back of her head—Brooklyn would've never spoken such awful things about her.

"I suppose I should start with an apology…" she began

hesitantly.

"You're damn right," I snapped, grabbing a large black trash bag I frankly didn't even remember picking up. As April turned toward me, I yanked the bag over her head.

"Ed—!" Her scream was cut off to muffled moans as she clawed at my hands, tearing at my flesh. The sharp pain and oozing blood didn't stop me.

I tugged the bag tighter until the chair tilted on its legs. April's feet kicked as she tried to rip the plastic from around her neck.

The shiny black plastic pressed into her mouth. I held on until she took her last breath.

My eyes squinted open as I emitted a sick moan, trying to rise, though my head and body felt buried alive. I rolled onto my back, the rustling of the leaves beneath me the only sound.

Leaves? I jolted upright. I was in the backyard—could *that* explain the strange dream?

"Eddie?" Wes shouted from inside. Standing in the doorway with panic etched on his face, he dashed out. "I— I woke up and couldn't find you." He shuffled through the leaves and knelt beside me. "Are you alright?" His eyes, puffy from lack of sleep, searched mine.

I tried to speak, but my throat was dry. Instead, I nodded

and cleared my throat hoarsely.

Wes sighed in relief, settling beside me on the leaves. "You scared me to death. Then I couldn't find the car key— I thought you'd driven off in your sleep. Remember Dr. Kenneth said—"

"Wait. What?" I spun toward him as he lifted my wrist— I was clutching his car key. What the hell?

"You must have grabbed the key but didn't get past the yard, thank goodness."

I couldn't fathom why I had the key. I dropped it as if it were searing hot.

"Hey!" Wes caught it, gasping. "What happened to your hand?" He inspected it carefully.

Dirt caked my nails, and scratch marks marred my skin—the same marks where April had scratched me in my nightmare. I staggered to my feet, my stomach lurching though I had nothing to vomit. "How is that possible?" I managed to choke out.

Wes kneeled beside me. "Eddie—are you okay?"

I wrapped my arms around my middle and shook my head. "It makes no sense."

"You're damn right it doesn't. What the hell are you talking about, dude?" He rose to his feet.

I blinked at him. "I—I dreamed that April came over late last night. But when she got here, I…" I leaned in and whispered, "I killed her."

Wes eyed me skeptically. "Are you sure that didn't actually happen?" He rolled his eyes. "Not the killing part—but you sure you didn't talk to her about something important?"

I shook my head. "I don't remember. It felt so real, but I could never do something so…" I recalled the memory of tugging on that plastic bag as April struggled. "…callous." I raised my trembling hands. "Yet somehow, I have these scratches."

Wes shook his head. "Eddie—do you hear yourself?"

"Look, I know how it sounds, but…"

He sighed. "Stop. You were asleep in a yard full of leaves. Anything—maybe a cat or a squirrel—could've left those marks. They're busy storing food this time of year, right?"

I rolled my eyes and then smiled ruefully. I *was* being ridiculous. If I'd really hurt April, wouldn't she be lying nearby? And where was the plastic bag?

Wes patted my back. "Come on, let's get back inside." He headed for the house.

I followed but paused at the door, scanning the yard one more time as if I'd missed something. But nothing was there.

30

EDDIE

NOW

My foot tapped nervously that morning as I stared at the empty seat where April should have been. Where was she? I kept stealing glances at Wes, checking if he was as worried as I was, but he stayed glued to his books—his best behavior on display.

Just before lunch, Principal Marriot's voice came over the intercom: "Wesley and Edward Hawkins, please come to my office. Wesley and Edward, my office, now." I slowly rose, and Wes and I exchanged worried looks. Whenever you were called to the principal's office, you knew you were in trouble or that bad news was coming. And why both of us? Could it have something to do with Hank? I couldn't help but feel a twinge of fear for the bastard.

"Is everything alright?" Miss Harper asked.

Wes paused at the door and scowled at her. "Are we psychics? How would we know what she wants?" He shoved open the door and stormed out. I watched him go, mouth agape—apparently that detention had really set him off. I offered Miss Harper a sheepish smile and carefully closed the door behind me. There was no time to get on Wes's case, as Principal Marriot was already waiting outside her office, silently ushering us in.

"What's this—?" Wes froze when he caught sight of Detective Brody. My body stiffened too. Why was he here? "Morning, fellows," he said with a curt nod, seating himself a few chairs over. Principal Marriot parked herself behind her desk, while Wes and I lingered near the door in tense silence.

"I suppose you're wondering why I want you here…" Brody began. Wes crossed his arms, and silence hung between us. After a moment, Brody cleared his throat. "It's about your friend, April."

Wes's knee bumped against mine, his hands balled up while he chewed his lip. I longed for him to speak his mind, but neither of us said a word as we rode in the back of Brody's car—a ride that seemed to last forever until we reached the police station.

"Well, if it isn't the Hawkins boys," Sheriff Owens remarked as we stepped inside. Without a word, Brody motioned for him to pipe down, and led us back to the room with the mismatched chairs.

"Is April alright, or not?" Wes demanded as he collapsed into a folding chair.

Brody took a deep breath. "Campers discovered her body in a creek this morning." In an instant, Wes tumbled from his chair and hit the floor. "You're lying. Tell me you're lying." His voice broke apart into agonized sobs as his fists pounded the floor. I blinked rapidly, panic fluttering in my chest. How could it be that I'd dreamt of murdering April, only to now learn she was dead?

Wes's wailing tore through my thoughts, and on impulse, I moved to console him, gently helping him back into his chair. Brody slid a box of tissues our way, though neither of us accepted them—I feared if I let go, Wes might collapse again.

"It appears April drowned," Brody said. "Do you know what she might have been doing out in the woods by herself?" Wes groaned, shaking his head weakly. Brody pressed his lips together as he reviewed the file before him. "April reached out to you last night, correct?"

Wes slowly met his gaze. "Her phone records show she sent you an urgent text: *'I'm in trouble, Wes; come over ASAP.'* But you never replied. Did you see her at all last night?"

I glanced at Wes. He nodded, tears streaking his chin.

"What did her texts mean?" asked Brody.

Wes sniffled, straightening while meeting my eyes. I was desperate to know—had April and Wes talked about *me*?

"I shouldn't say," Wes replied hoarsely.

"I need to understand what happened. What was she doing in the woods? Was she meeting someone? Was it you?"

"*No*," Wes shouted. "I met April at her house. She needed money."

Brody relaxed in his seat slightly. "Needed money for what?"

I edged away from the tension, waiting for his reply. "April cheated on her SAT exam. Some guy was selling answer sheets for around a thousand bucks or something. Either he was trying to squeeze more money out of her, or she owed him more—I'm not entirely sure. But she was trying to get money from me, and I simply didn't have that kind of cash." His voice broke into another sob.

"What's this guy's name?" Brody asked after a pause.

"Mario Rossi."

I was stunned—Mario was involved in selling test answers? How did he get them, and why had I never heard of it? Brody scribbled a quick note as I reached for a tissue to comfort Wes.

"What happened there?" Brody asked, pointing his pen at my scratched hands. I stared at them in disbelief, as if seeing them anew.

"The neighbor's stupid cat," Wes interjected. Brody fixed his gaze on me, and I simply nodded.

"He attacked me while I was doing yard work," I said. I couldn't tell if he believed me—I had no idea how it had truly happened. It couldn't have been from April, as I'd dreamt earlier. But...there we were.

"So, after you two talked, what happened?" Brody pressed.

"Well," Wes thought for a moment, "she was pretty distraught, trying to figure out who else she could turn to for money. She was so unhinged that I couldn't stand being near her—I just left." His head hung in shame.

Brody's eyes then met mine. "What about you? Did you see April?" Wes grabbed a tissue and blew his nose loudly— a subtle sign that didn't go unnoticed. But why if I hadn't seen her?

"No," I replied. "I didn't see April at all."

Brody nodded and continued scribbling on his pad. "I'm really sorry for both of your losses." He appeared to have more to say but then bit his tongue. "If you remember anything else, call me," he instructed Wes. He offered to drive us back to school, yet Wes insisted we take a cab home—there was no way we could concentrate on schoolwork after this.

In the back of the cab, Wes turned to me, fresh tears still glistening.

"What?" I whispered.

"Are you sure you don't remember seeing April last night?" he whispered back.

My heart pounded erratically. "Why?" I murmured.

"Oh, no," he groaned, squeezing his eyes shut and turning away—the words too painful to speak.

"Wes, what? What aren't you telling me?" I pressed.

He sniffled. "Before I left, April told me she was going to meet you. She had something important to say."

I gasped. "What do you mean? *I* didn't see her. It was just a dream, remember?"

Wes's eyes were bloodshot as he cried. "It's just—it's not adding up. None of it makes sense."

I shakily held out my hands, staring at the ugly red marks. I heard the chair creak as it tilted under the strain of my grip on the bag covering April's face. I kept my hands outstretched, imagining them soaked in blood. It reminded me of the night I killed JoJo. Suddenly, the seat dropped from beneath me. I slowly turned to Wes and, in a trembling voice, confessed, "That's because it was me. I did it."

31

EDDIE

NOW

Wes and I were technically the same age, though I was three minutes older. I can't recall when or why he decided to take on the role of big brother, always feeling the need to protect and watch over me.

At the police station, he pieced it all together—I was the guilty one. I'd woken up that morning in the backyard clutching a car key, and I must have run into April in the woods. My palms and fingernails were caked with mud—marks from her self-defense scratches. That was why Wes had pointed the finger at Mario. He was shielding me, just as he did with Riley. And yet, there was no way for me to get out of it.

After I explained to Wes what I'd done to JoJo, he became a hundred percent sure I was the culprit. I even considered turning myself in. I thought if I came clean to Brody about my sleepwalking spells and how terrible they could get, maybe they'd be lenient. I wouldn't know unless I tried. But Wes was completely against it—he had to be my protective shield and even blamed himself for not keeping a closer eye on me.

So, if I turned myself in, he wanted to share in the punishment. In the end, we both decided to say nothing and simply carry on with our lives. And that's exactly what I did.

School was unbearable with everyone whispering about April's death. I kept my head down, haunted by the sensation of my peers' accusatory stares. After lunch, a commotion near my locker caught my attention, and I could hear Wes's furious voice. I weaved my way through the crowd.

"You backstabbing fucker," Wes roared as he landed a punch on Diego's face.

"Goddamn it," I muttered as I rushed forward to restrain him, pulling him aside. "Stop it, Wesley."

"You're a piece of shit, Diego," he snarled as he tried to lunge again, but I dug my heels into the floor and held him back.

"Stop it, Wes," I whispered. "We don't need any more trouble."

"He fucked Brooklyn," Wes spat through clenched teeth.

My grip loosened. "What?" I turned to look at Diego. Was Brooklyn really messing around with both Mack and Diego? That didn't sound like the Brooklyn I knew—she despised Diego, and he despised her. Or was it just a cover to keep me in the dark?

Wes let out a sharp cry and broke away from me. I expected him to go after Diego again, but instead he stormed down the hall, his shoes thudding heavily.

My fists clenched as I stepped toward Diego. "What the hell, dude?"

"Whoa—whoa," a girl interjected. It was Mack. "Don't do it, Eddie. Walk away, Diego." Her grip on my shoulder was firm.

I glanced from her to Diego—Brooklyn's two love interests. Did they know about each other? It hardly mattered since they both knew of me. I shrugged Mack off when Miss Harper's door suddenly swung open.

"Shouldn't you all be heading to class?" she demanded, glaring squarely at Diego.

"I'm on my way now," Diego replied while shoving past Mack and me. "You can give him back his balls." He nodded in my direction before strutting down the hall.

"He is fucking incredible," Mack commented as she stepped beside me. We watched Diego until he disappeared around the corner.

"Everything all right?" Miss Harper called from the doorway.

"Peachy," Mack answered with a sarcastic grin. Once Miss Harper had closed the door, she turned to me. "You looked like you were about to snap his neck."

I shifted nervously, unwilling to meet Mack's gaze—a gaze that, in my mind, always reminded me of her kissing Brooklyn.

"Hey, I'm really sorry about April, though," she said. "It's unreal how much your group has suffered while he's acting like a *jackass*," she spun around and shouted down the hall.

I shot her a sideways glance and managed a small smile. She was clearly going through it too, what with Mrs. Donahue's condition and Riley's revelations. My heart sank—I owed her an even bigger apology.

"How have you been? I'm sorry I missed Riley's funeral. I don't remember hearing anything about it."

She tucked her hair behind her ear. "That's because there was no funeral."

"What do you mean?"

"We didn't have one. With my mom's cancer

treatments, we couldn't afford it. My dad had Riley cremated as soon as possible—he just wanted to get it over with, probably also pissed about Riley doing drugs. Drugs are completely off-limits in our house, and Riley—" Her voice trailed off. "I don't know what to make of it. It doesn't sound like something he'd do. But he shut me out, so what would I know about a druggie?" Her eyes widened as she clutched her mouth. "I—I didn't mean it like that."

I shrugged, averting my eyes. "I didn't even know Brooklyn used, either."

She nodded, understanding. After a pause, the words tumbled out from my lips, "Did you love Brooklyn too?"

Her cheeks flushed. "Um, I guess. I mean—she was honest and genuine."

"Yeah, she was." Except not when it came to me.

WES

I held the hotel room door open as Libby rushed inside, jacket thrown over her head. It was a heavy downpour that evening—with lightning, thunder, the whole shebang. A gust of wind blasted rain at me as I stepped back to let her in.

"Someone's following me," she panted. She slammed and locked the door before scampering to the window.

I rolled my eyes. "Not that shit again."

"I really mean it, Wes," she insisted, wrapping her arms around herself and shivering.

"Well, then I'm putting an end to this nonsense now." I turned and unlocked the door.

"Wesley, no. You could get hurt," she protested.

I yanked the door open so forcefully I could've ripped it from its hinges. "Who the fuck's there?" I shouted into the deluge, as the rain pounded heavily on the ground.

"Stop it, Wesley," Libby called out, but I ignored her and stormed out, slamming the door behind me.

Squinting into the rain— my clothes were soaked in seconds. All I could see were the silhouettes of cars in the lot. I moved further out—I'd been itching to kick someone's ass all day. "Come out, you asshole," I shouted across the lot, scanning for whoever might be hiding, too cowardly to face me. Shortly, I jogged back inside.

"Get in here before you catch a cold," Libby snapped.

I stepped back in, shaking the water off. "I didn't see anyone. Did you get a good look?"

She hesitated. "I—I'm not sure."

"Well, hopefully I scared him off."

"Just drop it. Get rid of those wet clothes." She had already begun removing her damp top. A few moments later, Libby's fingers intertwined with mine as a flash of lightning briefly brightened the dim room.

I sank against the headboard with Libby in front of me. "You don't have any crazy exes chasing you, do you?" I asked suddenly, intending it as a joke. She shifted uncomfortably and released my hand.

"Well," she began hesitantly, fiddling with the heart pendant on her necklace, "my crazy ex is already in prison." Her voice was soft and distant.

"Yeah?" I leaned in to look at her face.

Thunder cracked overhead, making her jump and laugh. I wrapped my arms around her and rested my chin on her shoulder.

"He was a bad guy, Wesley—a real bastard. He broke my arm in two places," she said, raising two fingers.

"Sounds like my dad," I muttered, kissing her cheek.

She shifted closer. "Does your dad hit your mom?"

I kept pressing kisses to her cheek, eager to avoid thoughts of my parents. "I'm glad that jerk's somewhere he can't hurt you."

She settled against my chest. "What do you think about your friend—April?" she changed the subject.

My eyes widened and my body stiffened. "I don't really know what to make of it. It's—it's awful, of course."

"Mm. Some teachers think April was on drugs too, and even that the Candy Man might have killed her."

My brows furrowed—who the hell started that rumor?

"Have you heard anything about that?" she asked, tilting

her head to try to see my face.

"No, I'm not involved with drugs, remember?"

"And Eddie?"

"Absolutely squeaky clean."

"Good. I just hope no one else dies at Haywood High. It's turning out to be a sorrowful year for the students."

She said something else, but I drowned her out while eyeing the clock—I had to pick up Eddie from swim practice at six. In my groggy state, I reached to adjust the clock, accidentally knocking over Libby's wallet. I fumbled along the floor to retrieve it, and when I saw her driver's license photo, the name made me pause. Michelle Howard? Who the hell was that?

EDDIE

"You call that a pull-up?" I challenged Brandon, the newest member of the swim team. He grunted as he attempted one and, with a heavy sigh, let his feet touch the floor. "What are you doing? I didn't say you were finished," I said as I stepped over to him.

"What's the pull-up bar good for in swimming, anyway?" he demanded, wiping sweat from his forehead with the back of his hand.

I leaped onto the bar, retracting my shoulder blades and lifting my body to demonstrate. "A proper pull-up allows full extension through your lats, shoulders, back, and wrists. Notice how that movement mirrors a basic swim stroke? That full extension is exactly what you need underwater." I landed, then added, "By the way, trust your fucking captain."

Coach Donahue had originally planned to name Diego captain, but when Diego quit the team before the announcement, the title was abruptly given to me. And now my teammates were testing me.

Brandon adjusted his glasses with a finger. "You don't have to be a dick about it."

"What'd you say?" I edged closer.

"Alright—break it up," Coach Donahue intervened. "Good job, Brandon," he said before sending him on his way.

I blinked in disbelief—he'd never say anything like that to Riley, even after Riley had outdone the whole team. I waited until Brandon was out of earshot.

"Do you want us to win the swim meet or not?"

Coach Donahue chuckled. "Well, the kid had a point. No one's going to count your pull-ups at the meet. I understand you have your own training methods, but you can't impose them on everyone."

I fell silent, trying to figure out what I had done wrong.

"Brandon is excellent at the backstroke, and right now that's exactly what we need him for," he pointed out.

I nodded, running my fingers through my hair in embarrassment. Coach was right—Brandon excelled at what he did best. Not everyone needed to be an all-rounder like me… or Riley.

"What's this really about? Are you trying to blow off steam?" he asked, placing a firm hand on my shoulder. "I know you've lost two very dear friends."

"Three, if you count your son."

"Right," he slowly nodded. "It's devastating, I know. But let swimming be your outlet. Your teammates are your support system, not your enemies. And I'm here if you ever need to talk."

I managed a small smile. "Of course." Though he was the last person I'd ever turn to—he had completely shattered my trust by getting involved with my brother. I shrugged his hand off my shoulder.

He clasped his hands together. "Anyway, you guys are off for the next couple of weeks—the pool needs draining because of some TDS levels or something. They'll have it refilled by November, though."

I nodded disinterestedly. I was ready to get the hell out of there.

"You sure you're okay?" he asked, squinting at me.

"Yep."

"Alright. See you tomorrow, buddy."

I could feel his eyes on me as I gathered my things and

rushed out to meet Wes—the rain had finally stopped.

"How was it?" Wes asked as I slid into the passenger seat.

What kind of question was that? He knew what practice was like—same old routine. "Why?"

"Just checking to make sure everything's okay. No big deal."

"Does Coach Donahue hate Riley or something?"

"Huh? How would I know?" Wes glanced my way. I tilted my head in a questioning manner. His brows furrowed in confusion then relaxed. "Oh, Eddie, about that—there's absolutely nothing going on between the coach and me. I'm seeing someone, and I want to keep it hush-hush—it just doesn't feel right to discuss it after... after April. But I promise when the time comes, I'll tell you. Fair?"

"Wait a second—so you're not bi?"

His eyes went wide. "No," he replied with a laugh. "Trust me, I wouldn't keep something like that from you. Besides, if I *were* bi, Coach sure as hell wouldn't be my type. Have you seen the hair on his arms? He looks like a goddamn werewolf." He managed to make me laugh. "But hey," he added, nudging me with his elbow, "as for whether Coach hates Riley—every family has its quirks. I mean, can we say that Monster loves us?"

He wasn't kidding. Hank would probably break into a hymn if one of us died.

"But listen," Wes said, "I only care about us. We have to stick together and be honest with one another. You understand, right?"

"Of course. Why do you ask?"

"I just want to make sure you understand me. If Brody comes around questioning you and I'm not there, you can't handle it alone. We can't risk you slipping with your story." He glanced at me. "Brody hasn't questioned you without me, has he?"

Instantly, I recalled that moment after Brooklyn's death—when I nearly let the truth slip to Brody at school. If it weren't for Coach Donahue, I would have ruined everything for Wes and me. I couldn't possibly tell Wes that.

"No," I answered. Wes straightened, eyes fixed on the road.

When we arrived home, Hank was waiting at the door. "Well, there you shit-faces are. I thought you'd be out until curfew. Get in here."

"What the hell is he doing around?" Wes muttered under his breath just for my ears. We climbed out of the car, and I lugged my gym bag.

"I had swim practice," I explained as we ascended the stoop.

Hank gestured us inside. "I ordered an extra-large pizza with all the fixings."

Wes and I exchanged a glance.

"Pepperoni?" I raised an eyebrow.

"Yep."

"Mushrooms and onions?"

"Double yep."

"Arsenic?" Wes quipped. Hank glared at him, prompting Wes to raise his hands in mock defense. "Something's off, and I'm just making sure you're not forcing us to drink the Kool-Aid."

"Haha. No funny business here, but I do have great news. Come sit down and dig in, and I'll tell you all about it."

Wes met my gaze again. With a shrug, we joined Hank. It felt strange sitting around the table as a family of three—a scene we hadn't seen since Mom was around.

A large pizza box and a six-pack of Cokes sat on the table. We let Hank dig in first and only helped ourselves after he had taken a bite, chewed, and swallowed. That put Wes's Kool-Aid theory to rest. I tentatively took a bite as Wes popped open a soda.

After a long pause, Hank began, "So—what do you guys think about leaving Haywood?"

My food nearly went down the wrong pipe. "Huh?" I glanced at Wes, who was looking at Hank in confusion.

"I got an offer for the house," Hank announced.

"This corroded piece of shit?" Wes asked incredulously.

Hank nodded. "Yep. After a bit of fixing up, yes."

"What about school?" I asked. "I'm going to Nationals next year, remember?"

"I didn't mean we were leaving tomorrow. Selling and buying a new home will take months. Everything will be fine after Nationals. Besides, Ridgedale Park has an exceptional swim team too."

"Ridgedale Park?" Wes echoed.

"I've already started the process for buying a place there."

"So, regardless of what we decide now, we don't really have a choice?" Wes demanded.

I looked at him, puzzled. Didn't he hear Hank? We could finally leave Haywood—something Wes and I had always *dreamed* about.

"You're welcome to stay in Haywood if you want; you just can't stay in this house because I'm selling it," Hank explained.

"What's this really about?" Wes pressed. "Why the sudden change? We've been stuck in this time loop for ages, doing the same shit day in and day out. What's changed, Hank?"

My eyes widened, bracing myself for Hank to lose his temper. Hank took a sharp breath, growing impatient with Wes's attitude. "They reinstated me," he declared, staring at us as if expecting congratulations. Clearing his throat, he continued, "But they need me in Ridgedale, so I've got to move. You both are welcome to stay in Haywood if that's what you want." With a shrug, he stood and left.

I lobbed a piece of sausage at Wes. "What is your problem?"

"My problem? What the hell is wrong with *you*? Just because he bought us a fucking pizza doesn't mean everything's all peaches and cream. I'm not going to Ridgedale with him," Wes retorted, slamming his fist as he got to his feet.

"Wes?" I tried to grab him, but just like Hank, he kept moving. I frowned in confusion. What was Wes holding on to?

32

WES

NOW

I opened Libby's car door and plopped into the passenger seat.

"Thanks for meeting me," she said. Her voice was soft, and her gaze was fixed ahead.

She didn't need to thank me—she was exactly who I needed. I'd been thinking about her non-stop for days; especially the name on her ID. Of course, she carried another identity, tainted by an abusive boyfriend from her past.

I leaned in for a kiss, but she turned her face away, so I could only peck her cheek. I pulled back, frowning. "Everything okay?"

"Yeah," Libby replied, shifting in her seat yet avoiding

my eyes.

Something was off. I took a deep breath and sat in silence for a moment before slipping my hand into hers. She closed her eyes. "Wes—" she began.

"How do you feel about relocating?" I asked.

"What?"

"I might move to Ridgedale, if you'd come with me. Maybe you could transfer to one of their schools, and I could just drop out."

"Drop out?" she spun around, pulling her hand free.

I raised my hands. "Let me finish. If I drop out, I can get my diploma online—and take my college courses online too. We won't have to hide anymore. What do you think?" My voice wavered as I stared at her.

She looked shocked. "Bloody hell, Wesley. You've really thought this through."

"Of course I have," I replied as I reached for her hand again. I could hardly believe what I was about to say, but she needed to know. "I'm in love with you, Libby Harper."

She covered her face with her free hand and bowed her head as if trying to shield herself. "What's the matter? What is it?" I asked but she only shook her head. "Come on. Just say it already. You don't like the idea?"

"It's—it's a brilliant idea, actually. And the fact you're willing to do that much for me is…" she choked.

"Babe—" I pulled her closer and held her tight as she

cried into my jacket, breaking my heart. "Don't cry. This is a good thing, right?"

She pulled away, wet strands of hair clinging to her face. "You don't understand, Wesley."

"So, tell me."

"I can't—we mustn't do this anymore."

"Do what? Have this conversation? Meet here? What?" My eyes searched her face, desperate for any sign—was she calling it quits?

"We can't see each other anymore."

"But I'm figuring out a way to make it work. We're almost—"

"It's wrong. And I should've never," she swallowed, "abused you like this."

My face twisted. "Abused me? Don't talk to me like I'm some goddamn victim."

"You can't even understand that's what's happened…"

"That's not what this is, Libby. Somebody's forcing you to say that. Just tell me who it is." She pressed her lips together, tears sliding down her cheeks. "Are you afraid of that stalker guy?"

She closed her eyes. "I can't say."

"Look at me and tell me you don't love me back then. Tell me that."

Her chest heaved, her eyes tightening. "Wesley, don't make me say that."

"You're the one lying to yourself."

"Go…"

"Libby—don't do this to me, please." We stared at each other—her face full of dread, mine twisted in pain. "Please?" I reached for her, but she moved away.

"Go, Wesley."

"You don't mean that." I hated the whine in my voice—I just couldn't lose her.

"We can't, Wesley. Please, don't make this any harder."

"Well, what am I supposed to do? Just forget about you? How's that going to work in class, Miss Harper?"

She sucked in a sharp breath. "I won't be teaching anymore. I'm leaving Haywood. Gosh, Wesley, just go…" Was she *seriously* skipping town? I kept searching her face. She blinked at me, then nudged me toward the door. "Leave."

"You know what? *Fuck* this." My shoulders heaved with each hard breath, yet I couldn't leave. I believed she'd come around—tell me she was just kidding and make love to me like that first night. But she didn't. Instead, she shoved me forcefully. With an angry cry, I turned and pounded the passenger window repeatedly.

"Stop it. *Wesley, stop.*" The glass shattered into a thousand pieces, some embedding in my bloody knuckles. I shakily cupped my hand to catch the dripping blood. Libby gasped. "Look what you've done to yourself." She moved to console me, but I reached for the door handle. "Wait. Let me take you to the hospital. You might need stitches."

"Just fuck off, Libby." I stumbled from the car.

She clamped a hand on my shoulder. "Sweetheart…?"

"Don't fucking call me that. I'm not your kid, and I *don't* need your pity." I slammed her door hard, dislodging the last shards of glass from its frame. Without another word, she started the vehicle and sped away. I stepped back, glass crunching beneath my shoes, and screamed into the night. Tears streamed down my face, my throat ached, and my hand throbbed, yet nothing compared to the stabbing pain in my heart.

The phone rang in my back pocket, startling me. For a split second, a glimmer of hope told me it was Libby. Trembling, I pulled out my cell—it was Eddie.

"Damnit! Couldn't I have a minute to myself?" I hissed as I punched the ANSWER button. "What?" I listened to Eddie's even breathing. I sighed, my insides trembling as a sob welled up. "Eddie, do you need something?" I asked, moving the phone away from my face, sniffling.

"I need you. Can you come?" Eddie's voice was flat, monotone.

"Yeah. I'll be home in a sec."

"No. School."

"School? Eddie, why are you there?" The call abruptly

ended.

"Eddie?" Shit! I hung up. Was he having another episode? I hobbled toward the car, clutching my injured hand to my chest.

I probably needed stitches. So. Fucking. What. No doctor could mend my broken heart.

The side door to the gym was ajar. I hated being at school during the day—who in their right mind wanted to attend night classes? My brilliant twin brother, of course.

I rolled my eyes. "Ow!" I winced as my throbbing hand reminded me of the earlier chaos. What was I thinking? It was all Libby's fault. I'd believed she was so different from everyone else—but in the end, women were all the same, just like Mom. I refused to cry for either of them again.

"Eddie? Where are you?" I whispered as I stepped into the dark gym, lit only by moonlight and streetlamps. I didn't have to search long—there, near the pool, stood Eddie, his silhouette stiff. Yes, he was definitely having another episode.

EDDIE

Wes's screams jolted me awake. "What the fuck did you do?" he wailed, on his knees and rocking back and forth amidst his sobbing.

"I—I don't know how I got here. I—what's *wrong?*"

Wes, still on his knees with a bloody, swollen hand pressed to his chest, ordered, "Turn around."

Swallowing hard, I did as instructed, drawing in a horrified gulp of air. Lying face down in the center of the pool was a body—I recognized the red baseball cap. It was Diego. I spun around; Wes's forehead met the floor.

"Wes, I promise you, I don't—know what happened…" My words choked as my chest tightened. "I promise, Wes. I don't remember. I don't know why we're here or how I got here." My chest constricted so much I could barely breathe. Collapsing hard onto my knees, I struggled for air. "I'm calling…the police…I've got Brody's number—" I scrambled for my phone. "I'm gonna—tell Brody…"

Wes slid over and wrapped his arms around me. "Shh. Inhale, silently count to three, and exhale."

Obeying, I blinked tearful eyes at my twin. "I can't keep doing this, Wes. I don't understand what happened. I…I dreamed that Diego and I were fighting underwater, that I drowned him. But this—"

Wes glanced toward the empty pool and trembled. "Somebody pushed him. Why the hell were you two even here?"

"I don't know, Wes. I swear I'm not lying," I murmured, my head lowering and my throat tight. "I'm going to call Brody." I stood, but Wes tugged me back to his side.

"*No*. We're getting out of here."

"Wes, this is wrong."

He rose, hesitating. "Did you drop anything in there?"

"Drop anything like what?"

"Evidence. Anything that could lead back to you."

I shrugged. "I don't know, and I don't care anymore. The truth has to come out either way."

Wes removed his shoes and hopped into the pool, stooping as he shone the light of his cell phone around. "Wes, please—just let it go. It's over. I'm calling Brody." I reached my feet.

"No…" Wes choked as he struggled to climb out after me. I pulled out my cell phone, and he swatted it away, wincing. "Fuck." He gingerly cupped his injured hand with his other.

"What happened?" I asked, staring at his bloody, swollen hand ragged with embedded glass.

"It doesn't matter. We need to get the hell out of here, and we're *not* calling Brody. Come on." He tugged at me. "Come *on*."

We grabbed our things and dashed to the car.

"Why won't you let me do the right thing, Wes? How long are we going to keep covering up crimes? I'm a goddamn serial killer. I need help."

He laughed maniacally. "Do you really think you'll get help? Do you think they'll help when the truth comes out about Wright and Riley…and now April and Diego? It'll look like you're tying up loose ends. They won't give a shit about your sleepwalking bullshit."

I glared at him. "Is that what you really think? That I'm making it up? April and Diego were our friends—I had no reason to kill them."

"Didn't you?" He fixed his gaze on me. "That night when I went to see April, she told me something—and I held out, because Brody might see that as a motive. He's already trying to connect us to Wright and Riley."

"What did April say, Wes?"

He shifted uncomfortably. "You have to understand— I'm only trying to protect you."

"What did she say?" I grabbed his shoulder.

"That she photoshopped the picture of Mack and Brooklyn."

I exhaled in loud wheezes. "How could you keep that from me?"

"For this very reason, Eddie. April was spreading rumors about your girlfriend. If I'd told Brody, you would have been suspect number one."

"Right now, I don't give a shit what Brody thinks. I should've known Brooklyn wouldn't cheat on me."

He scoffed. "Well, you're forgetting that Brooklyn did exactly that, only with—" He shook his head. "Brody doesn't need to know any of that. It's motive after motive, Eddie. I promised I'd protect you no matter what. I'm sorry if you hate how I do it, but I refuse to see you locked up for this. It's too bad they're dead, but we have to move on. We'll keep our heads down until we get to Ridgedale. You got that?" He sniffed, biting back tears. "I should've been with you tonight."

"It isn't your fault—"

"It doesn't matter. It's over now."

My eyes narrowed. "What are you talking about?"

He pulled the car over and turned to face me. "I've got you, bro. I promise. We'll get through Nationals and get to Ridgedale, just as planned. All this Haywood shit will be far behind us. I just need you to be with me—let me protect you." He opened his arms, and I hesitantly stepped in.

Because who was going to protect Wes from me?

33

EDDIE

Haywood High was a scene of chaos when we arrived that morning. Students huddled outside in groups while cops and teachers talked on the stairs, keeping everyone away from the building.

Wes kept his arm tight around my shoulder. "What's going on?" he asked a girl ahead of us.

It was Savannah. "I think they found a body or something." She gave me a sympathetic smile and a small wave.

I nodded and moved further under Wes's arm, still wondering why I let him talk me into coming to school.

"We'll look suspicious if we don't," he'd insisted.

After we got home last night, the harsh reality hit me:

I'd just killed Wes's best friend. I remembered hearing him cry in the bathroom all night.

I couldn't understand why or how I'd killed Diego. Sure, I never liked him and had dozens of reasons to despise him—he'd been with my girlfriend behind my back and given her the drugs that killed her. Still, I'd never wished him dead. I never wanted to see Diego like that...face down in his own blood.

"There goes Principal Marriot," Savannah noted, nodding in her direction.

"Settle down, everyone," the principal said. "There's been an accident inside the school. Authorities are still investigating and need to speak to each of you individually."

I couldn't face Brody today. "We should go..." I whispered.

But Wes shook his head. "It'll be okay."

At the police station, we sat across from Detective Brody, who tapped his pen in silence for a moment before taking a sharp breath. "I'm going to be direct. Your friend, Diego, is dead."

I blinked and looked down at my lap, unable to cry—even if I wanted to. Maybe I'd already cried all I could.

"We found his body in the school," Brody explained. "We're still piecing together what happened, but it appears it was an accident."

Wes's shoulders slumped. "What do you mean? I just saw Diego—we…" He slammed his hand onto the table. "Goddamn it."

"What is it, Wesley?" Brody asked.

Wes looked away, ruffling his hair. "I fought with Diego the other day."

My head whipped up. What was he trying to do—shifting the focus onto himself?

Brody leaned forward. "Is that how you hurt your hand?"

I glanced at Wes's wrapped hand. He'd joined me last night injured, but hadn't explained what happened. Wes nodded solemnly. Clearly, he was lying; if the fight had been that brutal, they would have expelled both him and Diego.

"So, tell me. What were you boys fighting about?"

"Because—" Wes hesitated. "I don't want to rat anyone out or anything, but…"

"It's alright, Wesley. Just be honest."

Wes exhaled shakily. "Diego—well, he dealt drugs to kids at school. I fought him because I found out he'd given Brooklyn the drugs she took the night she died. It pissed me off, yeah, but I didn't want him to die. What happened to him?"

Detective Brody cocked his head. "It's pretty tragic. We found him in the empty pool at school."

Wes squinted. "You mean he fell in and—split his face or something?" Then his hand shot up to cover his mouth. "That's messed up. You don't think he did that on purpose, do you? Based on what I just said?"

Brody shrugged. "That's exactly what we're trying to find out. Your information has been useful. If…" He eyed me. "How are you, Edward? You've been quiet."

"I don't know what to say. The past few weeks have been weird. When you really think about it…" My eyes flicked to Wes. "We're all that's left."

Wes hooked his arm around me. "We've got each other, bro," he whispered softly.

"Where are they?" A familiar voice boomed. It was Hank. Wes and I separated and stared anxiously at the door. "Wesley? Eddie?"

Detective Brody stood up. "Let's go," he said, motioning for us.

As soon as Hank saw us, he strode over to Wes and slapped him hard across the face. "What kind of shit have you gotten into this time?"

"Now, Hank—" Sheriff Owens started, but it was Brody who intervened as Hank's fist rose for another strike. Brody pinned Hank against the wall, the two of them breathing heavily.

"What the hell are *you* doing here?" Hank demanded.

"My job," Brody replied evenly. "And you are not about

to lay another finger on those boys. Do you hear me?"

Hank gritted his teeth as Brody slammed him harder into the wall. Hank said nothing, simply lowering his arms while glaring. With one final death glare, Brody released him. Hank's eyebrows knit together in a giant M as he turned to the Sheriff. "Are they done here?"

Sheriff Owens's mouth fell open. "Well, uh—" he looked from Hank to Brody; the tension was almost suffocating. "I called you Hank because you should know how often your boys have been talking to Detective Brody."

Hank glared at Brody. "That's right. I'm supposed to be present when you're interviewing *my* boys. Are we done here?" he snarled. Brody nodded. "Then excuse me while I get my kids home. Come on," he called over his shoulder before bumping into Brody while passing.

"Hank?" Brody stopped him at the door. "You heard what I said."

Hank huffed, shoved the door open, and stepped outside. I was certain Hank would be ready to punish us for the embarrassment, but when we approached his truck, he did nothing. We quietly climbed in and rode home in silence. It wasn't until we pulled over that he finally spoke.

"What do you boys want for dinner?"

34

EDDIE

Something flicked the top of my head, jolting me awake during English class. I quickly scanned the room. No one seemed to notice, but a crumpled sheet of paper rested on my lap. I hadn't slept well the night before. I heard Wes sobbing intermittently, and when I finally managed to sleep again, he woke me, directing me back to bed because I was rummaging in the kitchen and making noise.

I was lucky I didn't disturb Hank. The thought of him reminded me of the animosity between him and Brody—even though they had once been partners. What the hell happened between them?

The bell rang for lunch. I scrambled to my feet and gathered my things.

"Eddie, wait up," Savannah called from behind.

I smiled. "Hey."

"You were completely zoned out in there—even snoring," she giggled.

I covered my face. "Was that you who tossed that paper?"

She pinched her fingers. "You were getting just a tad too loud."

"Thanks for the heads up." I sighed heavily, feeling as though I weighed a ton of bricks. Hank had all the supplies ready to repair the house—paint, tools, drywall, even lawn equipment. He expected Wes and me to work on it after school every day. I could easily guess what my job would be—lawn work.

"Hey, I'm really sorry about your friend," she said, snapping me back to reality as her hand rested on my shoulder.

I hadn't thought about Diego all morning. Part of me didn't want to, knowing he was the reason Brooklyn was gone—not to mention he'd slept with her. How could I get mad at either of them when they were dead? How does one even…?

I pressed my lips together and turned to my locker to put my things away.

"You want to get lunch together?" Savannah asked.

I shrugged. "That'd be great."

We grabbed a turkey sandwich, an apple, and some

carrot sticks, and made our way to the park across the street. Since the gang's last private chat, I hadn't been there—now everyone was gone. A stabbing pain began in my chest. I shut my eyes tightly, willing it away.

Savannah arched an eyebrow. "You okay?"

I cleared my throat. "Uh, yeah. Just had a long night."

She took a bite of her apple. "Couldn't sleep much?"

"I—I have a sleep disorder. Sometimes I sleepwalk and wake up in odd places without remembering how I got there. I take medication, but…" I shook my head. Why was I telling her all that?

She returned her apple to the tray and stared at me, concern etched on her face. "No, go on," she insisted.

I chewed on my bottom lip. "It's too much. I'm always tired. And—"

"You're worried about swimming?"

If only she knew… "Yeah, that's it."

She brushed her hair behind her ears and then untucked her necklace from under her shirt. "Are you familiar with hypnosis?"

I laughed nervously. "A little."

"Well, this is my pendulum. And this," she said as she ran her fingers over it, "is an opalite. It's said to help with depression and keep anxiety at bay. If you're okay with it, I'd like to try something with you."

I hesitated. "I—I don't know."

She took my hand. "I promise it won't hurt. If it feels weird, just tell me, and we can stop."

What did I have to lose? "Let's do it."

"Alright." Her eyes shone. "Face me, keep your back straight, relax your shoulders, and take deep breaths."

"Like meditation?"

"Exactly. Just relax and clear your mind." Her voice became soothing as she raised her necklace, the opalite crystal, to chin level. The pointed, animal-tooth shaped crystal had creamy, opaque swirls of blue and orange as it swayed back and forth.

"As you focus on the pendulum and my voice, I want you to visualize everything I say."

I nodded, my gaze fixed on the tip of the crystal.

"You're stepping into the water. It's the clearest, purest water you've ever seen, warm and soothing. You're wading through it, sending ripples across the surface.

"It smells fresh. You can taste salt on your lips. Your feet slip away as you float—you're as light as a feather. Free."

My eyelids drooped, my shoulders relaxing. My breaths became deep and controlled. I faintly saw the crystal—was the tip on fire?

That was the last thing I saw before slipping into darkness.

My eyes drifted behind my shut lids. Someone was yelling. Through my muffled ears, I could make out what they were saying.

"*Eddie*." Someone shook my shoulders.

I blinked awake. It was Wes. I caught a glimpse of Savannah behind him, her eyes wide and fearful. What had Wes done to her?

"What's going on?" I mumbled, my eyelids fluttering in the sudden brightness.

Wes tugged me to my feet. "Let's go."

I tried to look at Savannah, but Wes kept pulling me away. "What are you doing?" I glared at him.

"You shouldn't be talking to her or doing that weird shit." He turned on her. "Stay away from my brother."

"Wes?" I nudged him. He gripped my arm tightly and pulled me across the street. I glanced back at Savannah, frozen in shock.

"What the hell were you thinking?" Wes spat, his eyes burning with anger.

"What are you so angry about?"

"Eddie, don't you understand? You need to be discreet with your secrets. Why would you let someone hypnotize you when you have no clue what you're even saying while under?"

My chest sank. "Shit. I—I wasn't thinking. You don't think I said anything, do you?"

"Maybe not. I was looking all over for you at lunch. I thought you went out to the car and saw her waving that—thing in your face. You were out of it."

"Wow." I took a breath. What was I thinking? I stopped once we got back inside the school. "Thanks, Wes."

He silently patted me on the back.

After school, I raked the leaves on the front lawn and was preparing the mower when I thought I saw someone run around the side of the house.

Someone in a white dress with dark, flowing hair. Was that *Brooklyn*?

I took off running around the house and caught her ducking behind a tree. Her pale blue irises peeked out as she playfully hid behind the thick trunk. "Eddie..." her soft voice floated on the wind.

My heart swelled—Brooklyn was back. I dashed toward the tree, my blood pumping anxiously. "Brooklyn, I've missed you so—" I stopped. She wasn't there. I blinked in confusion when an icy hand gripped my neck, followed by a familiar giggle—it was Brooklyn's giggle.

"I can hear you, Brooklyn." I spun around. There was no one. I felt a grip on my ponytail, yet she still wasn't visible. I collapsed into the leaves, exhausted. "Brooklyn?" I whispered, inhaling her citrus perfume. I closed my eyes, trying to hold onto that scent.

The aroma grew so intense I could almost taste it. I grinned as my eyes flew open, and there, Brooklyn lay beside me, intertwining her fingers with mine.

"Eddie..." she murmured, stroking my cheek before straddling me. Her touch was soft, trailing from my jawline to my neck. But then her fingers tightened around my neck, making it hard to breathe—she was choking me.

I clawed at her wrists, which felt as solid as stone. "Brook...?" I couldn't finish as I thrashed my arms, searching for something—anything—to knock her off. My fingers wrapped around a rock, its edge sharp. I gripped it tight and thrust it into the center of her stomach. She toppled off, and blood spread quickly across her white gown.

"Eddie?"

I jolted awake with something heavy sprawled on top of me.

"No. No. No!" I heard Wes repeat over and over.

Panic surged. What had I done now? "Wes—? Help." My voice squeaked as I stared up at the kitchen ceiling. "*Wes?*"

Within moments, he appeared, tears streaming down his face. "I can't..." he muttered, shaking his head, a hand covering his mouth.

I struggled beneath the dead weight, realizing I was pinned by someone's body. I squinted down and saw

Hank's shiny brown head. A sharp gasp caught in my throat.

"Hank?" I called softly. Wes shut his eyes, trembling. "Hank? Wake up." I nudged him, but his lifeless eyes stared back, lips slightly parted. A wail tore from my throat as I screamed until my voice was raw. "Get Hank off me. Get him off, Wesley, *please*. Please?" I kicked frantically.

Wes lifted Hank away. Hank hit the floor face down with a hard thud.

Shakily, I pulled myself up, every part of me aching. Blood drenched my clothes as I dropped the bloody screwdriver I'd been clutching.

"I—I don't—I don't—" I stammered, wrapping my arms around my sore midsection and rocking back and forth until the police arrived.

"Can I get you some water?" Detective Brody offered.

At first I shook my head, then quickly nodded. Water might soothe my aching throat. We were at the precinct now—we may as well had moved in with the frequency of our visits. I was dressed in navy blue sweats and a matching T-shirt, courtesy of the department. After taking dozens of pictures, they allowed me to shower and change once they bagged my clothes for evidence.

Brody disappeared and returned with a water bottle and

an ice pack for my bruised face.

I shakily unscrewed the cap, spilling water into my lap, and took a small, painful sip. Wes tried holding the ice pack to my jaw, but I pushed him away.

Brody sighed. "Can you tell me what happened?"

No—I couldn't tell him everything. I could only repeat the theory Wes and I had concocted.

I coughed. "When I got home from school, I was supposed to do chores—lawn work and stuff—but I was so tired." I paused, my lip trembling as I closed my eyes. I couldn't lie any longer. I killed Hank. *My father*. Wasn't it time I told the truth?

I opened my mouth, ready to confess, but froze as I looked at Wes—all he had done to protect me. I wasn't the only one in trouble. They'd send Wes to jail, too, and I couldn't allow that.

"I took a nap. Hank was furious when he came back and found me sleeping. He just went crazy..." I shut my eyes again, replaying the many moments Hank had dragged me from bed, punching, kicking, and stomping me. "We ended up in the kitchen because he was trying to force me outside." I took a deep breath that pained my left side.

"He started choking me. Normally, when that happens, Wes is there to stop him..." My voice broke as tears poured—not just for today, but for all the times I'd feared Hank would finally kill Wes or me.

"I was so scared. Hank was on top of me, squeezing my neck until I could hardly breathe. I saw the toolbox, but I didn't mean for this to happen. I just wanted him to let me go." I looked Brody in the eye. "I'm sorry."

"So am I. We all watched Hank's altercation yesterday. We knew his background. I shouldn't—I shouldn't have let you two leave with him."

Wes sniffed. "Well, it's too fucking late now. What's going to happen to my brother?"

Brody shook his head. "Nothing tonight. We're not filing any charges. But I will have a lawyer contact you in the morning with more details. Do you guys have somewhere else to stay? Your home is now a crime scene."

"Yeah," Wes replied. "We'll just grab a few things and head to a hotel."

Brody nodded. "Just don't go too far, okay?"

"Got it. Can we please go?" Wes asked.

"Sure," Detective Brody said with a sympathetic nod.

Back home, yellow and black DO NOT ENTER tape blocked off the kitchen with a large X. I peered at the dried blood still on the floor. Wes came up behind me, and I collapsed into his arms as we both sobbed. Even though Hank was a monster, he was still our dad—something we never forgot.

"Let's just leave Haywood tonight," Wes said once we'd calmed down. "We can head to Ridgedale as soon as tomorrow."

"But Brody said—"

"Who gives a shit what he said? I want to get you out of here. Hank already has a place in Ridgedale. We can search his room for information and map out the location. There's nothing left for us here. Tomorrow, there's a major drug drop, and my cut's gonna leave us loaded."

My stomach soured. "Wesley, we shouldn't—"

He gently took my face in his hands. "I'm gonna find a doctor to treat your sleep disorder. Everything's going to be okay, Eddie, I promise. We'll stay at the cabin tonight and head for Ridgedale once I'm done. Okay?"

I shook my head slowly. "I don't like this, Wes."

"Trust me." He hugged me tightly. "Let's search Hank's room first. Then we'll pack up and head for the cabin."

"Alright."

Hank's room was a disaster—a scene straight out of a hoarding documentary. Where did we even begin? I stepped over beer bottles, cans, piles of trash, and dirty clothes.

"Damnit, Hank. And I thought I was a slob," Wes said, making me smile. He moved over to the dresser to check its drawers while I headed to the bedside table.

On the floor beside the bed lay one of Hank's old

champion boxing belts. I stared at it for a moment before moving on.

A photo of Mom rested on the nightstand. She looked beautiful in her favorite green dress. I tucked the picture frame under my arm, deciding to keep it—this was how I wanted to remember her, not as the frail, delusional woman I'd seen in the window of Angel Wing Asylum.

"Zip." Wes scoffed as he shut one drawer and moved on to the next.

I slid open the drawer on the nightstand. It was empty except for one ragged photo lying face down. Hank must have crumpled it and then folded it to keep, leaving crease lines. I flipped it over. There was Mom, gorgeous and young, holding me—I looked about two or three years old. Beside her, clutching a laughing Wes, was Detective Brody.

35

EDDIE

Not a single word was exchanged between us during the ride to the cabin. Ever since that photo, Wes had been jittery—constantly bouncing his knee or drumming his thumb on the steering wheel.

What did it signify? Was that why Hank was furious with Brody—because Brody had been secretly seeing Mom? Could any of that be related to Hank's abrupt resignation? And is that why Mom kept insisting it wasn't Hank's fault, because she felt guilty for cheating?

The drive took just over half an hour. Once we arrived, we left our belongings in the car. Inside, Wes kindled a fire before stepping out to gather more wood, while I prepared our sleeping bags. Afterwards, I found myself fixated on the room from which I'd pushed Riley out the window. It felt like a lifetime ago, even though barely over a month had passed. So much had transpired since then—so much death. Murder.

Was there any hope left for me? Could a doctor truly fix my problem? Even if he could, the damage had already been done. No one could erase the guilt.

The front door slammed as Wes stomped back inside. I hurried down the stairs. "Do you really think a doctor can—?" But it wasn't Wes entering; it was Detective Brody. "What are you doing here?" I demanded, chilled by the realization that he'd tracked us down to our secret hideout.

"We need to talk," Brody stated.

Like hell we would.

"Brrr," Wes muttered as he entered. "It's chilly—" He glared at Brody. "Why the fuck are *you* here?"

"I needed to talk to you, boys. This place doesn't exactly scream hotel room," Brody said, eyeing the dim cabin.

"No, but it's cozy enough for a rest, which we'd gladly take if you don't mind," Wes retorted. He flinched as the floor creaked outside the door. "Who else is here?" he demanded, spinning around to face the door. It swung open, and Savannah stepped inside.

"Savannah?" I squinted in recognition.

Brody raised a hand. "This is my partner, Detective

Rojas."

I blinked in surprise. She hardly resembled the pony-tailed, dress-wearing teenager I'd known yesterday. Now, before me stood a stern woman in her twenties clad in a grey pantsuit.

Wes's eyes swept over them. "What's this *21 Jump Street* bullshit?"

"You said some interesting things, Eddie, while under hypnosis," she interjected, glancing at Brody. "Should I tell him?"

My heart pounded anxiously, my eyes widening. Wes was right; I should have *never* allowed her to hypnotize me. I shouldn't have trusted her.

"No. We'll discuss that in a moment. Thanks, Rojas, but you can wait in the car. I need to talk to the boys alone." She nodded and slipped out silently as Wes continued to watch the door.

Brody cleared his throat. "Before we delve into what my partner overheard, I want you all to know—we've finally caught the Candy Man."

And? What did that have to do with us? Wes shifted, mirroring my confusion. "And?"

"Don't you want to know who it is?" Brody asked, locking eyes with me. "It's Coach Donahue."

My jaw dropped. "*What?*"

He nodded, then turned to Wes. "But you already knew

that, didn't you, Wesley?"

Wes gritted his teeth. I'd completely misunderstood—I thought Wes and Donahue were romantically involved. In truth, Wes was *working* for Donahue.

Brody clicked his tongue. "Donahue shared an interesting story with me. I'm giving you the chance to tell it, Wes."

My eyes flicked between them.

Wes's breathing quickened. He closed his eyes for a moment, and when he opened them again, he glared at Brody. "Not until you share *your* story first."

Detective Brody offered a half-smile, blinking. "What story of mine?"

Wes laughed as he reached into his pocket. "Trying to play dumb?" I assumed he was pulling out the folded photo, but instead, he produced Hank's nine-millimeter.

"Wesley!" I recoiled. *"Put that down."*

"Shouldn't we know the truth, Brody? Or should I call you… *Dad?*"

"Wes?" I stammered.

"Think about it, Eddie," Wes shouted, keeping the gun tremblingly aimed at Brody, his gaze never faltering. "That's why Hank hated us so much—especially me. You were Mom's favorite, and I was his." He motioned toward Brody with the barrel of the gun.

I slowly looked at Brody, whose face was as pale as snow.

"Is it true?"

"Yes," Brody whispered.

"So, tell us… the fucking… story. Then I'll tell you mine," Wes spat.

Brody took a deep breath. "There's no need for a gun, Wesley."

"Uh-uh," Wes clicked his tongue. "Don't you worry. Spill the goddamn story. We deserve to know the truth."

Brody nodded, and after a moment of hesitation, he began.

"I was as young as Kira when I became Hank's partner. I thought Kira was the most beautiful woman I'd ever seen, but Hank had broken her—had complete control over her. Whenever he'd succumb to his drunken rages, I'd calm him down until he passed out, and then I'd stay with Kira to make sure she was okay."

His head dropped. "We fell in love. When she got pregnant, I wanted her to run away with me—to leave Haywood and escape Hank for good. But she was terrified of him hurting her, so she stayed with Hank until you were born. You all looked so much like me that I was certain Hank would kill me. Yet, he only demanded a paternity test. I thought that once he learned the truth, Kira could finally leave him."

He paused. "But when the test results confirmed that I was your father, not Hank, he couldn't accept a divorce.

The shame was too unbearable. To spite me, he abused Kira even more. When you had grown old enough to understand what Hank was doing, I'd had enough. I pleaded with Hank to let you three go."

He gestured toward the scar on his cheek. "He smashed my face through a windshield. I was in a coma for weeks. By the time I recovered, Hank had resigned, and Kira had been admitted to that asylum. I returned for you, but he threatened to kill you two before allowing me to have you."

He paused again, swallowing hard. "I'm sorry. I should have fought harder for you—and for Kira. But it wasn't that simple."

We had spent our whole lives forced into loyalty to a man we believed was our father, suffering abuse because our real parents had abandoned us. I squinted at Wes, who had lowered the gun to his side.

"Everything that's happened is my fault," Brody murmured. "I failed you. So many of the adults in your lives—your parents, your coach, Libby—failed you."

What did Miss Harper have to do with this?

"You son of a bitch," Wes gasped amidst tears, "*you* were her stalker?"

"What are you two talking about?" my voice came out small.

Wes took a deep breath. "I loved Libby."

"Wesley, you were sleeping with her?" I squeaked.

He wiped a tear from his cheek. "It went beyond that. What exactly did you say to her?" he demanded, glaring at Brody.

Brody raised his hands defensively. "I only did what I believed was right."

"*What* did you say?" Wes roared, lifting the gun once more.

"I identified myself as a cop. I told her to end whatever was going on, and to get as far away from Haywood as possible before I could have her arrested."

Wes spun around and screamed, "She was my only piece of happiness. And you took that away." My heart ached for him—why hadn't he told me?

"I'm sorry, Wes, for everything. And I have to tell you that Donahue was attempting to flee the country tonight."

"You're lying," Wes insisted.

"He was. He told you the drop was scheduled for morning, but he actually handled it at the hotel tonight. We apprehended him at the airport. He deceived you, Wesley."

Wes broke down, sobbing. "He wouldn't do that. He promised me."

Brody stepped in to console him. I hoped he would disarm Wes, but he didn't. Instead, Brody wrapped him in a tight embrace. "I'm sorry, son," he whispered. As he stepped back, he stared at Wes with sympathetic eyes.

"Now, tell us everything, Wesley."

Wes nodded, sniffling. "Yeah. You're right." His head dropped. "I did it. I killed them all."

36

EDDIE

NOW

"No. *I* did it," I admitted, my voice raw with shock. I couldn't let Wes shield me any longer. I fixed my gaze on Brody. "I have a sleep disorder. I do terrible things in my sleep—and when I wake up, I find myself somewhere else, with someone always ending up dead. Murdered by me." I drew a deep breath. "Wes has only been trying to protect me."

"I know that, Eddie," Brody said. "You told Rojas."

"I did?" I asked.

He nodded. "But I know you did nothing wrong." He then looked to Wes, silently urging him to speak.

Wes blinked, his eyes watering. "You were dreaming

about me while I was committing the murders."

My stomach tightened. "Wh-what are you saying?"

"I'm saying I killed April, Diego, and Hank."

"Wesley, why?" I shoved him. "You made me believe I was the one. I thought I was a monster!" Tears streamed down as I closed my eyes, torn between relief for my innocence and horror at realizing my own twin, my brother, was the real culprit.

"I did it for *you*, Eddie. Everything I've ever done has been for you."

Was he serious? "How? I never asked you to do any of that."

"Start at the beginning," Brody suggested. But Wes shook his head.

"How far back does it go?" I demanded.

Wes licked his lips and glanced at me. "All the way back to Mr. Wright."

My jaw dropped. "*What?*"

"Mr. Wright suspected Donahue and the swim team were up to something. Somehow, he found out Donahue was pushing drugs and planned to tell the principal."

"When he kicked you off the team? That was it?"

Wes nodded. "Donahue made us confront Wright that weekend. He wanted us to scare him, but it backfired."

My heart felt like it was being ripped from my chest. "How could you go along with something so—so wrong?"

"Coach offered the others money, but I refused to do it. He promised to get you back on the swim team—that's what changed my mind."

Sobbing, I turned away. "You should've talked to me. I didn't need the swim team that badly."

"Yes, you did. It was your ticket out. I was already damaged goods."

"Don't say that."

"It's true, Eddie, and you know it." His dark eyes flashed. "You've always been better than me."

"What are you talking about?" I squinted at him.

"What really happened to Riley?" Brody interrupted.

I glanced at him. "I shoved Riley out the window," I admitted, nodding toward the stairs. "He was assaulting Brooklyn, and I only shoved him to stop him—he fell to his death."

Brody stared at Wes. So did I.

"That's partly true," Wes conceded.

"You're kidding!" My voice shrilled.

"Oh, come on, Eddie," Wes replied with an exasperated roll of his eyes. "You knew what Riley was like. He'd gotten out of control—obsessed with his own power. Not only was he blackmailing us, but he also threatened to out his dad. It was Donahue who told Diego and me to handle him. We were all fed up with his bullshit. He'd burned each of us—you, Brooklyn, and April. Brooklyn was the one who insisted that something had to be done about him too."

I stared at him in disbelief. "Are you saying that weekend was staged? That you all drove here knowing we'd leave without Riley?" He nodded. "But why drag *me* into it? I ended up killing Riley."

"We figured that if you believed you'd killed him, you would keep our secret—for Brooklyn's sake.

"So Brooklyn drugged Riley, led him on, and then cried wolf so you could knock him out cold. No one expected him to fall out the window."

"That's just…*sick*, Wesley." I couldn't bear his presence any longer. Shaking my head, I stepped back. "That sounds nothing like the Brooklyn I knew. She wouldn't…"

"Yes, she did. Obviously, she would do anything to cover her secret—just as you would do anything for her."

"Why do you keep saying that? What's that supposed to mean?"

"It means you cared about Brooklyn more than anything. If you thought she was in danger, I knew you'd move heaven and earth for her."

"You don't think I'd do that for you too?"

"I would, but I can't say the same about you."

"Tell me about April and Diego," Brody demanded.

Wes sighed. "April confessed to drugging Brooklyn the night she died. She dumped the pills into her glass."

I yanked his arm. "Why wouldn't you tell me that?"

"Wait—did April say which drug?" Brody asked.

Wes nodded. "Adderall."

"So, Brooklyn's death *was* an accident," Brody said. "She overdosed because she took speed, unaware she'd ingested Adderall. It wasn't suicide."

I blinked; he spoke as if that changed everything. Brooklyn was still dead.

"That's why I killed April," Wes continued. "She was such a mess after Brooklyn died—I didn't trust her with our secrets. She was bound to spill them eventually.

"You were so broken up about Brooklyn, I didn't want to reopen the wound. I tried to help you get better, Eddie."

I shoved him. "Bullshit. You made me believe I was a murderer. How did I get those goddamn scratches on my hand?"

Wes shifted, running his fingers through his hair. "Well…" He cleared his throat. "…that happened while I was dragging you out into the yard."

"You lying bastard—" I spat, grabbing a fistful of his shirt.

"Stop it. Stop," Brody yelled, seizing my shoulders and pulling me away from Wes. Our eyes locked fiercely. Even though Wes and I were identical twins, at that moment he looked like a complete stranger. Brody gestured to Wes. "Carry on, son."

Wes shrugged vigorously to straighten his shirt. His eyes flicked to Brody. "Anyway, Diego committed the ultimate betrayal. Not only did he supply Brooklyn with drugs, but he was also sleeping with her. That bastard crossed every line imaginable. And as for Hank—" Wes fixed his gaze on me again.

My jaw clenched.

"He was really beating you during your sleep spell—you were so out of it that I feared he'd already... murdered you. I just couldn't handle it. I saw the screwdriver and jammed it into his fat ass. That was the only murder I'd *ever* fantasized about."

"Wesley, you don't mean that."

"Of course I do. Hank hated me with a passion. He always held you in higher regard, even if it changed nothing." He laughed bitterly, his eyes brimming with tears.

"Don't twist things around," I hissed.

"It's true. Hank despised both of us, but he would never dare seriously injure you—especially not your face. You were his star swimmer. I was merely the breadwinner."

My lip trembled as a tear trailed down my face. He wasn't lying. Hank was always careful around my face. But Wes—

I noticed the scar on his brow. "Wes, I'm sorry—for everything. You've spent your life looking after me, and maybe…maybe I took that for granted…" I swallowed hard against a sob. "But I'll always be there for you. You know that."

Wes turned his head away, biting his lip. He exhaled shakily and faced me with teary eyes and a crooked smile. Stepping forward, he rested his forehead against mine and whispered, "You're safe now, Eddie." As he slowly backed away, he raised the gun.

"Whoa, *whoa*," Brody called from behind me. "Put the gun down, Wes."

"Wes, please, we can fix this, I prom—" I started, but then a blast erupted and my brother's warm blood splattered across my face.

"*Wesley?*" Brody screamed. He dropped beside Wes, merging into the chaos. My gaze fixed blankly ahead.

"Oh, my God. He's gone..." Brody staggered in front of me, breathless, gripping my shoulders. "Listen to me. I'll take care of you, son. I promise they'll tie none of this to you, okay?" He cradled my face in his hands. "I failed you once, but I won't fail again. Eddie, do you hear me? *Eddie…?*"

GO GRAB YOUR FREE BOOKS

When you subscribe to my mailing list, you'll instantly get *The Perfect Daughter* and *The Perfect Ride*. Plus, you'll be the first to know about my new releases, special offers, and other fun stuff. (Rest assured, I will *not* flood your inbox. ☺) Visit **nikikeith.com** to get your download.

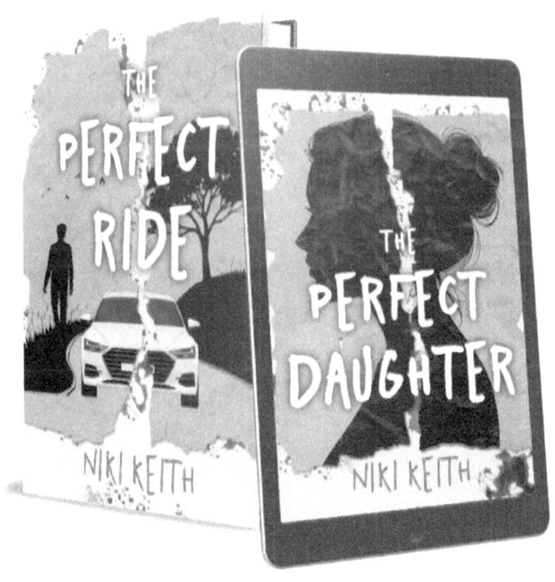

DON'T MISS THESE THRILLING
READS

CRUSH
NIKI KEITH

ONLY
THE
PRETTY
ONES
NIKI KEITH

I'D LOVE TO KNOW YOUR THOUGHTS

Reviews mean everything to an author. I would be really grateful if you could share your honest opinion about *Keep Your Friends Close* (it can be as short as you like.) And if you *did* enjoy *Keep Your Friends Close*, be sure to check out **nikikeith.com** for what's coming next.

I can't thank you enough for giving my book a chance. Take care! ☺

ABOUT THE AUTHOR

Niki Keith writes twisty young adult thrillers about broken teens doing bad things for all the right reasons. These days she prefers tea over coffee, dreams of going outer space, and is still searching for the best rice crispy recipe. When she isn't murdering fictional characters, she's cuddling with her affectionate love-biting kitty, pondering what to read next from her TBR pile.

You can connect with Niki on her website—nikikeith.com.